Singapore Trap

Susanne Bellamy

SUSANNE BELLAMY

ISBN: 978-0-6485275-4-1

Dedication

For Steve, who grounds me, supports me,
and sets me free to fly.

Chapter 1

Sydney, present day

Agent Paul Rimmer walked along the wide, brightly lit hall that led to Jake Harris' office in the Sydney headquarters of the Bureau. Relief at being summoned to a private meeting with his former partner put a spring in his step. As much as he loved surfing, two weeks away from the rush of work was enough holiday.

A crisp white door, open most of the time thanks to his former partner's open door policy indicated Jake was expecting him. He tapped lightly on the door and entered. Two years into his job as second-in-charge at the Bureau and Jake looked right at home, although Paul knew his one-time partner escaped to remote camping sites with his wife, Marcy, most weekends. But the trade-off from active fieldwork suited him and meant Marcy had been able to continue her medical research at the university laboratory.

"You wanted to see me?" Paul dropped into a chair and got comfortable.

Jake tossed a folder across the desk and leaned back casually. "Tell me what you think." Jake's dark gaze was hooded, but his tense jaw spoke volumes.

Paul flicked the folder open and looked at a long-distance photo, shot with a zoom lens, enhanced and cleaned up, but still lacking clarity. The background was out of focus, but clear enough to see the wall behind was grimy, with security grills over a pair of windows.

He picked the photo up and peered at the three-quarter-face image. A thrill raced down his spine like a perfect wave building beneath his surfboard.

Finally!

"I spy with my little eye . . ." Paul tossed the photo down. It slid across the desk and stopped halfway between them. Their gazes met and any attempt at humour vanished. "This is Chan, and yes, I'm sure, if that's what you were going to ask. Where and when was this taken?"

"Geylang district in Singapore, two days ago."

Paul frowned. "Geylang? Isn't that a red-light district?"

"Pretty much. Fitting for Chan, although the source of this photo doesn't believe he's living there. It was a chance sighting."

"But he's finally surfaced in Singapore?"

"That's the intel."

"Are you giving me this assignment? Please tell me you are." Losing Chan two years earlier churned his gut. He needed to make things right, especially for the dead girl they'd arrived too late to save. Her image haunted his nightmares. Some nights he was sure her ghost followed him, demanding vengeance.

"Yes. But before you ask, not with Tamsin. She told Marcy and me last night—she's pregnant. Fairly early stage, but her doctor has some concern about her health. Marcy didn't elaborate."

"So she's out of contention. Damn." Paul liked working with Tamsin. They understood one another's moves and thinking—apart from the Chan fiasco when their cover had been blown. Despite a mole in their department, they had succeeded in breaking up the Chan cartel, stopping most of the drug manufacture and distribution, and one of the nastiest illegal prostitution rackets in the country.

"I know you work well together. However, Tamsin's doctor has put her on desk duty for the next few weeks. Would you work with a local officer in Singapore?"

Exciting as picking up Chan's trail after all this time was, a wash of disappointment hit him. He wouldn't be on the case with Tam and would have to break in a new partner, someone whose thinking and reactions he didn't know. "Not keen, but I'll do it. At least he—"

"She. I requested their best female operative. I like the different perspectives. You and Tamsin convinced me of the benefits of mixed gender teams."

Paul was less certain their partnership worked so well because of gender. Tam was in a league of her own and he was happy to admit he'd learned plenty from her. Would partnering with another woman be easier because of his time working with Tam? Not that it mattered what he thought. Jake had decided, and Paul either accepted her, or risked losing the chance to bring in Chan.

"I suppose *she* will have local knowledge. That's a bonus. My experience of Singapore is limited to transiting through Changi Airport on my way to and home from Greece."

"Good. I'll set up a meeting with Tamsin for tonight. See if she remembers anything about Chan that isn't in the reports."

"Do you really think the queen of thoroughness would have omitted anything?"

"Fair comment. See you at Tam's place, eight sharp."

***

Paul stepped in and hugged Tam when she opened her door. His sisters had taught him well when it came to displaying affection and Tam was almost as precious to him as his siblings. "How are you, and congratulations, by the way." She looked peaky. The oldest of his sisters had *glowed* when pregnant with his niece.

"Thanks. Jake's already here," she said and led the way into the comfortable lounge room where they'd shared countless beers and family sagas.

Jake rose and extended a hand. "You're not late. Marcy sent me across early with some things for Tamsin."

"Like an Ikea cot for starters." Tam curled her legs up on

her armchair, picked up a bright green cushion and, holding it against her still-flat stomach, sipped a cup of steaming green tea. "Thanks for moving the meeting to my apartment, Jake, Paul. I can't seem to move far without either wanting to throw up or crawl back under the doona."

"No problem, Tam. Your reports were comprehensive. You always were more thorough than me, but I'm looking for any small, personal details that might help locate Chan. Odd preferences regarding food, recreation . . . You know the sort of thing I mean."

Tamsin's nose wrinkled and she set the mug down. "Perversions. That's what he likes, and the more awful you might think it, the more he'll like it."

"So the girl in the brothel—"

"Yes. Perverse, extreme, highly dangerous, although never to himself. He's a psychopath, which you know from the report and personal encounters. What you might not know is, he's fascinated by creatures that kill with poison." Tam rolled a shoulder as though an insect had crawled down her spine.

"What, like scorpions?"

"Probably not exotic enough for him." Jake scrolled through the file on his iPad and enlarged an image. "The search of his Sydney apartment yielded a large aquarium of highly dangerous tropical fish in his bedroom. Look at this." He passed the device to Tam who passed it on to Paul.

"Ugh, is that a tiger fish?"

"The big ugly thing with razor-sharp teeth? I believe so. It's like an African piranha. There was no evidence that Chan brought it into the country legally." Jake took his iPad back from Paul. "Singapore caters to all tastes. Trying to trace him via his taste for the perverse will need local knowledge."

Tamsin met Paul's eye and grinned. "I wonder if your new partner will be as willing to role play as me?"

"Hey, I only proposed when Chan got suspicious."

"It was your fault for hanging around so much. Should I warn your new partner? Those pet names you stuck me with were the pits."

"What's wrong with Baby cake?" Paul grimaced. Maybe he *had* been pushing Tam's buttons with some of the rubbish he'd dished up. "Anyway, it won't come to that. Chan already knows who I am."

Tam's gaze settled on him and she reached out to touch his arm. "Be careful, Paul. Chan's more likely to feed you to his tiger fish this time."

"Thanks for the vote of confidence, partner."

Jake was typing with two fingers on a fold up keyboard, muttering something about big fingers and small keys. Finally he looked up. "Anything else, Tam?"

Her lips pressed together and she turned her head away, but not before Paul caught a flash of an unfamiliar emotion in her eyes.

"If you're thinking of using female agents in undercover roles to get to Chan—don't." Her shoulders wriggled, as though someone had walked over her grave.

"You worked undercover, Tam. Up close and personal, and you came out okay. Why not another operative?"

"I was in the sweep team at the Sydney brothel, Paul. I saw what he did to that girl, and I saw another body at the morgue. Same cause of death, but . . ." Tam pressed a hand over her stomach and, for a moment, Paul wondered if she was going to throw up. He half-rose to look for a bucket, but she waved him to sit down.

Tam drew a deep breath and moistened her lips. "What he'd done to her before she died was inhuman. He thrives on cruelty. It's a power trip, an aphrodisiac to a mind like his. Do you want to expose another woman to that situation?" She looked from Paul to Jake, and back to him. "Call it a woman's intuition if you like, but I don't believe that's the way to trap him."

Paul shook his head, certain there was more to Tam's warning than she was letting on, but she was a top agent and if she wasn't sharing, it was because she thought he didn't need to know. Still, he filed her observation away. Tam, his sisters, his mother . . . different times, different observations, and they'd each been right. Who was he to knock a woman's instinct?

Twenty minutes later, Jake stowed his iPad and rose. "Thanks for the insights, Tam. Something there might give Paul the break he needs. Now, Marcy told me to ask if you're free for a barbecue on Sunday. She said to just show up if you're feeling up to it."

"Thanks, Jake. If it's in the afternoon, there's a chance I'll make it."

"Am I invited too?" Paul collected their empty mugs and carried them through to Tamsin's kitchen.

"No. You'll be in Singapore."

Chapter 2

Lin Tan slotted incense sticks into the altar in front of a photo of Kim. Pinned next to an image of the Buddha, the camera had caught her younger sister in a typical moment of joy. A breeze had lifted Kim's long hair and she wore that smile she always seemed to be smiling, the one that lit her eyes and said she hadn't a care in the world.

Lin lit a candle and set it in a holder within a circlet of orchids. Reaching behind her, she lifted a small tray of sliced pineapple and mango, Kim's favourite foods, and set it beside the flowers. Bringing her hands together, she bowed her head.

But try as she might, the image of Kim as Lin had last seen her intruded on her prayers. The welts on her wrists and neck told of her sister's last hours. Violent, frightening, tortured hours in which her sister had been subjected to unspeakable terrors.

If Lin had been home when she'd promised, none of it would have happened. Kim would still be alive.

How could she pray when Kim's death was her fault? Lin was the older sister; she was the one who should have seen if her sister had a problem. She was the one who should have been looking out for Kim.

Should have gone out looking for her sister earlier.

Lin opened her eyes and sat back on her heels.

Impossible to pray. Impossible to forgive herself.

As impossible as bringing her sister back to life in this world, but now Lin had a chance to bring the man responsible for her sister's death to justice.

Justice, or revenge?

One and the same.

She rested a hand on the urn containing Kim's cremated remains. "I know what I will do is not the way Mama taught us, but I swear I will find those who did these terrible things to you, who stole your life and deprived me of the joy of my sister, and I will bring them to justice."

Or death.

Lin would not voice that dark thought, even to her sister's ashes.

She picked up a fine gold chain and clasped it around her neck. Kim's leaf pendant, a violet and green jade Lin had never seen until a month ago, felt warm against her skin, as though Kim had only now taken it off and handed it to Lin.

Her fingers touched the pendant, feeling the fine tracery of veins carved into the stone leaf.

Good luck stone, meant to bring peace and harmony to the wearer.

Not for Kim. Who had given it to her, and why?

Lin hadn't succeeded in extracting answers from her little sister, and what did that say about Lin's ability as an undercover officer?

Turning her back on the altar, she pulled her satchel over her head and settled it on her shoulder, picked up her keys and locked the door of her apartment. She glanced at the lift, the light unmoving on the seventh floor, before heading down four flights of narrow concrete stairs to where her moped was parked. Unfashionable it might be, but it was a breeze to park, allowed her to bypass traffic snarls, and had earned her a reputation for always being on time at work meetings.

And why was she thinking about something as trivial as reputation when Kim was dead? Dragging her thoughts back to the mundane, she weaved through morning traffic, her subconscious guiding her through brief gaps that emerged until a horn honked loudly from the vehicle in front of her.

She swerved away from the now-stalled delivery truck with inches to spare and a catch in her breath.

Focus, Lin. How many times had Grandfather's patient voice challenged her to do better, to be better?

Setting aside such trivialities as the distraction from grief she knew they were, Lin kept her eyes on the traffic and concentrated on what the early morning call from her boss meant. Joe Wang had taken her off the high profile case she'd been working and assigned her to a new one with an overseas agent.

"It's huge, Lin. The Australian Bureau wants our top female agent to team with their man and lead a joint operation to find and capture John Chan and close his network for good. You're the best we've got, but I realise it's a big ask given that your sister—"

Disgust and grief in equal measure rippled down her spine, churned her morning coffee in her stomach.

And then, larger and darker than both those dark emotions rose a primitive need for revenge. It towered over her like a giant wave that would either dump her, or that she could ride to shore and claim vengeance.

It had taken all her self-control, but one glance at the photo of Kim and she'd swallowed the bitter grief choking her and pushed out a response. "I accept, Joe. I will not let you down."

Or Kim.

How could she fail her sister when the legally sanctioned power of the Bureau gave her the right to take down Chan?

Power, right, and the resources of two countries' agencies.

For the first time since Kim was murdered, Lin felt the rush of blood through her veins and a tingling in her fingers. She was alive and she would exact vengeance and if it was thinly disguised as justice, she didn't care.

She parked her moped then walked towards the domed gardens. "Meet the Australian agent beside the first dragon on the right." Joe's directions replayed in her mind and she wondered about her boss' weird sense of humour. Weird and inconvenient when she considered how useless that direction would be if the agent entered via a different path to the one she had taken.

Whose bright idea was it to meet in the Cloud Forest Gallery? This Paul Rimmer, or Joe's?

She parked her moped and strode towards the soaring glass dome set beside the marina. Mid-morning light bounced off the structure in brilliant pinpricks that left her blinking. A horn tooted from a boat leaving the marina and she stopped to watch it. Shading her eyes she followed the line of the marina around to the distant Merlion statue, remembering the first time she and Kim had seen the half-lion, half-fish. Kim had run right up to the statue and laughed in delight when the wind changed direction and spray from the mouth-spouting fountain drenched her.

Everywhere Lin looked reminded her of Kim.

Gripping the strap of her bag, she turned her back on the Merlion and hurried towards her rendezvous. Entering the structure she checked off her exits before turning right to the dragon sculpture designated by Wang, one of many such artworks. Paul Rimmer should be waiting there for her.

Slowing her steps as she approached the empty viewing space beside the dragon, Lin pushed aside her annoyance at his tardiness. Emotions clouded caution and diminished situational awareness. She could afford neither luxury. She stopped beside the dragon and pulled out her phone, a useful tool when she had time to fill and places to reconnoitre.

Turning slowly as though taking a panoramic shot, she assessed every tall, brown-haired male. Few in the right age range were around at this time of morning. Completing one pass, she trained her phone camera on the viewing platform above the waterfall and zoomed in. Amid the groups gripping the handrails, a lone male stood near the rear end. She couldn't see enough detail beneath his peaked cap to be sure, but, if that was him, he was waiting near the wrong dragon sculpture.

Uncharacteristically dithering, Lin lowered her phone and scrolled back to the text message from her boss. It had to be the Australian who had made the mistake, not her. Not cautious, detail-focused Lin Tan, whose mistakes could be counted on the fingers of one hand.

"Hi. I'm wondering if you can tell me—"

Lin snatched a quick breath and glanced at the tall, olive-skinned man at her side. Engrossed in working out if she'd mistaken the meeting place, she hadn't noticed the approach of the stranger. Damn, she needed to get her brain back on task, and quickly.

Was this her contact?

Brown hair and an accent, but he looked different from the unsmiling photo Joe had sent.

And the accent seemed—off. More American than Australian, although Lin wasn't certain. He looked older than his thirties too, but in Lin's experience, foreigners were often older than the age she thought them to be.

The man held open a map of the garden complex and leaned towards her.

Too close.

"There are lots of dragon sculptures in here. Like this one next to you. Can you tell me anything about him? Or is he a she? How do you tell a boy dragon from a girl dragon?"

"I'm sorry but I do not know about dragons."

"Neither do I, but I know a place where they serve great drinks all day. What do you say, sweet thing?"

The man crowded her, filling her senses with an overpowering cologne that did little to mask a potent, underlying body odour.

Please don't let this be my contact. If this is Wang's idea of a joke . . .

Lin contemplated her options. A knee to the groin might be sufficient; but now she thought about it, he looked too soft for an agent. "I'd say—"

"She'll tell you to rack off, same as me if you keep annoying my friend. Hello, Lin. Sorry I'm late."

The voice was deep and the accent, now Lin compared it with the first man's, was quite different. Flatter, and with more of a drawl. More menacing in a steel-wrapped-in-velvet kind of way.

"Hi, Paul. You're late."

Paul Rimmer was taller than the pest now slinking away from her, and more like the agent she had imagined. Muscular, with a craggy, lived-in face and, if she were honest, rather intimidating. Blue eyes looked down from a six-foot-plus frame, but it was the look in his eyes rather than his height that flashed out a warning.

No wonder the sleaze had fled when Paul glared at him.

"Did you go to the wrong sculpture? There are many dragons within the dome."

"No. I knew this was the right one, but I don't hang around so obviously waiting for someone. Do you get hit on often?"

"Hit on? What is this?" A sneaking suspicion that he thought her skills lacking burred up Lin's fragile sense of self. Fragile because she'd just lost her only sister, not because . . .

Toughen up, Lin. Be a big girl and admit when you are wrong.

Her mother's words, years old but still relevant, brought Lin's head up. Truth was important and it began by being honest with herself.

"If you mean I wasn't paying attention, you are right."

Paul tipped his head. A small frown flickered across his forehead and vanished. "You weren't, but I meant do you have to put up with blokes like that pestering you all the time?"

Her gaze slipped away along the path taken by the other man. "Ah, bloke is a man, yes?" She nodded and filed the new word away. "Sometimes. And getting hit on is a common problem for women everywhere. Is it not the same in your country?"

"Sometimes." Paul echoed her response and glanced along the path.

Her gaze followed, spotting the man who had accosted her lurking at the furthest point of the curve.

Paul dropped a casual arm across her shoulders and stepped out of the lay-by area onto the main path. "Let's walk and talk. I hate staying in one place for long."

Lin lengthened her stride to match his long-legged steps. "Is it really necessary to put your arm around me?"

"It sends a message to that man. He was still watching you."

"And you thought I needed help?" The idea riled her. Just because she was slender, men often underestimated her—on occasion, to her advantage. "I'd have dropped him with one knee and an elbow. Maybe he was just wary of you. You're big and scary with that fierce look on your face."

"What look? I maintain a neutral expression when I'm on the job."

"You call that neutral? Even I'd be tempted to back off if you showed me that face, and I don't scare easy." Oddly, there was something about this stranger with whom she had to work for the next however long that reassured her.

And riled her. His glare on her behalf had been protective, but Lin needed no one. "I look out for myself."

"Great. But if the shit hits the fan, I'll have your back. It would be good to know I have a partner who also has mine."

"I am reliable, but I will show you. You don't have to take my word." Glancing at the water on her left, Lin decided it was time to take control.

My turf, my turn to lead.

"We need to share information and work out our approach. Where do you want to go? My office or a café?"

"Your home, my hotel room, I don't really care which, but don't read that the wrong way. Either is probably safer than your office."

Lin stopped and glared. "What are you suggesting?"

***

Paul turned and watched his new partner's expression as he asked the hard question. "Don't tell me you haven't considered the possibility of one or more of your colleagues being on Chan's payroll?"

Lin frowned and gripped the shoulder strap of her satchel while her gaze wandered up the graceful triple-legged structure of the casino up ahead. The elegant curving upper floors reminded her of a sailing ship. "I have considered this, but only in an abstract way. There has been no reason to consider it for real."

"Then consider it now. Is anyone spending above their income? Has anyone bought an expensive vehicle or home or been on exotic holidays beyond the reach of most agents? That's just for starters."

Lin tipped her face to the sun and half-closed her eyes. "There is no one who stands out as having more money than the salary earned by agents in my department, but I am aware it could still happen." She resumed strolling along beside the water.

He shoved his hands in his pockets and strolled beside her. Lin was nothing like he'd been expecting. Dark hair piled in a messy bun added a couple of inches to her height, but the top of her head barely reached his shoulder. Despite knowing size didn't matter, he had serious doubts how she would manage in close combat. But maybe the system here operated differently to what he was used to back home?

"Do you do much field work?"

Lin shrugged. "Yes. I prefer it to paperwork." She stopped and raised her phone towards the water, turning in a lazy three-sixty degrees rotation.

Paul ducked as the camera swept towards him. A hint of admiration mixed with concern about the partner he'd been given. She had the casual surveillance technique down pat, but was she really capable of having his back in a tight spot?

An image of Marcy slamming a knee in his groin at Jake's home popped into his head. With minimal training from Jake, she'd eluded him when neither knew if they could trust the other.

He eyed Lin's diminutive figure. Time would tell.

Or a workout session to test her mettle.

With the phone held to cover her mouth from passers-by, she asked, "Why do you ask about corruption in my office? Do you have information?"

Paul straightened once the camera passed him. "Nothing specific, but our target has eluded international efforts to capture him for the past two years and suddenly, last week, he's spotted here. Did you find an entry date, immigration details, anything to show when he arrived?"

"No, which my boss—"

"Wang?"

"Yes, Joe Wang. He believes the arrival was by way of Malaya. Covert marine, which is not impossible but it's difficult, unless—" Her mouth closed, tightened.

"Unless you've paid the right people not to look."

She nodded. "Can we continue our discussion at your hotel?" She walked a little faster in a direction of her choosing.

"Sure. I walked. Are you happy to—"

"I drove."

"Okay. Then we can take your car. Where did you park?"

Lin threw him a glare that dissolved into a smile. It tugged at the corners of her mouth, as she looked him up and down. "*Sia la*. This will be funny."

"Please tell me you don't have some puny little Smart car?"

Lin snorted and covered her mouth with her hand, but he was sure she was grinning and he was about to become the butt of her joke. "No Smart car. But you *can* ride with me."

They reached a tiny laneway hemmed in by tall buildings and Lin pointed at a spot behind an industrial bin. "Our ride is there."

"You couldn't fit a broomstick behind that—" Paul stepped past the end of the bin and stared in horror.

Worse than a Smart car, tinier than the VW he'd imagined her owning, a diminutive faded blue and white moped was tucked behind the bin.

"No one even thinks of looking for a vehicle to steal in such places." Lin giggled.

The sound was unexpected, small in itself, but huge in what it implied for the operation.

Great. Just fricking great.

Not only did he have a new partner to break in, but she was giggly, inexperienced, and their wheels—if it was possible to apply such a meaningful term to such a minuscule two-wheeler—was a moped. He'd be laughed out of the Bureau.

If he lived to tell the tale.

Chapter 3

Conscious of the big Australian perched precariously behind her Lin eased off the clutch and sent the moped rolling down the laneway. Paul Rimmer dwarfed her little moped. Fearful its acceleration would be compromised by her tall, broad-shouldered passenger, Lin waited longer than usual for a bigger break in the traffic.

The stop-start-stop of traffic—movement she seldom noticed when riding alone—was different with a passenger.

And not just any passenger.

Her new partner's long legs were like brackets holding her on the moped. She ran out of seat trying to edge further forward but each time they stopped, Paul dropped his feet onto the road. The action rolled him against her backside. Never had she felt more firmly balanced on her moped and yet so off her emotional balance at the same time.

Aware of her partner in ways that disturbed her, the ride to his hotel felt ten times longer than it was, and when she finally parked between bollards flanking the front door, she couldn't tell which of them jumped off first.

"That wasn't too difficult, was it?" Flicking a glance at him, there was some small measure of satisfaction at his grimace. Even if it probably had more to do with the challenge of perching on a machine dominated by his size than riding pillion behind her.

"I'll find out about a rental car before we do any more driving."

Some perverse desire to push his buttons took hold and her question slipped out. "Weren't you comfortable on Minnie?"

He ran his fingers through hair barely long enough to be

ruffled. "Don't tell me you named that excuse for transportation after a cartoon mouse?"

She shrugged. "Minnie—minimum space on the road. It fits, and Minnie got you here safely."

"True, and I can see it works for you, but I prefer a full size motorbike to that kiddie toy. I'll hire a car."

The doorman slid a glance at Lin and the hint of a sneer crossed his face. He wiped it off before he opened the glass door and smiled unctuously at a tourist couple exiting the hotel.

Recognising that look and hating it, Lin knew she should ignore what it implied. *Prostitute.*

Anger ripped through her and she took a step towards the man before common sense prevailed. "Maybe you should go in first. Tell me your room number and I'll follow you up."

"Is there a problem with us going in together?"

Her gaze flicked to the doorman.

Paul's followed. His nostrils flared and his big hands clenched by his side.

Was he annoyed with her? She'd already made one rookie mistake in allowing that man in the Cloud Forest Gallery to approach her unnoticed. Lin clasped her hands. She was off her game today. Wang had cautioned her about returning to work so quickly.

I need to work. It helps me forget.

How stupid that comment was. As if work could make her forget Kim's death. On the other hand, leaving her mind flapping like a landed fish could get her killed.

Schooling both mind and expression, she met his gaze. "No problem."

Paul draped an arm over her shoulders and this time, she slipped her arm around his waist as they entered the building, ignoring the doorman.

***

Paul hadn't imagined the doorman's reaction. Anger had flickered in Lin's eyes, but she'd remained poised and graceful.

Graceful? Where did that come from?

He set the random thought aside, attributing it to missed sleep and feeling antsy about working with a new partner. And not just any new partner, but one who was supposed to be top in her field. One who, from her reactions so far, was far from experienced and was also, if he was noticing her grace and slender figure, a distraction.

Distractions were dangerous but now he'd acknowledged its existence, he could control his reaction. Keep his focus where it needed to be. But despite Lin's claim, "I prefer it to paperwork", and the neat use of her phone as she surveyed the area, he'd seen little evidence of field experience. And that made her a liability.

Reserving judgement until she'd brought him up to date on the local situation, he walked into the hotel. If he still thought the same after their information sharing session he'd phone her superior and demand a replacement partner . . .

He tweaked his tired brain. Perhaps *requesting* a new partner would be a more diplomatic first step.

Stepping on the toes of the local station chief on his first day wouldn't win him the right sort of assistance.

As they passed beneath a line of air conditioning vents blasting cool air into the lobby, strands of Lin's hair rose, wafting a sweet, delicately spiced perfume towards him. The scent had teased his nose during their ride to the hotel, another part of the distraction Lin posed. They crossed to the bank of lifts and stood to the side, waiting. He glanced at his new partner, but already his mind's eye could fill in details.

Almond-shaped eyes the same brown as the dark chocolate he loved, but rationed for himself, looked back. Her lips were a soft pink with a hint of gloss, currently tipped up in a socially polite smile as she turned her gaze to the floor number display. The lift pinged softly, announcing its arrival. The doors slid open and a couple exited.

He dropped his arm from her shoulders and put a hand on the inner edge of the lift door and held it open. "After you."

Once inside, the doors closed. He reached past Lin, pressed his key card to the reader and stabbed the button for the seventh floor. Her scent tickled his nose, a little exotic and perfectly suited to this woman—if she wasn't his new partner and he wasn't depending on her to have his back.

Pushing back against his growing awareness of Lin's total femininity, he breathed through his mouth and watched the digital floor number display creeping higher.

She's a damned nuisance, and a distraction. This will never work.

But it had to. He had a job to do and a partner whose moves he didn't know, and couldn't anticipate. Of course he was watching her closely. The sooner he learned what made her tick and how she thought the more chance they had of not getting each other killed.

Get into her mindset or get rid of her.

Familiarity required time and getting close.

He breathed in, a deep breath laden with his frustration and her perfume.

Either that, or tomorrow he'd have a new partner, preferably male and to hell with Jake's preference for mixed gender teams.

"When we're done here, is there somewhere we can work out?" His tone was growly, but minimum civility was all he could manage.

He needed to work off some of his pent up, frustrated energy. How did Lin's self-defence skills stack up?

Despite her delicate appearance, he wouldn't underestimate another woman in a hurry. Tamsin had always taken care of herself, and even Marcy had been able to catch him off guard. Would Lin manage to drop him if he let his attention stray?

Her expression gave nothing away, but her gaze bore a hard edge.

Was she still thinking about the doorman? Christ, if she carried a grudge like that, she'd be no use on the job.

She pinned him with a hard look and he realised she'd moved into the front corner of the lift, beneath—*and out of direct line of*—the security camera. And now he thought about it, she'd kept her head down or turned away from the camera when they entered. Maybe she had some skills after all.

"Official workout, or would you prefer to stay off the radar as much as possible?"

Gratified by this acknowledgement of his concerns about the security of her office, Paul leaned against a poster advertising happy hour drinks and nibbles in the rooftop lounge. "Off the radar. So you agree there's a possibility someone on your force is compromised?"

"It is always possible. Dealing with the cartel is like wrestling a giant octopus. You think you've got it in a chokehold and an arm grabs you from behind. The less visible you are, the better."

An electronic voice announced their arrival at the seventh floor and no more was said until they reached his hotel room.

Setting a finger to his lips, they stepped into the room and he closed the door behind them, pulled out a pocket-sized bug detector, switched it on and swept the room. Lin remained out of the way beside the door. Reassured the room was clean, he drew the curtains across the windows. "Help yourself to the mini-bar."

"Not on duty thanks."

He raised an eyebrow, shrugged, and took out two bottles of water. Opening one, he chugged down half the contents before setting the bottle on the small breakfast table beside the unopened bottle. "Me either."

Lin frowned and moved to sit at the table.

With a sigh, Paul leaned on the back of the other chair and pinned her with a look, half-frustration and half—*nope, it's all frustration*. "Look, Lin, I'm guessing being tasked with an assignment like ours and getting dumped with a new partner doesn't fill you with joy either."

Her eyes narrowed the tiniest bit.

Welcome to my world, sister.

He dialled back the grouchy tone, aiming for conciliatory. After all, they had been selected by their respective department chiefs. He would give her a chance.

One chance only.

"But for better or worse, we're in this together. Our goal is to make this partnership work smoothly so we catch the bad guy."

"This, I understand, and also, I understand we don't have much time to learn each other's methods."

"I'll help you all I can, but you can't let anything else distract you."

Her gaze didn't waver from his but her chin rose. "I will help you. Singapore is my home, my city. I know its odd places and dark spaces, and I know the people. I am also up to speed on—John Chan."

"Local knowledge helps, but are you clear that I'm lead here. I call the shots. What I say, you do without question. Do you understand that, Agent Tan?"

He watched a tangle of emotions cross her face. Had she expected to take the lead? Was she one of the new intake of agents who thought they knew it all in their first year out? Christ, how old was she? Twenty-three, twenty-four?

Looking at her lovely face marred by a mutinous downturn of her mouth, he felt old and jaded. And pissed off at having to lay down the law on what should have been clear to her when she agreed to the assignment.

"Agreed? Because if you don't, we end this arrangement now and I'll request a new partner."

Mutiny morphed into a flash of surprise before she composed her expression and nodded once. "I agree."

Holding in his sigh of relief, Paul sat at the table and unfolded a map of the city, spreading it across the table.

"I agree—unless you make a wrong call. I will tell you if that happens."

There wasn't a giggle or a grin in sight. Just a professional, neutral expression, anchored by an intense gaze. And that worried him almost as much. As bad, if not worse than partnering a rookie would be babysitting an overzealous, ambitious rookie with an agenda that threatened to derail his assignment. Damn the computer glitch at HQ that had sent him her photo and failed to attach information about her.

"Is there something you're not telling me?"

Her eyes widened a fraction, but her gaze didn't falter. "Like what?"

"Like, are you planning on using this case to make a name for yourself or try for a promotion? Because looking for glory takes your eye off the ball. With a target like Chan, it's deadly."

Anger flickered through her eyes. She slapped her hands on the table and stood. Faced him down. "You think I'm some rookie because of that man at the dome and a single moment of inattention. That was poorly done, true, but nothing for you to worry about. How old do you think I am, hey?"

"Twenty-two or three?"

"I've been in the department for ten years. If I was chasing *another* promotion, Joe Wang would have to retire and he's not about to. I'm his deputy and I'm good at what I do. And what I do, what I *want*, Agent Rimmer, is to find John Chan and bring him and his filthy cartel to justice. You remember what that is,

Rimmer? The reason both of us do the work we do."

His jaw tightened, and irritation slithered through his empty stomach. But there was passion and a tense focus behind Lin's anger. It shouldn't have reassured him, but they were qualities he could work with. He wasn't about to say he was happy to be working with her. But respect crept up on him. "Just so long as we're on the same page."

"I do not expect you to trust me, not yet. Nor do I trust you. We must show through actions that we can depend on each other as equal partners. Agreed?"

"I expect nothing less. Now fill me on Chan's activities and known locations."

Lin perched on the edge of her chair and drew the map closer. Unerringly her finger settled on a section of dense streets and lanes. "I'll start with the Geylang district . . ."

Chapter 4

The room Lin had chosen for their training session lacked air conditioning. It was private, but, in the tropical early afternoon heat, the air lay thick and heavy. Paul's foot slipped on the wooden floor. He blinked, trying to clear the sweat from his eyes.

Thwack!

He landed on his backside, rolled and felt the swish of Lin's leg rushing past his ear. He grabbed her foot and flipped her over. By rights she should have landed facedown, but where he expected his knee to land in the small of her back, he hit the wooden floorboards.

Lin was back on her feet and in a fighting stance, her right foot forward.

He'd have sworn she was right hand dominant, but she had switched sides and thrown him off. And if he couldn't keep up with her tricks, he was getting old.

Tricks, be damned. She's better than me.

Paul blinked sweat from his eyes and eyed off the distance. Taking into account her speed and shorter height, he feinted to her offside, spun back and grabbed her foot as it shot out to clip his ear. He tipped her onto her back and pinned her to the floor. "Oldest trick in the book, Lin."

Beneath his body, hers was slim and her skin was slick with sweat. She looked delicate, but his ear still rung from the flying kick she'd landed early on. A kick he should have seen coming, but once again, he'd underestimated his opponent.

His small and very feminine opponent whose skills in combat surpassed his. The knowledge would have lowered his mood when he started training and had everything to prove. Now, he was pleased to discover her skillset.

Pleased. And momentarily distracted by the way their bodies aligned as he held her captive.

She wriggled trying to escape his pinning hold and the faint fragrance of lily-of-the-valley with a hint of spice tickled his nose. Perfume that was somehow familiar, but richer, more tropical, more vibrant.

Like the woman whose body writhed beneath his.

Writhing. He liked writhing and skin slick from exercise. Distracted by inappropriate thoughts of Lin, his grip on her wrists slipped.

Her knee hit his groin. His grip barely loosened, but Lin slipped out like an eel and stood looking down at him. "Older trick from an older book, Rimmer."

Her skin glistened and her singlet top clung to sweet curves, none of which made it any easier for him to concentrate. Loose strands of hair had fallen from her untidy bun, but her eyes were bright as she bounced on both feet. "More, or you had enough?"

Too late, he realised an inconvenient truth that reflected poorly on him. While Lin's victory in their bout was largely due to her superior skill set, he'd given her an extra advantage when he lost concentration, lost focus, and started thinking about bedding her.

Not going to complicate the assignment like that.

He'd never thought about previous partners like that—not even Tam with whom he'd shared a fake engagement as part of their undercover roles—and he wasn't about to start now. Shaking his head, he rose and extended a hand.

Lin looked at it like she had no idea what to do with it.

"Good session." He waited. "Don't you shake hands with your opponent at the end of a bout?"

She frowned and lowered her hands from their defensive

position. "No. We bow, like this."

Paul half expected her to offer a *rei,* a Japanese bow, but Lin gave him a Chinese hold fist salute. He noted her graceful movements before the significance of her choice of bow registered. Accepting her compliment that they were equals while knowing her skill set was superior, Paul returned the bow. "Where did you learn to fight like that? Not at the academy."

Lin picked up her towel and wiped off her face and arms. "My grandfather is a master of martial arts. He trained my uncles and aunts, and my mother, and he trained me and my sister."

"I underestimated you. You gave no clue what you're capable of. That's clever."

"Showing off is the fool's idea of glory."

"Bruce Lee said that." Paul mopped his face, tossed the towel aside and reached for his shirt. "Are you a fan of his movies?"

"Yes. I have watched them many times. My grandfather knew him. They were both students of Yip Man. They learned together, practised together, and remained friends until Lee's death. Are you hungry?" Lin tossed her towel into her training bag and stood, hands on hips watching as he pulled on his joggers and double-knotted the laces.

He picked up his watch and checked the time before slipping it on. Nearly two o'clock. "Food would be good. Your choice." He stood and looked at Lin.

Slender and graceful. Now he knew she had steel springs in her limbs and a flexibility he couldn't begin to match. Not that he impressed easily. He'd never considered himself sexist, but Lin was the third woman to surprise him with her abilities. After working with Tamsin, he should have known better. And after being bested by her twin, Marcy, with no field training other than a few moves Jake had taught her, he *really* should have known better.

Did underestimating beautiful women make him a slow learner or a bad agent? Or had his eldest sister been right when she'd told him that growing up with only sisters for playmates had made him overprotective of all women?

That he could live with.

"We'll get street food. You like hot and spicy?" She pulled on a loose flowery pink dress and cinched it with a narrow belt before tugging off her hair tie. Flipping her dark hair forward, she worked the shining inky mass into tamed sleekness and tied it back up into a high ponytail.

It was a small, intimate action, one that meant nothing in itself, but it was also a sign of trust.

Nothing like bonding over a training session. He grinned. *Bonding, or getting beaten?*

"Hey, Rimmer, you get hit in the head or something?"

Paul pulled his mind back to the present. "Hotter and spicier the better. Bring it on."

Lin's lips quirked up and a hint of a smirk flashed across her face before she turned and grabbed her satchel. "You talk big, but let's see if you know what spicy really means in Singapore."

He had a feeling hot and spicy food would have nothing on Lin Tan.

***

Usually Lin felt energised and relaxed after a training bout, but working with Rimmer had left her tense and with a thrumming awareness of her new partner.

Rimmer. That name suited him better than his first name. It sounded like the big motorbike he preferred, purring along an open road.

She could see it in her mind. Rimmer would drive and she would ride pillion and hang onto him, sitting close no matter how big the seat was. Sitting close, and leaving her grief behind in a stream of dust.

Because, for the hour they had trained, and for the seconds he'd pinned her to the floor, she hadn't thought about Kim, or the grief clawing up her guts like a black devil creature. Something about the big Australian sidestepped all that raw emotion and sparked an attraction she longed to embrace.

Longed for, but knew she mustn't.

But how alive he'd made her feel for that brief window of time.

A scooter came towards them down the narrow laneway. Lin dodged out of the way and collided with Rimmer as he ducked around a protruding canopy so far above her head she hadn't noticed it.

The contact sent tingles down her arm and a ridiculous impulse to put her arm around his waist as she had back at the hotel.

She stepped away.

"*Paiseh.* Sorry." Grateful she didn't blush, still she felt heat creep into her face.

Silly woman to be giving such awareness to a brush of skin on skin.

Especially after Rimmer's body had pinned hers to the floor not long ago.

Now she was right back at the point where her distraction had started.

"Turn right here." Her short tone bordered on rude, but the *Rimmer distraction* was potent. Neither of them could afford it. Not with stakes as high as they were playing for.

Not when this chance to trap Chan was her best shot at avenging her sister's murder.

Attraction was fleeting.

Revenge was forever.

Chapter 5

As street food went, Lin's choice was a winner. Paul reached for the last chilli prawn on the plate, paused and looked at Lin. "Are you sure you don't want it?"

"Sure. I'm impressed you haven't broken a sweat. These are the spiciest prawns in the city."

"I'm sweating, just not from the food, but it's good. Does the humidity get much worse than this?" The air hung heavier than before, so thick he imagined chopping a pathway through it to escape. His shirt stuck in a line down his back and sweat prickled on his scalp.

"Maybe a storm's coming, but it won't get any cooler until late, and then only a little." Lin meticulously wiped her fingers on her paper serviette and scrunched it onto the empty plate. She picked up the small cardboard container of pineapple juice and finished the contents, then set it on its side on top of the serviette. "So, where do you want to start looking for our man?"

Paul swallowed the last mouthful of prawn. If only all assignments came with food this good. He wiped his fingers and thought about possibilities. "Have you established any patterns of movement for him?"

"Not yet. It's frustrating because we've had only a couple of sightings and not a single completed journey."

"Do you mean your agents lost him?"

"He disappears. Last stakeout we had both front and back exits covered, but he never came out."

Paul rubbed his thumb across his bottom lip. "We lost him in Sydney two years ago in a multi-sting assault. I'm as sure as I can be that he was in the brothel when we surrounded it. No way out, all exits covered, but when we got to his playroom—"

Damn, he'd sworn never to use that term after finding the young dead girl in that chamber of horrors. Paul cleared his throat. "We think he escaped through a secret passage behind a mirror. Left a young woman dead. The passage led to a sheer drop into the harbour. Nobody heard or saw him leave, but unless he's a ghost, that was the only possible way out."

"Unless you were wrong and he wasn't there in the first place." Lin rested one hand on top of the other on the table, but one finger tapped small double beats on her bottom hand while she gazed past his shoulder. Was that how she processed information? "Maybe that's where we need to start."

"What? In Sydney?"

Her gaze snapped back to his, pinned him and drilled in for every nugget of information he had. "Am I right in assuming the dead girl died during a particular sex act?"

"Yes. Plastic bag over her head, and not the first time he's done it. The madam of the brothel spilled details about his— predilections. BDSM at the violent end of the spectrum, she said. Have you found evidence of that here too?"

Lin's lips parted and a suspicion of moisture gleamed in her eyes.

Fascinated, he noticed a convulsive swallow ripple down her throat. But now wasn't the time to go easy on his new partner. He leaned forward, refusing to let her look away. "You have, and it was pretty rough, wasn't it?"

Pressing her lips together, Lin sat straighter. Her chin rose and an awful premonition that she'd known Chan's latest victim made Paul's gut clench.

"I'm sorry to push you on this, but—"

"John Chan killed my sister."

***

She'd known this would happen at some point. Had thought

she was prepared for the question to arise. Had thought about how to share the revelation about Kim's death.

It shouldn't have been so difficult, but the words fell like stones into a pond. They fell into a pool of silence with one giant splash that faded into ripples, disturbing the surface briefly; forever changing what lay below.

A landscape of loss.

There was no other way to frame her sorrow.

Sympathy followed shock in Rimmer's eyes and all but undid her tenuous self-control.

His hand reached over and covered hers. Hot on her suddenly cool skin. "I'm sorry, Lin. When did she die?"

"Ten days ago."

Surprise.

Frown.

Hand tightening its hold.

"Ten . . . Should you—I mean, are you okay to be back at work—especially on *this* case—so soon after her death?"

Her boss had posed the same question and worn a similar look of concern when she fronted up for work the day following Kim's cremation.

Her stomach clenched, her lungs worked double-time, starved of oxygen. No, she wasn't fine, and doubt hovered on the edge of her mind like a typhoon on a summer horizon. Doubt would lose her this chance to atone. She stiffened her spine, stilled her unquiet hands, and met his gaze. "I'm doing something useful."

"But he killed your sister. How can you focus on the investigation?"

"Who better than me? Chan killed my sister. I will track him down and make him pay." She pulled away from Rimmer's hand. Anger—righteous, dark and all-consuming—whirled in her mind.

"Listen to yourself. You sound like a character in a Bruce Lee movie vowing revenge. Chan needs to be caught and brought in to face all the charges against him. There are outstanding warrants for his arrest in Australia as well as here. You can't kill him, Lin."

"Who said anything about killing him? I want justice for Kim."

"Naturally. But your desire for vengeance might blind you to danger where Chan is concerned."

Rimmer's concerns were legitimate. A personal vendetta against Chan could turn dangerous for her partner as well as her if she stopped paying attention for even one moment. But Rimmer and this joint co-operative assignment were her best chance of winning justice for Kim.

She couldn't lose this chance.

Hot on the heels of her doubts, aware of anger and fear rising within like a tsunami, threatening to swamp her control, Lin pressed her hands against the cool table top. If she lost control now when they were simply talking about Chan, Rimmer would quickly reassign her and find a new partner.

I'd dump a partner blinded by personal connection to a target.

Sucking in a deep breath, slowly breathing it out, she met his eyes. "I can keep a cool head, but understand this, Rimmer. Kim is the reason I will move heaven and earth to bring Chan to justice. My grief will not make me lose focus. I will use it to make me strong and I will not give up."

He sat back and folded his arms, watching her without speaking for what felt like forever. Eventually he leaned forward and rested his arms on the table. "Maybe. Grief is sneaky. It slides in and trips you when you aren't expecting it. With an enemy like Chan, grief can be a dangerous distraction. You have to be mentally tough to overcome your grief and, at the same time, not lose focus. Tell me honestly, Lin. Do you *know* you can do this? Could you face Chan and not pull the trigger?"

"I can and I will." For several long, heavy beats of her heart, she held Rimmer's hard gaze.

"I'm holding you to that promise." But his expression put her on notice. One slip up and she'd be off the case.

Relief coursed through her now Rimmer had given her the chance to continue. Turning the conversation away from her, she tipped her head to one side. "You sound like you know about grief from personal experience? Who have you lost, Rimmer?"

His gaze flicked away and a muscle in his cheek twitched. "My grandma. We were pretty close."

"Was she sick or very old?"

His gaze locked with hers. "Old enough to know better." Bitter words, bitter tone, and then he sighed. "No, I shouldn't say that, but she was killed in a damned stupid accident."

"What happened?"

"To celebrate her eightieth birthday she decided to go tandem sky-diving. The parachute malfunctioned. Both Gran and the instructor were killed."

Lin set her free hand on top of his and shook her head. "I'm sorry for your loss, Rimmer."

"It's almost five years ago and sometimes I still find myself reaching for my phone to call her and share something that's happened." His gaze dropped to their joined hands and hers followed.

A hand sandwich. The silly thought floated through her mind, which was better than the idea that she'd never truly get over her sister's death. It was too hard to think about the lonely years ahead. Better to focus on Rimmer's hand between hers. The comforter comforted.

Except the tingling in her skin had nothing to do with comfort and everything to do with attraction.

Startled by the discovery that Kim's memory had slipped from her mind at the touch of Rimmer's hand, Lin pulled away. Her hand rose to rest on her sister's jade pendant. She hadn't been able to save Kim, but she refused to let anyone distract her from avenging her sister's death.

Surging to her feet, she slung her satchel over her shoulder. "We're wasting time on things we cannot change. Come. We'll start in Geylang."

"Lin?"

"What?"

"Remember what I told you this morning?"

"I am focused and—"

"Not that. The other point I made—I lead, you follow?"

Away from Rimmer's touch, Lin could think, and feel. Away from Rimmer, she felt annoyed. He was right, but still . . . "You're one bossy man, you know that, Rimmer? So what do you want to do?"

"I want to see where your sister died. If you aren't up to doing that with me, just take me there and point me in the right direction."

Her breath stalled in her chest.

Where Kim died. Where she breathed her last.

Did she cry out for me? For Mama?

A hand touched her shoulder and she looked up into Rimmer's blue eyes. Both his touch and his gaze grounded her. Reassured her he'd be there.

"You don't have to do this, Lin. I can request another operative if you've changed your mind."

He's going to take me off the case if I don't. I can't let that happen.

Breathe in—hold. Breathe out—and look him squarely in the eye.

She shook her head. "I will not change my mind. I will take

you, show you where—"

"I don't think Wang should have put you on this case. He shouldn't have put you in the position of having to relive finding your sister."

"He wouldn't have assigned me if he didn't believe I can do this. He has given me his trust."

Meeting Rimmer's gaze, conscious that she must not fall at the first hurdle, she dug deep and pinned her resolve to a spine of steel. "I gave you and him my word. I will not fail Wang, I will not fail you."

She took a step, stopped and looked back at Rimmer. "I will not fail my sister."

He nodded. "Where do we start?"

Part of her mind registered the irony, but only a very small part. The rest of her body and mind was consumed with bricking up the gaping hole grief had punched through her heart. She held Kim's jade pendant and silently begged her sister for strength to carry her through.

"Where I said—in Geylang."

Chapter 6

"This is Geylang. A red light area. I found Kim in there." From the opposite side of the narrow street, Lin nodded towards number sixty-five.

A pair of bulbous red Chinese lanterns hung either side of a plate glass sliding door, but the building looked shabbier in the late afternoon light than in the early hours of the morning when the call had come in. She'd taken little notice of her surroundings at the time. Looking at the place where her sister had died, it made even less sense that Kim had been here, let alone in that room, doing—

She ran her hands over suddenly chilled skin. The thought of what Kim had been doing with Chan was unbearable.

Wrong way around. It's what he was doing to her that makes me sick.

"And that building is one of Chan's brothels?"

Lin struggled to push the monosyllable past the lump in her throat. "Yes."

"Is it legal?"

Rimmer had been right to worry. Simply standing in the laneway outside the building had sent her mind jumping straight into the ugly past.

Dragging her imagination from the awful scene replaying like a horror movie in her mind, Lin reverted to facts.

She could forget, or at least drown out the ugliness of that night in a sea of facts. Unemotional. Quantifiable. Boring.

"The Geylang trade is legal in Singapore. Sex workers get a licence to operate, but they have to attend monthly check-ups to make sure they are free of sex-related diseases before the licence is renewed."

He raised a hand. "I'm not planning on visiting as a customer, Lin."

Two potbellied men exited from the brothel next door to the one they were observing. "Those men, they would never get sex for free, but you, you wouldn't ever need to pay for sex or go to a brothel anyw—" She slapped a hand over her mouth and waited for Rimmer to tell her off. "I'm sorry. Please forget I said that."

Rimmer chuckled. "No way I'll forget you said that."

"I didn't mean to offend."

"Lin, you just told me—in a roundabout way—that you think I'm hot. What man would take offence at that?"

His grin remained in place while Lin's face flamed. "I cannot think of you as hot. You are my partner."

"True, and it's not a good idea to act on an attraction when we're on the job, but for the record, I think you're hot too."

Her gaze slid away. A curl of heat licked in her belly. Heat that was sensual and promising . . . And distracting.

Just like that, with a smile and a hit of humour, Rimmer had made her feel better, made her forget her awful memories. For a moment she'd felt almost—normal.

Had he played up to her like that deliberately?

"You're a nice guy, Rimmer—" Out of the corner of her eye she spotted a familiar face exiting the building they'd come to check out. Grabbing Rimmer's arm, she pulled him until his back was to the building across the road.

"What have you seen, Lin?"

His gaze appeared to be on goods on display inside, but she was pretty sure he was watching the reflection in the glass of the shop window.

All credit to Rimmer, he was quick on the uptake. "The man in the yellow shirt, he drives for Chan."

Rimmer drew his phone from his pocket and held it up.

"Smile, sweetheart."

Lin pulled a face and played along.

Rimmer turned his attention to the window as he fiddled with his phone. "Got him."

Lin moved closer and peered at the screen. "Want to follow him?"

Rimmer nodded but paused to look at the reflection in the window. "No, he's coming back. Looks like he's going back into the brothel. Make like you want something from the shop." Aloud, he said, "Want something to eat?"

Raising her voice she took his hand and tugged him towards the shop door. "Sure. Come on, babe."

Once inside Rimmer picked up a packet of mints, barely seeing the promotional tag: 'Top quality for best Singapore Sting' – and carried it to the counter by the door.

The cashier took Rimmer's money and grinned at Lin. "Sure you only want one packet? These are very good, satisfaction guaranteed."

Busy tracking the driver's return to the brothel, Lin barely turned her head. "One packet's plenty if you know what you're doing."

Slowly they left the shop and paused on the footpath while Rimmer put away his wallet and fiddled with his phone.

She counted the seconds until the driver re-emerged carrying a small gift box tied with a red bow, and then they followed him, keeping to the footpath on the opposite side of the lane.

Rimmer ripped open the packet of mints and offered it to Lin. "Want one?"

She took one without thinking and put it into her mouth. It fizzed on her tongue with a sweet heat. "He's headed towards that silver limo. Come on."

Rimmer popped two mints into his mouth. "Not bad.

What's the Singapore Sting that bloke mentioned? Sounds like a cocktail."

Suddenly aware of the mint in her mouth and the use to which prostitutes put it, Lin couldn't meet Rimmer's eyes. "One of the specialties of the district."

"I'm intrigued. Tell me about it over dinner. Our man's getting into his car. Can you see if anyone's inside?"

Lin peered at the back window and shook her head. "The window tinting is too dark. There could be an orgy going on inside and nobody would know." Crunching the mint, she swallowed and prayed Rimmer would forget to ask about the specialty. Thinking about sex was one thing. Describing the intimate act using the mint to Rimmer—out of the question.

Rimmer took her hand and tugged her along the narrow footpath towards where he'd parked his hire car. "The driver picked something up from the brothel. We'll work on the assumption that he's delivering it to Chan's home. We'll follow and hope this is the break we've been waiting for."

***

Sweat trickled down Paul's back and he thought longingly of a cold beer. He didn't foresee downing one any time soon. "Aren't you glad we've got air conditioning in the hire car?" He fished in his pocket for the keys and unlocked the doors. Hotter than Sydney when he flew out, and more humid than Gran's home outside of Townsville, Singapore's heat weighed heavy on his mind and body. Frankly, he preferred winter and snow to tropical heat unless he was surfing.

"Yeah, well, you might be pleased with your air conditioning when we're sitting in peak hour traffic, but I'll bet you'll soon regret not letting me bring Minnie. She can cut through the traffic and we wouldn't lose this guy."

Paul slid into his seat and waited for Lin to shut her door before turning the air-con on full blast and then pulling out into the lane. He couldn't imagine being crammed behind Lin on her tiny scooter while they tailed their quarry. Not even the thought of her slim body pressed against his would entice him back onto steaming bitumen roads amid the traffic fumes. "That was lucky, you spotting Chan's driver."

Lin folded her arms and hunched a shoulder.

So what if she's annoyed? But the rental car was better camouflage for a tail. "We won't lose him. Besides, the size of me on Minnie . . . we'd stick out like a sore thumb."

"We're going to lose him. Have you ever driven through Singapore at peak hour?"

"I've never visited Singapore. Just transited through the airport. Odd, I know, but work took me more often through Bangkok."

"Huh. Well, believe me, Minnie would have been much better for this job." She pointed at a solid bumper to bumper line of cars filling the road ahead. "You'll never break into that line of traffic."

"Want to bet?"

She snorted. "Sure. You do that and next training session, I'll take you on with one hand tied behind my back and I'll still beat you."

"Hmm, oh ye of little faith; watch and learn." He rolled the car forwards, angling in behind one car and inching the bumper bar into the narrow gap between two cars.

"What are you doing, Rimmer?"

"Merging."

A horn honked from the car he was cutting in on, but Rimmer kept edging into the slowly widening space.

"But you don't have a right of way."

"How is that relevant? Chan's driver didn't either and he's four cars ahead. Keep your eye on that vehicle." Offering a casual wave of thanks to the driver he'd cut off, he slid his car into the line of traffic and glanced at Lin. "You were saying . . ."

"That is not polite."

"But it's effective. Do you drive *politely* when you're on Minnie? I'll bet you weave in and out of traffic, don't you?"

"Yes, but I slip into small gaps. I don't take someone else's space."

"Would you rather I let our link to Chan get away by being polite?" Stirring Lin was light entertainment as the line of traffic crept forward and stopped him drumming his fingers on the steering wheel. Sure they weren't going anywhere fast, but neither was Chan's driver.

She half-turned in her seat and opened her mouth to reply, but shook her head. "Of course not."

Suddenly she thumped his shoulder. "Left. Turn left now, quick."

Rimmer spotted the rear of the silver limo as it turned up a side street and passed the building line out of their sight. "Damn it, I can't turn. There's two cars in the way."

And no space to get around.

Lin pushed open her door and jumped out. "Pick me up when you get out of the traffic." She slammed the door and bolted, leaving him to follow.

He had to give it to her; her reaction might make the difference between losing the trail and finding Chan. It was the sort of thing Tam might have done. What he would have done if she'd been the one driving.

The sense of familiarity in her reaction was reassuring as he edged closer to the car ahead.

"Come on, you lot, move." For all the good his growling did he might as well not have spoken.

Ahead of him, the mint-green Smart car inched forward. Through the rear window he watched as the young female driver opened the mirror on her sunshade and applied her lipstick.

Rimmer eyed the gap between a street sign and the parked car beside him and the tail of the Smart car in front. Hanging back while it made a kangaroo hop forwards, he waited, taking slow breaths, assessing the gap. "Come on, sweetie, stop farting around with your makeup and roll forward just a little bit more . . ."

The green car moved and Rimmer swung the wheel, clearing the Smart car, the parked car, and the sign by bare centimetres. His wheels bumped over the kerb and the side mirror snapped closed with a sharp crack, but then he was through and accelerating down the side street.

Scanning both the pedestrian path and street ahead, he exhaled a gusty breath. There was no sign of either Lin or the silver limo. If the driver had taken off, Lin should be waiting nearby.

Unless she'd found another way to stay on their tail?

What would she do?

He'd worked with Tamsin for a while before he'd been able to predict her reactions. He'd only met Lin this morning and had no idea how his new partner might think, her pursuit on foot notwithstanding.

His gaze passed over a rack of bright yellow rental bikes and snapped back to an empty space on the far end. He glanced at the passenger side floor. Lin's daypack sagged in the corner, but she'd grabbed her satchel before she bolted from the car to give chase. She had her bag so he could assume she had her credit card and phone. Loving her scooter as she did and praising its ability to negotiate traffic, the next best thing was probably an electric bike.

Accelerating along the side road, Paul mused. Maybe he did know something about Lin after all. Keeping a lookout for both a yellow bike and a silver limo, he pulled up at the red light at the next crossroads. Heavy traffic made his chances of seeing either low to nothing.

Damn it. Now he'd lost both Lin and Chan's driver. He

waited for the lights to change and drove straight ahead for want of a better direction. Cruising along the side street, he was looking for somewhere to pull off the road and check his whereabouts when his phone rang.

He pulled it out of his pocket and glanced at the screen. Lin. "Where are you?"

"Rimmer, it's me, Lin."

"Where the hell are you?"

A horn honked through the phone speaker and cut out some of her reply. ". . . did you?"

"I lost you. Say again."

"Turn left at the first set of lights and then first right and keep going." Scraping sounds of metal on metal shrieked through the phone, followed by a clatter and a grunt.

Like a bike crashing on the road. And a body hitting the ground?

"What's happened? Lin, are you okay?"

Lin's soft "Damn it," was followed by a swiftly indrawn breath. "Sure, sure. Car pulled out in front of me, but I must stop and exchange details. Try to catch Chan's driver, Rimmer. He's still travelling straight ahead. Stopped at lights a block ahead. Hurry." The call ended abruptly.

He tossed the phone on the passenger seat. How lucky their timing had been.

Again.

His scalp tingled and his grip tightened on the steering wheel.

Or is this unlikely coincidence dressed up as luck?

If he turned left just ahead and then took the next right, he would be on the road behind Chan's car.

But the coincidence preyed on his mind. He could leave Lin behind and follow the car, maybe even catch up to it, but that would separate him from Lin.

'Divide and conquer' wasn't just some old saying. It worked, and Paul wouldn't put it past Chan's network—or a corrupt official in high places—to know of his arrival and partnership with Lin.

Was it possible this scenario was playing out as planned by their quarry?

Needing answers, needing to find out if he was being played, Paul accelerated around the corner against the red light. The engine roared, but he made it a whisker ahead of oncoming traffic. At the next intersection, he got around on the tail end of the changing lights, but seconds stretched into minutes when Lin might be in danger.

He cruised along the street, spotted Lin at the side of the road ahead, and slowed. Her rental bike lay on its side, the front wheel bent. Along the side of the car she'd run into, a scrape revealed what had happened.

Paul's gaze flicked over the driver of the car. Nothing about him seemed out of place. He was dressed much like the locals they'd seen in Geylang and those at the street food stall. The man turned away, reaching for something from the side pocket of the driver's door. Was that bulge beneath his shirt a gun?

Paul reached for the small pistol in his calf holster. His finger rested beside the trigger.

Lin must have said something to the other driver. He turned back to her with what looked like a business card. She grabbed it, shoved a piece of paper into his hand and then raced across to join Paul. Her right knee was grazed and a trickle of blood ran down her leg.

Her door slammed and Paul drove around the bike and car angled into the road. "You okay?"

She dropped her bag at her feet, took out a tissue and dabbed at the graze on her leg. "Fine. Did you see the limo?"

"No."

"So me giving chase was for nothing?"

"Not for nothing. Two scenarios could have played out here, Lin." The knowledge that he'd lost the first tenuous connection to Chan burned in his gut, but didn't stop him driving on, scanning the road and driveways and parking lots for the limo or the yellow-shirted driver alighting from the vehicle.

Lin thumped the dashboard. "Dammit, Rimmer, we nearly had him. If we'd been on my scooter—"

"The driver would have spotted us easily and probably headed in a different direction to throw us off. But we learned something important."

"Car chases work better if we're on Minnie?"

He snorted. "Only if we were riding something decent. Did it occur to you that your accident might have been deliberate?"

Lin's eyes widened and then narrowed as she shook her head. "But that would mean someone knew we were following Chan's driver. Not possible, Rimmer. We're not rookies. We weren't obvious."

"Normally I'd agree, but don't you think the coincidence of us seeing Chan's driver—a man you recognised immediately—coming out of the place where your sister was killed—" He paused and waited for the penny to drop.

"—an obvious place I would take you to start our investigation—"

"—and the enticement presented by that package to tail the driver in the hope he'd lead us to Chan, plus a convenient turn up a side street in heavy traffic to create a sense of urgency to our pursuit and force us to make an error . . . all too neat, Lin. Either we were going to be separated and the limo driver would have taken me on a wild goose chase, or we were going to lose him when I stopped to pick you up. It didn't matter which choice we made."

She frowned, folded her hands and double-tapped her

finger in the thinking rhythm he'd noticed at lunch.

It didn't matter . . .

He pinned Lin with the same look that made his team quail on the rare occasions he wore it. "Or maybe it did."

Is there a third alternative?

Nothing could be assumed with Chan.

Lin seemed not to notice his look or, if she did, she took no notice. The woman was one cool cookie, as Gran would have said.

Lin crumpled the bloodied tissue and tucked it back into her bag. "He knew what we were doing almost before we knew it ourselves."

"Probably. I think Chan's men know we're watching, and trying to find him. Someone, probably in your department, could be feeding him information. That happened to us in Sydney. Two moles, both dead now."

"Two?" Her eyebrows rose. Her surprise seemed genuine.

"At least two." Paul looked back at the road, spotted a street sign and turned onto Cluny Road. Ahead lay the Botanic Gardens, as safe a place as any to plan their next move.

But what if Lin was working for Chan? What if her sister's death wasn't real? What if it was nothing more than a cover story and she didn't even have a sister? As background went, a dead sister ticked all the boxes. Distraction caused by grief would cover any little slips she made.

Paul kept his mouth shut and turned onto the road to the gardens. He'd trusted other operatives who had turned traitor. Why should the fact Lin was beautiful—a total distraction, if he were honest—put her above suspicion? "From now on, trust no one."

From now on, he'd be watching Lin very carefully until he'd worked out where her true loyalties lay.

Trust no one.

Especially his new partner.

Chapter 7

He doesn't trust me.

The barrier flew up between them, snapping shut with a thud. Lin understood that look, the implication, the distrust that flickered in his eyes.

Rimmer's look had been meant to intimidate her, but she wasn't going to give him the satisfaction of knowing he'd succeeded. Her work was excellent—always.

Usually.

Honesty stung. She prided herself on doing her best, and it hurt to be off her game. Her boss trusted her, and she knew she was the right person for this job. The morning's brief distraction had been an aberration she would not allow to recur.

Nothing, not even active dislike or distrust would stop her tracking down John Chan's hiding place and seeing him brought to justice.

With or without you, Rimmer.

She glared back. Anger and hurt pride meant nothing, but she refused to let his distrust interfere with her investigation.

"I will keep your saying in mind."

"Do that, and put some effort into thinking about those people you work with, the ones who don't seem to spend more than an officer's regular salary." He parked the car, slammed the door and stabbed the button on the remote. The sedate single beep of the locking system engaging was at odds with the restrained violence of his actions.

They walked in silence past the visitor centre at the entrance to the gardens, the distance between them growing wider as they neared the black and white colonial building that was now an exclusive French restaurant.

"Do you want to grab a bite of dinner?"

Lin's stomach twisted at the thought of food. Conflict sharpened her focus, but robbed her of her appetite. "No thanks."

He grunted.

"Where do you think will be quiet at this time of evening?"

Her annoyance with Rimmer had blinded her to the sudden fall of night, a swift transition from day to dark in the tropics. Ahead, a greenish glow through the trees indicated they were near a pond. "I do my best thinking near water. We'll go sit there."

Spotlights, down lights—a meandering line of strategically placed lights picked out the green of the trees surrounding and reflected in the water. It was beautiful and peaceful and had been one of Kim's favourite places to picnic.

Had Lin's subconscious guided her here, knowing her need to dig deep for calm? She led the way to a bench and sat at one end, breathing in and exhaling—counting slowly to five.

Clever, vivacious Kim. Her sister's presence felt close here.

Rimmer sat in the middle of the bench, his arms splayed along the backrest, taking over the space.

Conscious of his hand resting next to hers, she edged towards the last centimetre of bench. Damn it. Why had she called him *hot* this afternoon? He was using her awareness of him to his advantage. He wanted to throw her off her game. He was testing her, but why?

And why the sudden shuttering of connection? After training and lunch there'd been a sense of camaraderie developing between them. What had brought back the cold, distant agent again?

Rimmer glanced casually back along the path they'd walked, rolled his head as though stretching his neck muscles and checked the other direction. "What do you suggest our next move should be?"

He picked up a loose strand of her hair and played with it. When had he moved closer?

With a nonchalant toss of her head, she pulled her hair out of his fingers. "What are you doing, Rimmer?"

"Nothing."

"Well do nothing without touching me."

"Just making us sitting on a seat by the water look natural."

"No, you're being a pain." Sitting with a straight back that would make her mother proud of her, Lin glanced at him.

His expression was unreadable, but his blue eyes had darkened into deep cold pools reflecting the lights behind her.

Cold eyes, hot man. Irritating, annoying, distracting man.

Turning her attention to the water, she sought focus and composure. He was lead on the case. Most likely this was a further test of her ability. "To answer your question—what next?—we work with what we know and make educated guesses about possibilities, then check and eliminate them until what we're left with leads us to Chan."

"You say that with certainty."

"We *will* catch Chan, no matter how long it takes. There cannot be any other outcome."

He leaned forward, resting his elbows on his knees, and clasped his hands loosely. "So what do we know for certain? Is that brothel owned by Chan? Does he frequent only that place, or does he have others? Is it possible he has already set up other illegal operations in Singapore?"

There it was again. *That look*. Intense. All-seeing. Lacking trust.

She felt like a worm on a hook. Tightening her muscles, she refused to wriggle. Wriggling was for guilty suspects and children. She met his eyes and kept her reply succinct. "Yes. Likely to be others. And possible, although he'd have to be paying off a lot of people. To the best of my knowledge he's only been in

Singapore for the past three weeks. That's not enough time to have made contacts and set up an operation."

Rimmer made no response.

Lin's mouth dried as though she'd eaten a sour plum. Worry that Rimmer would have her chucked off the case if he didn't like her answers made her want to box his ears like her uncles claimed her grandmother had done to them.

"Three weeks isn't much time, but what if he had someone setting it up for him while he was in hiding elsewhere? You said it was possible he entered illegally from somewhere nearby. Could he also have been directing operations from a base there?"

Visualising the narrow marine border between the two countries, Lin nodded slowly. "That makes sense. If he's working through an intermediary, he leaves no trace. Perhaps we have narrowed our search too much."

"We need to look for patterns of movement and a range of property purchases, not just sightings of Chan."

"Want to visit my office later tonight? Nobody's there after ten o'clock and we can search databases and online as long as we want."

"You're on. Things to look for—a pattern of acquisition of property in Geylang and similar areas, recent sales of properties at the top end of the market—"

"Why top end?"

"Chan expects only the best. He'll want somewhere comfortable, with plenty of luxury and high spec security. Preferably high walls with no sign of the house from the road."

Lin nodded. "I see where you're going with this. We should also look for missing women. He must have a supply chain if he's setting up illegal brothels and keeping off the police radar."

The cool gaze narrowed on her with a hint of thawing. A slight nod added to the impression he liked her suggestion. Liked. It was a bare half-step up from his former mood, but she would take it as a positive.

"His brothels in Sydney were mostly serviced by illegal immigrants, but there were a few who had been abducted from other countries and brought into Australia. They were unable to tell us exactly how, but we suspect container shipping." His tone held disgust, but it was the tension in his body that was most revealing. Something about this case was personal to him.

She'd read as much of his file as the Bureau had provided. He'd led the teams hitting the Rocks locations two years ago. She was willing to bet it was something about the brothel that angered and sickened him. Was that because he had four younger sisters and a stack of female cousins, or did it have to do with what he'd seen in that raid?

He continued. "We'll follow through on your idea. Abducted girls and illegal immigrants are caught in virtual slavery, but they're two of Chan's favourite staffing methods." Rimmer's gaze unhooked from hers and turned towards the water. His expression mirrored Bruce Lee's as he prepared to take on the bad guys.

Lin's certainty firmed. There was definitely something about that Sydney raid that had been so successful in shutting down the cartel, but which had failed to capture John Chan.

She jumped to her feet. "I want to start now."

Rimmer glanced at his watch then stood and stretched, as though he had all the time in the world. "No hurry. It's barely seven now. We'll eat and—"

"Sheesh, what is it with you and food? You're like an oversized stomach saying 'feed me' every couple of hours. We had a late lunch."

"After a strenuous workout."

"Well, I'm not hungry."

"I am. We'll eat now."

"You are one bossy bas—"

Rimmer set a finger against her lips and shook his head. "Chain of command, remember?"

The urge was strong to bite his finger and show him what she thought of his chain of command attitude. But if she did that, she would taste his skin again. During their training bout her lips had slipped across his skin before she evaded his hold. Of course she'd licked her lips and now his taste was burnt into her memory.

Salty, following their full-on workout. Both had been slick with sweat. But beneath that lay musk and sandalwood; the taste and scent were all Rimmer.

Much as she longed to teach him not to touch her like this, she couldn't risk lowering her guard. Turning, she strode off along the path back the way they'd come.

Annoying, bossy, full of himself . . .

For her sanity, touching Rimmer was off the table.

***

Paul easily caught up with Lin's angry stride and made a point of crowding her along the path. Stirring her about her Vespa had broken the ice. It was a shame recreating the connection he'd enjoyed with Tam—with whom he'd had the ideal work relationship—was off the table. He didn't trust Lin. But the idea of keeping her on edge was now part of his watch and learn plan. Clearly they both felt an attraction made obvious by the close-quarters training session. He'd make use of that.

What else he needed to sort out, and fast, was if Lin was playing a double game. He would not take the risk of another mole jeopardising this operation. Chan would not escape a second time.

Every moment of that operation was etched in his memory in minute detail. He'd replayed it many times, searching for a clue he'd overlooked. Who had helped Chan escape . . .

Sydney, two years earlier

"Blue team is in position. Green team, are you set?" Paul

spoke into the walkie talkie clipped on his shoulder. None of his team would know, but nervous tension zapped through his body. Tonight's takedown of the Chan cartel was too important not to succeed.

Having confirmed his teams were in place around the perimeter of the warehouse and the exclusive brothel owned by the Chan family, he gave the go-ahead. Power shut down, streetlights flicked off and the Rocks was plunged into darkness. Moments later, a rooftop generator kicked in and lights flickered on within the brothel, his team's target.

He glanced at his watch. One minute after twenty-three hundred hours.

Breathing slowly, Paul used his night vision scope to scan the shadows between the building and the dark rocky upthrust that had given the historic area its name.

No movement.

More teams awaited his signal to begin a combined multi-pronged raid on the Chan mansion and three sites in Sydney from where they knew the cartel's illegal businesses operated.

Focused on his entry point, he took several slow breaths. He and his partner, Tamsin Westcott, had risked their lives to get information that had led to tonight's raid. Tam's twin sister had also been caught up in their investigation and now, Bureau agents were about to close the net. Determined not to let a single member of the drug cartel escape, Paul checked his watch again, and raised his walkie talkie to give the signal. "On my word . . ." He drew a deep breath. "All teams are go."

Cordoned off and locked down, the dark streets around the warehouse and brothel exploded as dark-uniformed officers hit their assigned points of entry.

Paul led his team through the front door. A small and intimate reception area was unoccupied, but a security camera began tracking their progress before Paul shot it out. He took the entry into a spacious L-shaped club lounge. Blacked out windows were mostly hidden by heavy red drapes, while several decadently-padded couches were set at strategic points around the room. The furniture was all angled towards a low dais.

Two men seated on couches raised their hands. Considering the girls positioned beside and behind one man, with a third girl on the floor between the legs of the other, Paul dismissed them as clients. The third girl looked up at Paul and his team and the only sound in the room was the soft pop-slurp as her lips left her client's cock.

But the clients and the workers weren't Paul's primary target. Leaving them to be collected by the sweep team, Paul signalled his partner, Grant Perkins. They moved into position on either side of the dais, guns at the ready. A dark-green feather lay on the scuffed and polished floor.

Paul glanced back at the tableau of clients and girls and his gut tightened. The youngest of the three still knelt between her client's knees, a boa draped around her neck.

The girls servicing the two clients were little more than teenagers, and this dais was apparently a stage for clients to view a parade of women and make their selection. *Like a bloody meat mart.*

Perkins led the way along a short Besser-brick hallway with a single door at the far end. Unpainted and poorly lit, it was clear the hallway was only used by the working girls as a passage from the lounge to the rooms where they plied their trade. According to the building plans the door led to the business side of the brothel, which they knew to be a selection of theme rooms catering to all tastes and wallet sizes.

Paul put his shoulder to the heavy fire door and pushed. Ahead a small, tastefully decorated foyer with six heavily carved and painted doors intersected with another wider hallway connecting back to the lounge. Their informant had told them rich clients were given the royal treatment when they came into this part of the brothel. Upstairs, outraged shouts and banging doors revealed Green team's progress through the cheaper rooms.

Methodically the two agents separated left and right, each taking a set of doors along one side and working their way through the rooms. Paul pushed the first door wide. Two men attended by a single woman yelled at him to get out before one noticed his gun and pushed the woman away. The other grabbed the stumbling sex worker and held her in front of him as a shield. Neither of them was Chan.

The middle room, heavy with a spicy Oriental scent, was vacant. In the third room, styled as a dungeon, a leather-clad dominatrix whipped the buttocks of a bound and blindfolded client with a riding crop. "Who's there?" The man raised his head, and jerked it from side to side. The dominatrix, totally into her power role, stared him down. "I told you, no talking."

Paul rolled back around the doorjamb, caught Perkins' eye and tapped his chest twice. He'd take the lead into the last room.

John Chan's private room.

The final intel report had indicated he'd left home for an evening at the brothel.

Paul moved into position and waited until Perkins gave a jerky nod—*ready*—the only sign he was as keen as Paul to capture Chan. Paul gripped his gun in his right hand and pushed the door wide with his free hand. His gun rose, the tip synced with his searching gaze around the spacious, high-ceilinged room. A young woman sprawled naked and alone on the bed, her dark hair fanned across the pillow—beautiful and unmoving.

Cautiously he made his way to her side and set his fingers on her neck.

No pulse.

Her wide-open eyes stared sightlessly at the ceiling. Partly concealed beneath her shoulder, a ripped plastic bag confirmed how she'd died.

"Anything?" Perkins approached the bed. "Aw, shit."

Paul gently closed her eyes. "I want Chan in handcuffs before we leave."

"Sounds—"

"Not now, Perky."

Perkins flicked a glance at the dead girl. "Sorry."

They left the room and met up with the second team near the stairs, their search netting the brothel's Madam Wu, several employees and a handful of clients, but Chan wasn't among them.

Paul pressed the button on his walkie talkie. "Gold team, have you got John Chan? Was he with his father at the house? Over."

Jake's disembodied voice crackled over the walkie talkie. "Negative. Chan senior is in custody along with his very angry wife and assorted family members who were visiting the family home. She's screeching up a storm. Chan junior isn't here. What about at the warehouse? Over."

Perkins was already in contact with the warehouse team. He shook his head when their reply came through. "Not there either."

"Damn it." Frustration fizzed alongside adrenaline through his veins. In spite of the success of the rest of the operation, the loss of Chan left a sour taste in his mouth. "Jake, do you want to let Danton know, or do you want me to tell him?" Neither wanted to be the one conveying that news, but Jake would be more worried about getting home to protect Marcy if Chan had slipped the net. Given Chan's predilection for sex and revenge, and his pursuit of Marcy's twin, Jake's partner could be a target. Before Jake could answer, Paul dived in. "Forget I asked. I'll do it. Over."

"Thanks, mate. Over and out."

They returned to the room where the dead girl now lay beneath a sheet. One of the sweep team twitched a corner to cover the girl's foot.

Had Chan managed to slip out before the raid? But how, and why hadn't he been spotted?

"I can't see the benefits of this myself." Perkins' comment pulled Paul back to the room. His teammate stood in front of the oversized mirror, set so clients could enjoy watching themselves as they performed on the bed. "Unless you're a selfish, narcissistic prick."

"Not for me either, but intel indicated this room was the one most often used by Chan. His *private playground*." Paul tipped his head up. From the dark ceiling, hooks and chains hung down, indicating something of the darker sexual tastes of their quarry. His glance landed on the now-shrouded figure and disgust mixed with bile in his gut.

"I reckon Chan's gone." Perkins sounded disgusted.

"But how?" Paul nodded towards the dead girl. "That method's one of the violent, sick fuck's preferences. He was here, I'm sure of it. We're missing something."

"What, like a secret door out of here?" Perkins snorted. "Been reading crime novels, mate?" Sometimes Perkins could be so bloody flippant.

Paul's gaze landed on the dead girl and sorrow and anger filled him. This job had its good days, but this wasn't one of them.

He approached the mirror and studied the edges. "Could be a two-way mirror."

"Makes a sick kind of sense I suppose. One bloke pays to do it and another pays to watch."

"Instead of being impressed by the brothel's business model, try looking for that secret door *you* suggested might be—" Paul bent to examine the glass near his hand. Fingerprints smudged one edge on the otherwise clean surface, and Paul pressed his fingers over the same spot.

Click.

The mirror moved slightly away from the wall. He directed a light through the dark gap. There was no sweaty-faced Chan hiding in a cupboard, but a narrow, rough stone passage angled downwards. "Perky, I apologise."

Paul let his teams know what he'd found and then he and Perkins turned on their night-vision goggles and stepped into the passage.

Some twenty metres along, the passage took a right turn that ended at a heavy metal door. Flakes of rust dropped on his black gloves, but the door was solid and barred their exit. Paul set his shoulder against the metal and forced it partially open with a squeal of unoiled hinges. It stopped against a lump of broken concrete. He pushed harder and the lump tumbled into the water below as he stepped into the open.

Perkins dropped to one knee and examined the ground where the concrete had been. "The grass is flattened, but there's no sign the block was there before tonight." He joined Paul where he stood scanning the harbour.

Night breezes carried the scent of salt water and diesel. Ahead of them, the lights of Sydney Harbour danced across the water. Boats motored slowly past sending small waves crashing against a jumble of rocks below Paul's feet. The narrow opening was hemmed in on both sides by buildings that reached to the water's edge and Paul visualised their location as seen from the water.

Perkins stood by Paul's side looking out. "How the fuck did he escape? There's no watercraft close enough to pick him up."

Paul's grip tightened on his gun as he peered in vain at the nearest boats.

We should have had a boat out here.

"The harbour's the only way out. He must have been tipped off. Shit, reckon we've got another mole to ferret out." . . .

Paul took a wary, sideways look at Lin.

Was Chan's escape sheer dumb luck? An oversight in their planning, or was it another mole?

In spite of an intense and thorough intradepartmental investigation there had been no further discoveries of treachery. But the possibility of a repetition here plagued him. Was Lin the reason no real progress was happening?

Damn it, he was going to push her hard. If she was a double agent, he would ferret out her secret and send her to jail.

Keeping his tone light in this cat-and-mouse game, he asked, "How about that French restaurant we passed? Is it good?"

Chapter 8

Lin glanced at him and kept walking fast, as though she wanted to leave him for dead. "Yes, but you need a reservation. We'll never get in."

He stepped closer, crowding her against the hardy agapanthus plants edging the path. "Why don't we ask? It never hurts to ask, Lin."

The soft tap of her footsteps came to an abrupt halt.

He turned to her. "What's up?"

Lin was standing at the edge of the path, gripping the strap of her satchel. Behind her head, a light created a halo.

Scoffing at the illusion, he snapped out the first thing that popped into his mind. "What's the matter? Is your knee sore from that—accident?"

Damn. He hadn't meant to let that snide tone leach into his voice. Nor compound his slip by the insinuation in that brief hesitation. Giving away any hint of his suspicions was unacceptable. Why was he letting Lin get under his skin?

"As a matter of fact, it is, thank you for your concern. As for what you just said—tell me, Rimmer, why all of a sudden are you acting like I'm the enemy, like I can't be trusted?"

Paul raised both hands. "Whoa, where's this coming from?"

"You tell me. This afternoon we were getting on fine. After my bike accident, we're not. What happened in between?"

"Nothing is different."

"Bull dust."

He snorted and her eyes narrowed.

"Isn't that what you call it when someone lies?"

"So now I'm lying, am I?"

"You aren't telling me what you're thinking. Partners share their ideas and work together. I feel like you've shut me out and put me on trial and I have no idea why. Is it because I said you were hot this afternoon?"

Paul shrugged, but her question gave him an out. "You're right, and I did say giving in to any physical attraction while we're working together is a bad idea. We need to keep things professional." Would she buy that?

Why not? She was the one who'd suggested it. He let his gaze roam her body from head to toe hoping such blatant assessment knocked her off guard.

"I was being professional. You're the one who seems to be fixated on—"

Her lips pressed together and she strode past him, bumping him out of her way with her shoulder.

"On what? Think highly of yourself, don't you?" Paul shoved his hands in his pockets. Damn, why had he said that? Nothing he'd said was untrue, but Lin's question proved how necessary it was to draw a line between work and play. She was astute and if she were working for Chan, letting his guard down with her—and that's what it would be if they had sex—would be the ultimate stupidity.

And I just handed her the ammunition.

"Just so we are clear, I do not wish to go to bed with you, Rimmer. I was behaving like a professional. I'm sorry if my comment—which, by the way, *you* interpreted as sexy—made you think I wasn't. Being professional, that is."

Keen to leave this conversation behind, Paul nodded. "Glad we cleared the air. Now do you want dinner or are you going to just sit and watch me while I eat?"

Chapter 9

Filling in the time until they could slip into her office unnoticed by fellow operatives gave Paul a chance to learn more about the local operation. He was still mulling over Lin's observations as he turned the car onto the approach to the Singapore Bureau car park and rolled to a stop in front of a heavy-duty metal gate. Lin handed him her passkey and he opened his window and held it to the reader. The gate rolled back. Conscious of the security cameras tracking their progress, he parked the car and then followed Lin inside, through the security checkpoint, up several floors in the lift, and on down the corridor to her office. Thinking through lines of investigation, he wondered if she'd tipped anyone off about their plan when she'd slipped away to the restroom.

Conversation over dinner had initially stayed firmly around tourist type activities and places to visit before sliding into information about her workplace. The case was off limits until they were back in the car and away from any chance of being overheard. Silence reigned on the drive to Lin's workplace and continued until they stopped in front of a room with a window looking into a large, open-plan office.

Lin flicked a switch and lights came on. "This is mine. I'll log you in on my laptop and I'll use the desktop computer. What do you want me to look for?" She dropped her satchel on a utilitarian desk and turned on the computer beside it before placing a small laptop beneath the internal window. She pulled a cord and venetian blinds clacked shut.

"We need to check news reports, local and international police reports, real estate sites for high end property sales—"

"Newspapers are probably easier for you to access. There are personal log ins for the police sites that can make it—"

He held up a hand and she fell silent. "I know how tight security can be on official sites. I'll look through news articles in—what language is spoken here?"

"Several, including English, which fortunately for you is the main one. There're also newspapers in Tamil, Malay and Mandarin Chinese. I speak all four, although my Tamil isn't great."

"Mine is non-existent so anything other than English is all yours." Lin didn't need to know he'd studied Mandarin at university and was fluent, if a little rusty.

"Okay." She logged into the laptop and clicked into a news app.

He stood a little behind and to one side, watching her move easily around the screen, noting the icons she clicked, memorising them so he could search outside of what she selected once she was busy at her screen.

Lin stepped away and gestured towards the basic office chair in front of the laptop with such grace, she could have been offering him a throne. "These are the English language papers in Singapore. Where do you want me to start?"

He pulled the chair away from the desk and sat, swinging around to look at her. Seated, his eyes were on a level with her breasts. He lifted his gaze and looked her in the eye. No more distractions from his partner. "Expensive property sales in the past eighteen months."

"Didn't you say it was two years since Chan escaped from your sting operation in Sydney? Why not start then?"

"It's more likely he laid low for several months to be sure we couldn't pick up his trail, but if you want to go back two years, be my guest. You know what we're looking for?"

"Yes, large, luxurious, with high-level security. Do you

want me to concentrate on houses or should I include apartments too?"

Paul hesitated. Even though Chan had chosen to live in a luxury penthouse overlooking the harbour, Paul was inclined to believe he would go for a fully fenced, very private property with a large dwelling similar to his father's home in Sydney. A house and grounds had greater potential to accommodate his activities. "Spread the net wide for now. It's time consuming, but more likely to produce results."

"I'm on it."

She didn't ask what he was going to start on, just sat at her desk and focused on the screen. Beside her, a framed photo of a young woman, so like Lin it could have been her sister, sat in pride of place. A vivacious, younger version of Lin.

A twinge of uncertainty niggled in Paul's mind, but he dismissed it. For all he knew, she might have a sister in real life. Cover stories worked best when they stuck close to a person's truth. Easier not to slip up if salient details were real.

He sat in front of the laptop and typed into the search bar: Missing girls.

Illegal immigration ensured a steady replenishing of supply. Back home, Chan used covert arrivals from East Asia to stock his brothels and businesses requiring manual labour and little English. Covert arrivals were forced to work to pay back the costs of bringing them to a country they wished to live in.

Of course, Paul thought grimly, covert workers never paid back what they owed because their tabs kept increasing as room and board were added at a rate greater than they could ever pay back. Here, it was more likely that girls had been abducted and brought in from other parts of Asia to work in illegal businesses.

And abductions would be most likely to leave some kind of trail.

Paul added a time frame to match Chan's disappearance

from Sydney up to the present and watched as pages of links to stories of loss flashed onto the screen.

So many missing girls.

Refining his search to match the age groups favoured by Chan, Paul refreshed the page.

Still too many. He ran his fingers through his hair, considering how to get better results. Fingers poised over the keyboard, he began adding simple keywords to the search bar.

Some time later he heard the soft rumble of Lin's office chair being pushed back and looked around.

"Rimmer, any luck?"

"Depends what you call luck? There are way too many stories of missing girls in the past two years."

"People smuggling is huge business in many places. Do you have a minute to look at what I found?"

"Sure." A nerve-wracking squeal as he pushed his chair back across the blue linoleum set his teeth on edge. He glanced down. A thick paperclip was caught in one wheel. Leaving it for the moment, he joined Lin. "What have you got?" He leaned over her shoulder, eyes fixed on the screen, but that subtle sweet fragrance rose from her hair. He turned his head, just a fraction and breathed in her scent.

". . . so what do you think?" Lin tapped the screen.

Shit, what had she said?

Frowning, he leaned past her shoulder, turned the screen around and then moved to the side. "Tell me more."

"Most of these properties are on Bukit Timah Hill. The area is known as a rich man's paradise and many homes sell for tens of millions of dollars." She showed him a list of high-end sales and then clicked into a Google link for the first property.

A satellite image opened showing a heavily-treed property with a large dwelling near the centre.

Paul tapped the screen. "That's the sort of property I could imagine Chan purchasing. When was it bought?"

"A little outside our reference period. About twenty-eight months ago. The purchaser is listed as a company name, but I thought I'd check it out. The sales brochure describes it as having an underground garage for ten vehicles. That sort of space would have a lot of potential if you were bringing in a truckload of women you didn't want anyone to see.

"And look at this recent satellite image of the property . . ." Lin clicked on another tab. The same property appeared with a date stamp only three months earlier.

"What's that new building? Can you zoom in on it?"

"According to the details on the building application for the property, the owner built a second dwelling for his extended family to move into. The second dwelling is listed as having six bedrooms and four bathrooms."

"That doesn't fit with what we know about Chan. He usually prefers his own space. That additional building would mean he had other people close by. With a mother like his, I doubt he would build a home for her on the same property."

"What about housing kidnapped women? That flat roof would allow guards to patrol easily enough."

"Maybe." Paul checked the details and distance between the main house and the new building and shook his head "It's not his style to mix business and pleasure. Chan is the ultimate hedonist. Everything is about control and his pleasure alone. And given the time frame of the purchase, I think that one is unlikely. Set it aside for now."

"Okay, then what about this one." She clicked out of the multi-garage mansion and onto another image.

This one also had thick trees around the perimeter inside a high wall, but the house wasn't as big as he imagined Chan would consider fitting for his sense of his own importance.

John Chan slipped through the Bureau's net without any

sighting of him and I'm setting myself up as the ultimate expert on him?

Losing Chan still burned his gut, but the reminder was timely.

What did he know about what Chan would consider acceptable, especially considering the man's success at staying off the radar for the past two years? Would Chan see the cost of acquiring property in the exclusive area sufficient trade-off for a less spacious home?

Getting inside the mind of a narcissistic psychopath made Paul feel dirty and sick to his stomach, but it had to be done. He glanced across at the article on his screen: a fifteen-year-old schoolgirl missing for over a year from across the border with Malaya.

If Paul had guessed right, she and others like her were the reason he had to dive head first into the muck of Chan's mind and divine his whereabouts, find his businesses, stop him wrecking more lives. Leaning past Lin's shoulder, he reassessed the property on the screen.

"Possibility. Purchase date?"

"Six months ago. It's not as big as some of the others, but it's got some of the best security measures of the properties I've seen so far. High spec exterior cameras and alarms were added before the owner moved in. The fit out was done by the top security firm in Singapore." Lin looked up at him and a smile played around her lips. "Does size matter?"

Paul felt the tug of an answering smile and the attraction of light banter like a summer breeze. Delicious, energising, especially when offered by Lin. "Only in the important things in life. Like food."

Her laugh was surprisingly earthy. "So, upsizing your order at fast food places is important?"

"It has its attraction when I'm ravenous."

"And when you aren't ravenous for food? Is size important then?" Her voice dropped into soft huskiness, into an entirely too-welcome offer that he'd blindly walked towards.

Moments of weakness. Giving the enemy the upper hand by showing *his* weakness. Spy school one-oh-one.

Lin knew he liked her. Wanted her. There'd been no hiding his response when he'd briefly trapped her in training.

But did I trap her, or did she create the situation to trap me?

Was she playing a game, messing with his mind, playing on their mutual attraction? Was it even mutual, or was she on Chan's payroll?

Do not trust anyone.

His order this afternoon had been a warning for Lin, but he'd do well to apply it to himself. Trust, or the lack of it, was more important than attraction.

Or size.

Damn it, he'd better not go down that track.

He straightened, missing the scent of Lin's hair even before he walked back to the laptop. "Put that one on the maybe list. It has possibilities in spite of its lack of size. Keep looking. I've got a hunch we're onto something." He turned his back on her, and on whatever seduction she might have in mind.

Three hours later Paul stood and stretched, rolling kinks out of his neck. He eyed the pile of printed pages neatly stacked on Lin's desk. In his bones he knew they were onto something, but the connection remained elusive.

A yawn escaped and his stomach rumbled, the sound loud in the quiet office.

Lin grinned. "Again, Rimmer?"

She was making an effort to restore their new working relationship to a comfortable footing, but Paul refused to play. Not until he knew beyond a shadow of doubt that she was untainted by connection to Chan.

"What? Hours of research makes me hungry. Bring what you've got and we'll go find something to eat."

"How about sleep?"

"That too. We can go back to my hotel and order room service, grab a couple of hours sleep and then get back into it."

"Or we could go our separate ways and meet again for breakfast."

Her reluctance to stay with him pinged his wariness, and his lack of trust in his partner ratcheted up another notch. "Do you have a problem with working out of my hotel room?"

"It's not that. I'll meet you there if that's what you prefer?"

"It's better use of our time if we're together. No time wasted travelling."

Her tired smile melted away and she pushed to her feet. "True, but still I would like to shower and change and sleep in my own bed."

"Aside from changing your clothes, everything else is on tap at my hotel. I'd like you to stay."

Was he only pushing this because he didn't trust her? He wanted to believe that was his sole reason, but another part of his body knew better.

Still, her refusal niggled. What was the truth behind her determination to leave?

He rubbed both hands over his face. The overnight flight to Singapore and the long day of preliminary investigation with an unfamiliar partner combined into a crushing wave of fatigue, slamming into his body with the force of a tropical hurricane.

If she went home he'd have to tail her, or go with her under some pretext so he could keep an eye on her.

His eyes prickled with lack of sleep and his brain wouldn't come up with any reason other than the one that had lain at the edge of every thought about her since that damned training session.

He wanted Lin. Was it because she'd proved better than him? That was a bonus in a partner, not a motivation to have sex with her. Besides, he preferred an equal partner in all areas of life.

What's different about her home that can't happen in my hotel room?

King-size bed versus maybe a single or double bed if he was lucky?

No contest.

He pulled himself up. *That* wasn't going to happen under any circumstances.

Lin watched him without speaking before she picked up the pile of printouts and stuffed them into her satchel. "You look wrecked, Rimmer. Come on, I'll drive you to your hotel."

***

Lin drove thoughtfully through the quiet streets. Quiet by Singaporean standards, at least. Beside her, Rimmer emitted a soft snore. His confession about not being able to sleep on a plane meant he mustn't have slept at all in the past two days. Even in her grief, Lin had found refuge in sleep.

Until the nightmares hit.

Sneaking quick looks at his sleeping profile as she drove, she watched as street and shop lights cascaded in red, white, green, white across his face. Each change highlighted his aquiline nose, firm chin, and high cheekbones. Stubble darkened his face, etching him as a pirate.

Or could ugly handsome make a GQ cover model?

Kim had often drooled over the guys who made it onto those magazines, but it was always the stubbled, smiling-into-your-eyes guys she flipped over. Personally, Lin preferred stubbled broodiness. When Rimmer let his smile loose, the contrast was riveting.

Minutes later she pulled up in the hotel driveway and opened her door.

75

A young concierge scurried through the night door, blinking as though he'd been caught napping, his too-wide smile slipping as he caught sight of Rimmer, head pressed against the window.

"Do you need assistance with your passenger?"

Lin rounded the front of the car, tapped on the window beside Rimmer's head and opened his door. "All good, thanks." She put a hand on Rimmer's shoulder and shook. "You're home. Food! Come on, wake up."

Unlike the concierge, Rimmer's eyes shot open, his body on full alert.

Several moments too late if there'd been any danger. "Come on, sleepyhead, time to go to bed."

Rimmer got out of the car, reached for Lin and took the keys from her hand, and tossed them to the concierge. "We'll need it again in the morning."

"Yes, sir."

Rimmer handed over a tip before taking Lin's arm and heading towards the entrance.

"What are you doing?" She should have been prepared for some slick move like that, but she was tired and tomorrow . . .

I can't think about tomorrow. Not yet.

"Food, sleep, work, in that order. You can shower while the food is being sent up."

He'd just woken up and yet he looked ready for action. He looked good enough to— Lin gave herself a mental shake. Why the fascination with Rimmer? He'd behaved poorly, he didn't trust her, and he'd manipulated her into doing what he wanted. Coming back to his hotel was a bad idea when she had—

"I really have to go home. Mr Wang gave me the morning off."

Rimmer pushed the call button for the lift and leaned against the marble wall, his arms folded across his chest. His muscled, impressive chest. The one she'd both seen and felt in training.

"Is having time off during an investigation standard practice here? I've got to tell you, it doesn't look professional."

"Only when something is truly important." That damned lump of emotion rose, threatening to clog her words. She turned towards the floor numbers displayed in the panel above the button. The numbers blurred and she blinked away her tears. Should she wait for him to enter the lift and then cut and run?

"What's more important than this case?" There was a note of genuine concern beneath his gruff tone and his frown.

Afterwards Lin couldn't recall why she'd answered his question, or whether his concern was for her, or for the missing women whose stories he'd been lost in. Maybe it was that Kim was an integral part of their search for answers, therefore he deserved to know.

Looking up at him as the lift doors opened, she replied. "Tomorrow is Kim's funeral."

Chapter 10

Paul's mouth opened, but the words he should say—words he needed to find to apologise—wouldn't come.

If this is the truth, I'll apologise later.

"I'll come with you." He stepped into the lift, drawing her in with a gentle hand under her elbow. There had been a moment before she spoke when he'd thought she was going to run. And while crash-tackling her to the floor of the lobby offered certain compensations, he wasn't keen about the attention it would generate.

Lost in her grief—or a damned good facsimile of the emotion—she entered the lift at his side. "Rimmer, this is personal. The funeral is not the case. Kim is not your case. She is—was my sister."

"And she was found in a building owned by our target. You're my partner. I'll come with you. What time does it start?"

"Eleven. I don't need you to come with me."

"But I will be there with you. Now, what do you feel like eating?"

"I'm not hungry."

The lift doors opened on the seventh floor and they walked to his room without seeing another guest. He glanced at his watch. An hour to get food, eat and shower, and they could still grab a few hours of sleep and work before the funeral.

"I'll order a selection off the menu. Something might tempt you." Once in the room, he repeated the search for bugs while she stood, back against the door and her eyes dark. He'd have added stormy to the description, but not even pushing her buttons about eating had chased away the haunted look.

"You can use the bathroom first. I'll order room service."
For all his training and field experience, he couldn't decide if Lin
was genuine or giving an Oscar-worthy performance.

She pushed off the door and, setting her satchel on the
dresser, opened it and took out the sheaf of pages. "Here's the
printouts if you want to look over them." Without another word,
she disappeared into the bathroom. Moments later, the shower
turned on followed by the soft thump of the shower door closing.

With the phone tucked between his shoulder and chin and
the menu in his hand, he rang room service and ordered several
items. Lin had eaten almost nothing at the restaurant. One of these
might tempt her.

Who was he kidding? Ordering so much food was an
excuse to take his mind off the sounds coming from the bathroom.

Off the images of Lin wearing nothing but her silky skin in
his shower.

"Will that be all, sir?"

Paul bit off a groan. "Did I order a bowl of chips?"

"Yes, sir."

"That's all, thanks." He rang off and set the phone back on
the handset then moved to Lin's bag.

Glancing at the bathroom door, he tipped his head to listen.
The shower was still going full bore. He opened the satchel and
searched the contents. Nothing of interest, except for a business
card for a cemetery and memorial garden. On the back, neatly
written, was the name: Kim Tan, and the time Lin had given him
for her sister's funeral.

It proved nothing except that she was thorough in her cover
story.

But unease niggled at the base of his skull. Was it possible
Lin was telling the truth? And if she had, was there a chance she
wasn't working for Chan? That yesterday's coincidences were just
that—coincidence?

The shower was turned off and a moment later, the shower door thumped closed. He dropped the card back in the pocket where he'd found it and closed the flap of the bag.

The bathroom door slid open emitting a cloud of steam and Lin.

Wearing a hotel bathrobe.

With wet hair and her clothes draped over her arm.

His manhood stirred. Beneath that bathrobe, did she have anything on? Damn it, why was he staring at her like he was a randy teenager? He'd never obsessed over Tam like this.

"I've finished if you want to have your shower, Rimmer." She pushed wet strands of hair off her face. Turning to one of the chairs, she dropped the clothes on the seat before picking up her floral dress. She shook it out and then draped it over the back of the chair and smoothed a wrinkle.

Paul eyed the voluminous bathrobe. It hid everything, but his imagination filled in the details. Hadn't he had his hands on her this afternoon? He knew the shape of her, the curves and dips of her body, the heat and silkiness of her skin.

Lin glanced across at him and stood straight, her hand gripping the bathrobe tightly beneath her chin. "Is there something else, Rimmer?"

He hadn't moved. Not one inch towards the bathroom. And he was staring.

At her.

Hungry to know if his imagination had done her justice.

An uncomfortable tightness behind his zipper provoked him to move. He wrenched his gaze from her and strode towards the bathroom. "Food won't be long. I'm taking a shower."

A cold shower, dammit. A long, cold shower.

***

The bathroom door closed and Lin sucked in a breath, the first deep breath she'd managed since stepping into the bedroom.

Rimmer had looked at her like she was . . . like he wanted to . . . What? Slap a pair of handcuffs on her and throw her in a cell?

He doesn't trust me.

Fine by me. I don't trust him either. And I don't like him.

The last was a lie and she refused to lie to herself. What she didn't like was her awareness of him and the way her body reacted when he was near. For a man she'd just met, a partner she had to trust if she was going to achieve justice for Kim, such awareness was an inconvenience. More than that, a distraction like Rimmer could get them both killed.

Giving in to the attraction sparking between them would mean losing sight of her goal. Bringing Chan to justice was the only thing that mattered. She'd willingly sacrifice herself to achieve that, but she didn't have the right to put Rimmer's life at risk more than the job demanded.

All of which meant keeping a lid on their simmering attraction and staying focused on the job.

She lifted her satchel off the dresser and sat in the armchair. Her hand paused as she lifted the unclipped flap. Had she closed it after handing the pages to Rimmer? She glared at the wall separating them.

Blast him, had he looked in her bag?

Anger washed away the vestiges of fatigue, spiking her adrenaline levels as she delved into her bag until her fingers closed around the photo.

The last photo of her and Kim, right where it belonged, in the side pocket with her sister's ring, the one that matched Lin's. Their grandfather had given each of them a ring fashioned like a dragon on the occasion of their twenty-first birthdays.

Channel your power through the dragon, he'd told her. *Slow, fluid, then strike hard and fast.*

She set the photo on the table and picked up Kim's ring. The red dragon eye winked as it caught the light behind her and she slipped the ring onto her left hand. Holding her hands side by side, she lifted them higher, catching the light until two dragon eyes watched her—as though they were alive.

Why had she resisted wearing Kim's ring until now? She made a fist of each hand and closed her eyes, opening herself to the power of the dragon.

Conscious of the ring on her left hand, she moved slowly into the stance of the most powerful dragon move Grandfather had taught her and allowed the dragon to become one with her.

She opened her eyes. Her left hand flashed out, the right following like its shadow and her feet so fast they were a blur. Yes, Kim was with her in spirit.

Sisters, side by side.

Two dragons, one for each hand. Double the strength.

Enough to defeat Chan.

Chapter 11

The sun beat down and a drop of sweat rolled down Paul's temple. He stood at a distance from the family group standing in the quiet water at the edge of the inlet. An older woman, her hands shaking as though afflicted with Parkinson's disease, set a vase containing incense sticks on a natural rock ledge of a nearby outcrop before wading into the water and joining the others. Sweet smoke drifted towards Paul, tickling his nose. He sniffed and breathed through his mouth, willing himself not to sneeze and interrupt the prayers. The Buddhist monk's saffron robe was the single bright colour among the white clothing of Lin and her family.

Garlands of white flowers were laid reverently on the lapping waves. The ebbing tide carried the flowers slowly seaward. Lin waded deeper into the sea, opened the urn she'd carried carefully down from her apartment earlier this morning, and consigned her sister's ashes to the eternal waters. She handed the urn to a slim, upright, grey-haired man and turned back to the sea. Taking the white garland from her neck she dropped it on top of the ashes, brought her palms together and bowed her head.

Behind her, Lin's family—elderly grandparents, her mother and several uncles, their wives and children—followed her lead as the monk's chanted prayers rose on the breeze.

And Paul felt a right bastard for not believing Lin.

Once the idea of her as a double agent for Chan had taken hold in his brain, he hadn't believed her story. Not yesterday, nor this morning as he drove her to her apartment. When she returned carrying an urn, he accepted that her sister had died. But the presence of the urn didn't mean there wasn't some deeper game being played.

And then he'd briefly held the urn containing Kim's ashes while Lin slipped a white robe over her dress. He'd followed her to where her family waited on the shore, watched as a woman he assumed was her grandmother set the white flower lei around her neck, listened as the monk intoned prayers for the dead.

And knew in this, at least, Lin was genuine.

She'd lost her sister.

Paul's phone vibrated. He took it from his pocket and glanced at the caller ID. *Aunt Shirley.* An appalling pseudonym, but he grinned every time he saw it.

Smothering the grin, he turned his back on the ceremony for Lin's sister, walked a short distance away and stood beneath the shade of a tree before taking the call.

"What have you got for me, Jake?" Behind him, the monk's voice rose as his prayers changed and continued.

Paul's former partner paused before replying. "What's that noise? Where the hell are you, mate?"

Glancing at the group still focused on the water, Paul hunched his shoulder and turned away. "At a Buddhist funeral."

"That would be your partner's sister I take it?"

"You know about her?"

"Yes. Sorry about the balls-up sending the attachment. We had an attempted intrusion on our server."

"How the hell could anyone hack our server? It's supposed to be the most secure in the country."

"It's all good now. We haven't been compromised. How's your new partner?"

Distracting. Annoying.

Beautiful.

"She's the best martial arts operative I've come across."

He was beginning to think Jake enjoyed teaming him with strong women. Women who could kick his arse into next year if he let them. Women he respected, admired. Who challenged him when he was wrong.

He wouldn't have it any other way.

"Judging by your tone of voice I'm guessing you found that out the hard way?" He heard the laugh behind Jake's question.

"Yeah, well a little warning might have been a good thing."

"Mate, you have a history of underestimating beautiful women." Jake's voice took on a serious note. "The attachment should be on your phone now, along with some intel Tamsin dug up. She's been pursuing a line of research into purchases and forced acquisitions of land in neighbouring countries. It's thrown up some information she thinks you should pursue."

"Thanks, I'll check it out. Lin and I did some digging last night. She found several residential properties worth checking out. Mostly homes, and one apartment that might suit Chan's tastes. And I'm looking at cases of missing girls over the past two years."

"Any patterns showing up yet?"

"Nothing definite, but I reckon we're on the right track." He glanced back at the ceremony. Lin's family were wading out of the water onto the narrow strip of sand. Lin's gaze zeroed in on him. "Jake, I've got to go. I'll keep you posted."

He ended the call and strolled towards Lin, who stopped walking, waiting for him to approach.

An older man who Paul assumed to be her grandfather stepped up beside her. His body was wiry and his eyes looked into Paul as though he saw his doubts.

Shrugging off the fanciful impression, Paul offered a nod by way of greeting and waited to see what Lin wanted.

"Rimmer, this is my grandfather, Li Qiang. Grandfather, this is Paul Rimmer."

Li Qiang extended a hand. When Paul took it, Li bowed. "Thank you for accompanying my granddaughter today."

"It is a difficult time for your family. I'm glad I could come with Lin."

"How do you know her? From work?"

Paul glanced at Lin, preferring to let her answer in a way that suited what she'd told her family of her work.

"Rimmer is my new partner, Grandfather. Together we will—"

"Lin, a word with you."

Li Qiang's eyes pierced Paul with an intensity that made him feel foolish for cutting her off. "I understand, Mr Rimmer, words best left unsaid." He turned to Lin and placed a hand on her head. "Go, do what must be done."

"Yes, Grandfather." She bowed, low and graceful, before turning to Paul. "We have work to do. Let's go."

"My condolences." Paul nodded to Li Qiang and followed Lin to the car.

She removed her white robe, folded it carefully and set it on the back seat. Pausing with her hand on the open passenger door, she looked out over the placid waters.

Raw grief, tightly contained by Lin's iron will played out in front of him. Watching her profile, noting the rapid blinking and a soft sniff, Paul knew he was a bastard. He'd been wrong about her. Her throat rippled, swallowing emotion and whatever regrets she carried for her sister's death.

How focused on the job could she possibly be after sprinkling her sister's ashes?

"Are you okay, Lin?"

Lin pressed her lips together, sniffed once more and turned to him. "What do you think? Of course I'm not okay, but Grandfather accepts what I have to do. What I must do." Her breasts rose as she sucked in a deep breath.

With determination, he met her eyes. "Are you sure you don't want to stay for your sister's wake? Do you have a wake?"

"Not as you would know it, Rimmer." She stepped into the

car and pulled her door closed.

Paul joined her. "I'm sorry. I know very little about Buddhism. We had a wake after Gran's funeral and I thought maybe—"

"Don't worry about it. My family are performing religious ceremonies every day for forty-nine days, hoping their prayers improve the odds of a positive rebirth for Kim."

"Don't you want to be part of that?"

Her eyebrows rose and her disbelief pinned him. "For forty-nine days?"

"Hmm." He had no idea what to say to that. Five years had smoothed the raw edge off his grief for Gran, but he couldn't imagine how crazy he'd have been if he hadn't had work to occupy him in the early days after her passing. "I guess not."

"I offer my prayers each morning before I go to work. There is no prohibition on working during mourning. But I have anger inside me, Rimmer. Anger so great that I doubt my prayers are of any help. The one thing I can do for my sister is to bring the man who killed her to justice and stop him ruining other lives."

Paul understood her need to act. Doing something had kept him sane when his world was tipped on its head. He turned the key in the ignition, but didn't immediately pull out of the car park. "Lin, please accept my sincere condolences. I am truly sorry for your loss."

She looked at him, her face impassive. "Life is uncertain; death is certain. I have to believe that Kim will be reborn into a better life or else I'll—" Quickly she turned her head away.

Paul set a hand on her shoulder.

Her muscles tensed beneath his fingers. "We're wasting time. Let's go."

He dropped his hand and put the indicator on. There was nothing he could say to make Lin feel better. Last night and this morning, he'd been abrasive, rude, and disbelieving. Now, he offered sympathy that she seemed not to want, and why would she? She didn't know him, and she'd told him up front that he'd have to earn her trust.

As she has to earn mine. Yesterday's conversation played over in his mind. Was that a ploy to set him at ease, or the truth?

Did he trust her?

Not at all. Not yet. Not until she'd proved herself beyond doubt and Paul's need for certainty.

Life is uncertain.

He already knew death was the only certainty and love wasn't enough to keep those he held dear close to him.

The best thing he could do, the only thing, was to focus on catching John Chan.

***

Fragile.

Without Kim, she was like a piece of fine porcelain that had been broken and mended. Never the same, never as strong as before, but still useful.

Catching Chan and making him pay for Kim's murder was the only way to strengthen the cracks of her shattered self.

Her thoughts scattered like the floral leis they had set upon the water, falling apart, pulled in whatever direction the tide took them. She had to find a way to do her job without giving in to the fog of grief and the stabbing pain in her heart. Find a way, or fail Kim.

"So, I was thinking . . ."

Rimmer's voice interrupted her attempts to think. At least he wasn't touching her now. When he touched her, she couldn't think about work, about loss, about—anything. His touch wiped out memory, wiped out grief and filled her with sharp, hot need.

"With your input, I want to map out a plan to tackle the amount of information we're going to be dealing with. We need more human resources, and therein lies one of our key problems."

"Who we can trust." Grateful he was still including her in planning—grateful he hadn't rejected her and her distracted mind as dangerous—Lin sat straighter.

"What we'll do is keep the most sensitive materials in our hands, and hand out the legwork. I'm keen to set a trap to catch the mole in your department."

"You're so certain there's one in my department. What about in yours?"

His expression became shuttered and she recalled what he'd said: Two operatives dead and not knowing if there might be others.

"Anything is possible." His tone—so cold, so detached. Was he mercurial, or was her clouded perspective the problem?

She set aside the tangential thinking and focused on his idea. A trap—because anything was possible, and any operative could be swayed. It was only ever a question of finding the right motivation. Find a vulnerability and apply pressure. Like in martial arts.

What was his weakness? He'd loved his grandmother and missed her even now. He cared about people. That much had been clear yesterday, before her accident. The inconvenient, frustrating accident that meant they lost Chan's driver because Rimmer stopped to pick her up.

He could have left me and stayed on the tail of the driver.

But he'd stopped to pick her up and they'd lost their chance.

A connection zapped and snapped into place in her mind, and she stared at Rimmer, mentally pulling out details from the file she'd been sent on her new partner.

Betrayed in a previous mission, he'd barely escaped with his life. There were two dead agents from that same case. Had one of them been his partner? Did he have trust issues as a result?

It would explain his hot and cold attitude, and his demand

she stayed in his hotel room last night.

To keep me under observation?

Such a demand was definitely not in the department handbook, so why had she given into his request?

If she didn't count one scorching look when she emerged from the shower, a look that had sent heat racing through her body, Rimmer hadn't touched her. They were both clear that sex wasn't on the table. And yet . . .

Should she count that single inadvertent brush of hands when they reached across the table for the same page? Tension zapped between them before his "after you", delivered in glacial tones.

She shook her head and dragged her wayward mind back to the task at hand. "This is true. And because anything is possible, I'm wondering how my little sister ended up in that brothel. That is not who she was."

"What do you mean? Not a prostitute?"

Lin's breath caught in her throat. Anger flared, flowered, like red fireworks against the dark sky. Rage so all-consuming she clenched her hands into fists. "Did you assume that Kim was a prostitute because she was found in a brothel?"

"Lin, I make no judgement, no assumptions, but I want to understand. Tell me about your sister, and why you think she was in that place." He parked the car in a space overlooking the water and turned off the engine.

Without the quiet hum of the motor, she was conscious of his steady breathing and the strength of his tanned hands as he rested one on top of the steering wheel. His full attention was on her.

Struggling to rein in her burst of angry adrenaline, Lin took several deep breaths and pressed her lips together.

That was the thing about grief. It carried her emotions like a runaway rollercoaster, scattering anger here, loading up on grief there . . .

Lusting after Rimmer too, even as her anger with him subsided.

Keeping her eyes on the water rippling past them, she felt inadequate to the task. How could she convey to him the life and spirit that had been her sister? "Kim was beautiful and strong-willed, loving and caring. She was younger than me, and loved life, loved having fun. She poked fun at me for being too focused on my work and not going out enough. She used to guilt me into going out with her sometimes by saying how disappointed she was not to have prospects of becoming an aunty."

Quickly she slapped a lid on the realisation that neither would she ever be an aunty to her sister's children. Gripping the jade pendant, she reached for calm, reached for less troublesome memories to share.

"Sometimes she would arrive at my apartment out of the blue and drag me out to a party with her."

"She sounds like the oldest of my sisters, always mother-henning the rest of us, but in the nicest way."

A smile tugged the corner of her mouth. "Yes. Mother hen is just what she was, with a dash of showy feathers."

Silence sat between them for several heartbeats.

Mother hen Kim. Except when they'd faced each other across the mat under Grandfather's watchful eye. Then sisterhood gave way to fierce competitiveness that Lin usually won. Wrapped in memories, Lin relived moments of joy and sisterly love.

"Do you have any theories about how your sister came to be in Chan's brothel?" His question recalled her to the present.

"No." The word whipped out, harsh and full of agony. Why couldn't he leave off with such questions about Kim? She'd had nothing to do with Chan until the night of her death. Nothing to do with Lin's case. But Lin knew why Rimmer was tenacious, like a bloodhound on the trail of a fox. Horrible as it was to think about

Kim in that place, if he teased out even one detail that helped bring Chan to justice, Lin had to tell all she could remember.

Even if remembering flayed her with a thousand knives.

She sighed. "No idea. Men were attracted to Kim, but she managed to keep them as friends when they realised she wasn't about to settle down to marriage with them."

"Any chance she might have gone to the brothel with a male friend for—"

"No, no kinky stuff. Sex was private for Kim."

"So she never spoke of it with you?"

"Did you say you have four sisters?" His lack of understanding surprised her. "Haven't you ever overheard them talking?"

He grimaced. "I tried not to listen. Are you saying the two of you did talk about sex?"

Lin shrugged. "I shouldn't divulge the secrets of sisterhood to a man with sisters of his own."

He held up a hand and shook his head. "No need. I get the idea. But seriously, is there nothing about your sister to explain how she came to be in that place?"

"Nothing. But you know, we should be working out a way to ferret out any of Chan's moles within the department."

"What I said before. We keep hold of the sensitive material and farm out the legwork and—"

A familiar buzz started in Lin's mind as an idea, at once welcome and daring, frightening and empowering, pushed its way out of her subconscious. "I have an idea, Rimmer. You're not going to like it."

Chapter 12

"I hate it."

Not just hate. Lin's suggestion made Paul's stomach roil. "I won't sanction it, not with Chan."

"Told you you'd hate it, but it has a high chance of flushing out a bad agent."

"It has a high chance of getting you killed. No." It went against every protective instinct in his body, and then some. And Tam had specifically warned against the exact same thing.

"But, Rimmer—"

"But Lin . . ." He copied her intonation and held up one large hand like a stop sign. "I don't think you want justice. Acting as bait for Chan is a death wish."

Her gaze narrowed and she pursed her lips before nodding once. "Okay, we'll put it on the backburner for now."

Clearly his objection wasn't unexpected, but try as he might to contain the deep-in-his-gut visceral reaction, she must have noted his fear. Nothing else would have stilled Lin's tongue so quickly.

"We'll can the idea completely." Damn the gruffness of his voice and damn the nightmare that occasionally disturbed his sleep. But offering herself as bait to lure Chan out meant either that she had no real idea of the depth of depravity they were dealing with, or she was naïve beyond belief.

Fear goosestepped down his spine at the thought of sanctioning putting Lin in Chan's path. Tamsin had done something similar and her twin had almost been killed because of it. "Chan is a psychopath. He cares for nothing and no one."

"I get it. You're the boss. What you say goes." Lin's eyes

were wide and innocent.

Too innocent.

"I'm deadly serious about this, Lin." He didn't trust that look, or the need for revenge that was driving her.

"Okay, okay. Consider it forgotten. I have another idea, this one for more agent power."

"If it's anything like your last idea, forget it." He gave her a hard look, but Lin appeared impervious to it.

"Do you want to hear it?" She met his eyes, refusing to say more until he ground out a single word of willingness to listen.

"Spill."

"Our concern is that someone or more than one in the department has been bought off or manipulated into passing information to Chan, right? We can't be sure who is not compromised, so instead, we take a small group of promising final year interns, agents in training, and we give them the grunt work. Keep them separate from the main office and embargo communications with other operatives."

He rubbed his lower lip with his thumb. It wasn't a half bad idea, but damn it, Lin had given him a nasty shock with her suggestion of becoming bait to lure Chan. "I'll think about it."

Her half-smile, quickly suppressed, made Paul wonder if she'd played him. Thrown out an idea she knew he'd hate, followed by one less dangerous, less crazy, and with potential.

"Good. So, I can't believe I'm the one saying this, but—do you want lunch?"

Figuring her suggestion came as a sign she'd got the emotional weight of her sister's funeral in hand, he allowed himself to relax just a little. "Sure. My treat."

The sky was the deep, hot blue of the tropics and sunlight tipped small waves in the wake of a boat cruising past, its white paintwork gleaming, blinding him as the angle changed and rays bounced off the windows. Blue, white, and the lush green of well-watered grass—clean, fresh colours far removed from the darkness of Chan's world.

And lunch with Lin.

"Tell me where to go."

Mischief filled her gaze. "Do you really mean that?"

***

On the same day she'd consigned Kim's ashes to the sea, had she really smiled and teased Rimmer? It hardly seemed possible or appropriate, and yet this attraction disguised as annoyance was keeping her sane. If only she could talk it through with Kim.

But if her sister had still been alive, would Lin have been assigned to this investigation, or still working her previous case?

"Rimmer."

Her partner looked up from his lunch of Mongolian lamb, chopsticks poised to lift another mouthful of food. "What's up?"

"I'm wondering why I was taken off the case I was working and assigned to this one?"

"Because you're the best operative they've got." He scooped up a large piece of meat and chewed with concentration and appreciation.

"Sure, that's what Joe told me."

"Don't you think you are?"

She slid a finger down the bottle of juice and trailed the water condensing at the base of the bottle in a path along the paper-covered table. "I am."

"So what were you working on? I'm guessing the case wasn't as big as this."

"Maybe not. A missing socialite."

"I'll make another guess—it was high profile because her daddy is high up in government and could pull strings. Am I right?"

"Got it in one. But when Chan was spotted, Joe Wang took

me off the case of the careless socialite and gave me to you."

Rimmer's eyebrow quirked up and he grinned.

It took Lin a moment to work out why. "You're going to focus on my phrasing instead of asking me why she was careless?"

"It's more fun. Okay, was she the careless one, or was it an inside job? Did she disappear from the family home without triggering any of a sophisticated battery of security cameras?"

"She gave her security detail the slip while she was in a club in town."

"Careless of her security detail. Stupid of her. Chances are, she slipped away to meet a man. But why were you put on the case instead of the local police?"

"You were right about her father. He's a government minister who demanded the Bureau put their best female operative on it because, quote—only another woman could understand the thinking of his wayward, careless daughter and he wanted a professional—unquote."

"Not very complimentary of local law enforcement." Rimmer scooped the last of the lamb into his mouth as though still ravenous.

Lin eyed the two empty plates by his side. "Sure you don't want another serving of something?"

He swallowed and set his now empty bowl on the table. "I've had enough for now, thanks. Unless you've got another serve of Lin sarcasm to dish out?"

"I won't even dignify that with an answer. I've got a lot of calls to make if we want an active team ready to go tonight."

***

Paul continued working through pages of articles about missing girls while Lin set their intern investigators to work—three men and three women selected for their performance scores and specific backgrounds. Six carefully chosen young agents-in-training under their control and working through masses of information.

But Lin's concern about her reassignment niggled. He listened to those niggles, instincts. Call them whatever, but they'd saved his life on a handful of occasions.

He pulled the laptop she had given him to use while he was in Singapore towards him and searched for details on the missing socialite, Serena Masters and her father, Lew Masters. The newspaper reports were typically sensational and speculative, except for one left-wing publication that posed Serena's disappearance as having more to do with her father's covert and corrupt business deals.

Paul dismissed it as the usual socialist beat up and moved on.

Next he turned to police reports. Bare facts and a short report with a note of Masters' *request* to have Lin assigned to the investigation and not much else besides.

Not what he'd been expecting.

On a hunch, Paul also searched for earlier mentions of Lew Masters and widened the parameters to include the period before his appointment as a government minister. Several file numbers, contents redacted or labelled: Top security clearance, piqued his interest.

"Lin?"

She glanced across, held up one finger and called, "Give me a moment" from where she was giving directions to one of the women who looked barely older than a high school student. Wendy, if Paul remembered correctly, and she had placed first in several tests, although not in the physical elements of fieldwork.

Wendy nodded, adjusted her black-rimmed glasses, and turned her attention to the pile of papers in front of her.

Lin skirted the table. "What is it?" She stood beside him and bent down to look at his screen. "What has the minister got to do with—"

"Where are your file notes on Serena's case? Can you show them to me please?"

Frowning and casting him a wary glance, she turned the laptop a little way towards her and reached past him to open a new tab and enter her password.

Her scent filled his nose and her ponytail slid across his arm when she leaned closer to the screen. "That's odd."

Catching himself taking a too-deep breath spiced with her scent, her tone registered before Paul looked at the screen. "What's wrong?"

"My case notes—they've been archived. No one has been assigned to take over Serena's case."

Paul stared at the digital stamp across the file details. "Archived? Why would her father make such a fuss about getting you on his daughter's case and not make a fuss when you were pulled off it? Has she returned? Does he know the case has effectively been closed?"

Lin bit her lower lip. Her frown deepened, and she clicked into the previous tab Paul had left open.

He grunted, half-embarrassed. Of course, if his hunch proved right, he'd look clever to Lin.

"Why were you checking the minister's background before he rose to prominence in government?"

"A solitary reference in one newspaper at the time of his daughter's disappearance suggested shady dealings in his past. I dismissed it at first then decided any offbeat reference was worth following up."

"One reference in one paper sent you down this track?"

"You think I'm crazy?"

Slowly shaking her head, Lin stood. "No. Just because I know of nothing in his background doesn't mean you're crazy. This is a different line of inquiry. Do you want me to search through back channels? See what I can find out that way?"

The hair on the back of Paul's neck rose. "Can we get an interview with him?"

Chapter 13

Conscious of the closed circuit camera, Lin pulled her cap lower and bent her head over her phone. Caution ingrained during training was hard to change, despite this not being her first visit to Masters' mansion.

Rimmer gave their names when requested by a static-fuzzed voice over the intercom and closed his window as he drove through the security gates. Eight-feet high, elaborately decorated with incised tropical plant patterns, the metal barriers swung closed behind the car. Continuing around a circular drive, he drove past the thickly planted central garden.

The mansion came into view and Lin studied its graceful lines with a familiar eye. "Would you say the mansion has a 'wow' factor?"

"If you like that sort of thing. Or you could say Masters is compensating for something with that protuberance." Paul eased the hire car to a halt beneath said *protuberance*, a grandiose portico with Greek-style columns.

They climbed out and Paul pressed the remote control, locking the car.

"Reflex reaction, Rimmer?" She tipped her head towards the car.

"Can't be too careful in a neighbourhood like this."

His dry humour made her chuckle. He was different from the agents she knew and worked with. But then, Paul Rimmer was different from every other man she'd met. He didn't trust her, and that wasn't her imagination working overtime. One minute he annoyed the heck out of her, but the next, he did something to make her smile. Some of the time she downright disliked him. But there were also stretches of time when he took her out of her grief and pain and into the realm of imagined pleasure.

And then there were moments when she thought she glimpsed the inner man beneath his professional mask. Few and far between, but she liked what she saw then.

Side by side they climbed the wide, shallow, beautifully tiled steps to the oversized front door. Before Lin could press the doorbell, the door was opened by a Chinese Singaporean man in a beautifully tailored black suit. He was the epitome of an aristocratic British butler. Straight back, slightly supercilious air, and not an ounce of emotion in his expression.

"I'm Agent Paul Rimmer and Agent Tan, you already know. We're here to see Mr Masters. We phoned earlier."

The butler held the door open and stepped to one side. "Of course. I'll show you to the pool, sir, madam. Please follow me."

Madam. The old-fashioned title had sat awkwardly with Lin the first time he'd used it. It made her feel old, like her grandmother. Like she had to be on her best behaviour. But "Sir, madam" . . . It linked her and Rimmer. Like they were a couple—

She left more space between them as they passed through the central foyer with its soaring ceiling and massive arched window, and took a left past a lush tropical garden, emerging at—

"Did he call this a pool?" Paul's voice was low, for her ears only.

Lin's gaze roamed over a series of interconnected pools, a steaming Jacuzzi, and a ten-foot high waterfall, a part of the house she hadn't seen on her previous visit. "I guess as a government minister he couldn't afford anything more substantial."

Paul's mouth kicked up in a lopsided grin.

The butler stopped in front of a huge oval banana lounge unlike anything Lin had seen. "Sir, Agent Rimmer and Agent Tan to see you."

A peevish voice preceded Lin's view of Lew Masters.

"Fine. Bring coffee here." Masters pushed himself out of the lounge and reached for a robe, which he shrugged into but left unbelted, showing off a hairy chest and substantial potbelly above his swimming trunks. "What's this all about? I'm a busy man."

Working hard not to roll her eyes, Lin fixed her gaze on the minister. On her last visit he'd been dressed in a suit and tie and had remained seated. Standing, he had maybe an inch on her; no more than that. "We understand, sir. If you recall, I'm Agent Tan. At your request I was working on your daughter's disappearance and—"

"Yes, and now it's closed. You want a medal or something? Why are you here?" His feet were planted wide, hands fisted on his hips, taking up space and attempting to dominate those he confronted.

His stance reminded her of a bulldog, or maybe a cockerel. *Small man syndrome*, she thought, working through the possibilities thrown up by this new knowledge, that Masters knew the case was closed. Had he ordered it closed, or had someone dared to tell him it was going to happen?

Lin ignored his question. Questions were for her and Rimmer to ask. "And your daughter?"

"What about her? She's a silly girl. She gave her security detail the slip. I fired them. End of matter."

Masters knew the case had been closed, fine. But as far as Lin knew, Serena Masters hadn't returned home, so why had her father stopped pursuing his daughter's disappearance?

"I'm glad to know she's safe." Lin paused, watching Masters fold his arms, and taking note of other small shifts in body language. "Serena *is* safe, isn't she, Mr Masters?"

"She . . ." Masters glanced towards the house, his Adam's apple bobbing.

Not so cocky now.

Rimmer picked up the lead, their interchange as smooth as

when they'd planned their questions in the car on the way over. "No other agent was assigned to continue the investigation." Paul's voice was calm, official, but his intense blue gaze belied the bland tone. "We couldn't find any confirmation that your daughter returned home. She is home, isn't she?"

Fear flashed through Masters' eyes.

No, not fear. Terror.

Pure and unadulterated.

Excitement raced through Lin's veins. Rimmer's instinct was spot on, but could they induce the minister to reveal why he was almost shaking with fear?

"We're just tidying up loose ends since the case has been—closed." Rimmer paused, turned up the heat in his gaze and stepped towards Masters. "When did Serena return? The case notes are missing a resolution. I'm sure you understand the department has to dot all the i's and cross all the t's."

Lin wanted to cheer Rimmer on. Sweat trickled down Masters' face and his hands fumbled and shook as he tried to tie his belt.

"No need, all good. No need." Masters' gaze darted wildly from the pool house to the butler approaching with a drinks trolley.

"So your daughter is home safe and sound?"

"She's okay. All good."

The butler set the trolley at the side of the path and picked up the silver coffee pot. "Shall I pour, sir?"

Masters gestured, a vague wave the butler took as assent. He picked up a white cup and saucer and, raising the silver coffee pot, poured the coffee in an expert stream. Black, no sugar, he offered the cup to the minister.

"Put it on the table." The wobble in Masters' voice matched the shake in his hand.

The butler turned to Lin. "Coffee, madam, sir?"

"No, thank you." Lin offered a small smile and glanced at

Paul. "My partner doesn't drink coffee."

Paul continued as though the interruption hadn't occurred. He played bad cop so well, she felt like applauding. "When precisely did Serena return? We'd like to talk with her, find out if she can tell us where she's been? Who was she with? Did she leave of her own volition or escape? Was she unharmed? We need to know if—"

"Enough. She is safe. The case is closed. Now leave." He stalked away.

"Can we talk to her, Mr Masters?" Rimmer's question sent the minister scurrying into the pool house. A door slammed.

The butler gestured towards the path they'd taken to the pool. "Allow me to show you out."

***

The gates closed behind them. Security cameras at the gates followed their departure, and Paul drove slowly away from the mansion down the quiet street. "What do you make of him?"

"Scared for his life." Lin retrieved a voice file and pressed the play button. "Listen to how he says 'she is safe'."

Masters' voice had lacked conviction and the brief denial spewed out fast and high.

"He never specifically said she was at home; only that she's *safe*."

"So you don't think she's a precocious princess who's run off with the cabana boy to spite daddy?"

"Serena isn't there. My guess is someone's holding her to control him."

Paul turned the corner and pulled over to the kerb. "I agree. The question is, who? Why take her unless they've demanded a ransom?"

"There was no demand; at least none that Masters shared. But Masters is high up in government, so that opens other possibilities."

"Hmm. I've never worked a kidnap—it's not the type of case my Bureau is normally involved in—but do you think he's received a ransom demand since you were taken off the case and been told not to involve the police? Did his response strike you that way?"

Lin switched off her phone and dropped it into her lap. "Not really. When I first spoke with him it was in his home office. The way he told the story was that she'd probably allowed her head to be turned by some man he was certain was only after Serena for her father's money. He seemed angry more than anything and said he expected me to get her back unharmed. Unsaid but no less clear was that he didn't want to pay for her return."

"Would you say he and his daughter were close?"

Lin shook her head. "There were a few family group photos on the walls and one of his wife and daughter as a child on his desk, but I had to ask Helen Masters for a recent photo of Serena. She was genuinely worried about her daughter."

"Have you got a recent picture of Serena on your phone?"

"Of course." Lin scrolled through, found the file and handed her phone to him. "That's her."

Paul glanced at the photo and then stared. Long dark hair, fair skin, blue-grey eyes, tip-tilted at the corners. He enlarged the photo to focus on her features. He hadn't imagined the likeness.

Fear for the woman filled his gut, and dread as a possibility too awful to contemplate took shape. "When exactly did Serena Masters go missing?"

"Two weeks ago, last Thursday."

"And when was that sighting of Chan made?"

Lin's eyes narrowed as she tried connecting the dots he set before her.

"Coming up three weeks ago."

Paul took his phone from his pocket and scrolled through.

Was it possible that the Bureau's first sighting of Chan wasn't the first time he'd arrived in Singapore? He stopped at a photo of Tamsin and set the two images side by side. "Serena could be her twin. Perhaps triplet is more appropriate since she already has an identical twin."

Lin was silent for moments, looking from one to the other before meeting his gaze. She returned the phone and nodded at the image on the screen. "Who is she?"

"My partner, Tamsin. Chan tried to manoeuvre her into becoming his mistress. He was humiliated after Tam and I both escaped a trap at his family home, and word had it that his uncles wanted him killed because of the debacle we created. Tam's identical twin sister, Marcy nearly died in Nepal because Chan sought revenge."

Lin's assessing gaze met and held his. Was she already intuiting the connection his thoughts had jumped to? She was clever and quick, like Tam, but the way she tuned in to his thoughts was—spooky.

"Is it only seeing how alike Tam and Serena are that surprised you?"

"Maybe. At first, but—" He looked at the photo of Tam and his thoughts winged back to the dead woman in Chan's bed the day they'd raided the brothel. She'd had dark hair, and lighter skin and blue eyes, like the Westcott twins.

And there was that other photo he'd seen during their Sydney investigation into Chan that made bile rise in his throat. "A young woman's body was pulled from the harbour a short time before that raid. She was found upriver from the brothel. Not much skin remained intact by the time she was pulled from the water, but the coroner said her DNA indicated she was of mixed ethnicity. Dark hair, lighter skin. And the autopsy showed she'd been asphyxiated."

"Not drowned?"

"No. We had our suspicions but couldn't prove anything. But Chan likes his women young, dark-haired, and pale-skinned. Preferably with light coloured eyes, but that's not a deal-breaker when he's choosing his *bed-mates*."

"But your partner and her twin fit that description, and so does Serena and so did—"

"Your sister. Except weren't her eyes chocolate-brown like yours?"

"Kim had eyes like mine, but she wore contact lenses, sometimes clear, but sometimes in different colours." Lin sucked in a shaky breath and flicked through her photos with unsteady hands.

Paul hated the next question, even as it formed in his mind, hated asking as the words formed in his mouth. But he hated it most when he thought how the asking of it would focus Lin on her sister's death—in the worst possible way. "Was she wearing coloured lenses the night she died?"

Lin nodded, her head bobbing up and down like a sideshow alley clown until she stopped at an image of Kim and offered her phone to him again. Her hands settled into fists in her lap and she pressed her lips together.

His gaze lingered on Lin's tense body, and her drawn expression, and he worried about the emotional wringer this investigation was putting her through. Finally he looked at the photo she'd given him.

Times like this, Paul hated his work. Hated it with a passion, and yet a frisson of excitement raced through his veins as he studied the image. "The resemblance is uncanny—like seeing a ghost."

Had he stumbled onto the link between the dead girls in Sydney and Chan's pursuit of Tamsin?

"Is it possible Serena was taken because she looked like the twins? Do you think the same could be said about Kim?" He set the photos side by side and turned both screens towards Lin.

Her eyes darted between screens. "It's possible."

"We've got work to do, but first I'm going to buy you a drink."

"I do not feel like celebrating, Rimmer." Her voice was tight, squeezed out of a throat constricted by the darkest of emotions.

He knew much about such grief. He also knew that alcohol wasn't an answer, but Lin looked shattered. "We're not celebrating. You've had a shock. And while I still think Wang was wrong to put you on this case when you're in this early period of mourning Kim, I'm selfishly glad he did."

She looked up at his admission, surprise edging out some of the tension that had drawn her mouth into a straight line. "You like working with me?"

Like, yes. Trust? That was growing.

"Yep. Coming, partner?"

Chapter 14

Sunlight slanted across Paul's computer screen and the muted roar of late afternoon traffic hummed in the background as he opened a new tab. In the office, their team were busy at their computers. He was almost certain he'd found a connection between several of the missing girls. He just needed to—

"Excuse me, Agent Rimmer? Do you have a moment?"

Holding back a sigh, he looked up. He was the team leader and interruptions were part of his job. "What is it, Wendy?"

She set a photo in front of him. "This was taken within the past hour."

Paul pushed his Bluetooth mouse aside, picked up the photo and examined the man at its centre.

Chan had evaded international police for two years and now he'd been caught on camera a second time in less than a month. *Sloppy? Or overconfident?* The coincidence triggered Paul's gut response. It twisted into a bad feeling about improbabilities and piercing certainty about departmental corruption. Had Chan become careless after so long on the run, or were Paul and his team being played, drip-fed false information and red herrings?

"Where?"

"At the cemetery where Agent Tan's sister is buried."

Before he corrected Wendy, Paul looked across at Lin. She gave the tiniest shake of her head.

"Good pick up, Wendy, thanks."

"I've emailed a copy to your computer, but I took the liberty of printing it as well. You'll want it in your file, won't you?"

"Very helpful."

Lin waited until Wendy had returned to her workstation before she moved to Paul's side and peered at the photo.

"Care to explain what that was all about?" He kept his voice low and his head turned away from the group of interns.

Lin raised one shoulder in a careless shrug. "Grandfather agreed with my concerns about the circumstances around Kim's death. We chose cremation and scattering of Kim's ashes over interment and advised only family of the change of venue on the morning of the ceremony."

"You'll be sharing those *concerns* with me later."

"Of course." Lin reached for the photo. "May I?"

"Sure." Paul handed the photo to her and watched her expression as she examined it closely.

"It's the same cemetery we were planning to—" She tipped the photo towards the bright sunlight slanting through the windows. "Can you open a copy of this on your computer? I need more resolution of—"

Paul clicked on the new email, and then enlarged the photo. "What did you notice?"

Lin leaned over his shoulder and pointed at Chan's left arm held across his waist. The top of what looked like a container rested in the crook of his arm. "That's an urn he's carrying."

"Interesting. Whose ashes does he have in there?"

Lin slipped back behind her computer and he heard the keys clacking, much faster than his hunt and peck approach. "Anything?"

"There are announcements on the funeral home site for an interment of ashes today for a Japanese businessman who suicided recently, and two burials, neither under the name of Chan. Nothing that explains why John Chan and that urn were there."

"See if there is security footage from the funeral home."

"On a cemetery?"

"Why not?"

"It's fenced and locked at sundown. Security cameras will be directed towards the front gate. They'll only show cars arriving and leaving. No cameras will be set to scan the cemetery itself. Unless you think you're going to see ghosts rising from their graves after midnight?" Her eyebrow rose in a graceful arc above the first hint of humour he'd seen from her all day.

"So tell me, how did we get this photo of Chan?"

Lin raised her chin and tipped it towards the intern table. "Ask Wendy. She's the one who found it."

Paul turned to the table of interns and raised his voice to be heard over the clatter of keyboards and flurry of movement from their small team. "Wendy, can you join us please?"

Wendy rose and pushed her glasses up her nose, picked up a notebook and pen and joined them. "Yes, Agent Rimmer?"

"Where did you get that photo of Chan?"

Her gaze flicked to Lin, but other than that single look she kept a tight rein on her reaction. "My mother's cousin works at the cemetery. Sometimes he takes photos for a book he's been working on for the past few years."

"A book of photos of graves?" Her response seemed ghoulish, but it was unembellished and immediate. The truth therefore, but Paul sensed it wasn't the whole truth.

Wendy shook her head. "A history of death in Singapore. On occasion he also photographs mourners for the book. Those who catch his interest."

Lin tapped Paul's screen drawing their attention to Chan and the urn he carried. "Why did this cousin send you *this* photo? Have you spoken about our case to anyone?"

Wendy bristled, her eyes widened, seeming huge behind her glasses. She inhaled a deep breath and shook her head. "I have spoken with no one about this case, Agent Tan. Although the coincidence is strange—" She drew her phone from her jacket pocket, turned it on and offered it to Lin.

Paul leaned over to read the email that had accompanied the photo.

Wendy continued. "My mother's cousin knows only that I am studying psychology at the university. You can see his message says he sent this man's photo immediately because he'd never seen a mourner with such cold eyes and wanted to know what I thought about him."

"You're saying this is nothing more than a curious and strange coincidence?" Paul loathed coincidence with a passion, and for good reason.

Wendy lowered her gaze to her notebook and frowned. "It is never random. Sometimes coincidence is a plan in disguise."

"Twice?" The word shot out of his mouth like a bullet from a gun.

"Rimmer?" Lin's voice was strained, wary. Did she think he was going to speak out of turn in front of their intern?

He raised a hand, stopping further comment. "Tell me now, Wendy. What is the real reason this cousin sent you this photo?"

Wendy's gaze lifted and met Paul's, but she turned to Lin. "I am aware that the truth of your sister's funeral is—different from what belongs to public knowledge. I have not spoken out of turn to my mother's cousin, about this case or your sister. But I set up an alert for any mention of John Chan's name."

Lin set her hands on Paul's desk and leaned towards the intern. "There was no mention of John Chan on the funeral company's site."

"No, but there was a parcel that arrived two days ago marked 'Fragile'. It was sent to an address in Geylang, number sixty-five—"

Paul's glance collided with Lin's. It had to be the parcel they'd seen in the hands of Chan's driver, the one they had considered a decoy following their abortive attempt to tail the driver back to wherever Chan was living.

"That was good thinking. Why didn't you share this earlier?"

"I have been told often by my supervisor that I overreach myself. He tells me I'm too independent, self-reliant—conceited about my abilities . . ." Wendy's eyes glistened, but she sniffed, swallowed, and raised her chin. "I did not wish to earn reprimands from you for doing what I thought was logical. I am grateful for this chance to use my training in practical ways."

Sami, Paul's youngest sister had made a similar observation about a female teacher. "It still doesn't explain why you asked your mother's cousin to take photos."

"The description of the parcel's contents was human ashes. I did a search for a recent death in Chan's family. Two weeks ago his father died and was cremated. Then on the Dark Web I found a trail of messages between Chan and one of his uncles, a not-tech-savvy uncle. His privacy settings were poor—" Wendy glanced at Paul and cleared her throat before continuing.

"As the eldest son, Chan requested the ashes be sent to him. I asked my mother's cousin to photograph all mourners over a three-day period. I told him it was for a university assignment. He's been sending photos throughout the morning."

"Correlate the time this photo was taken with details provided to the funeral home. Find out what name and address was used. And Wendy—"

"Yes, Agent Rimmer?"

"Good work, but in future, run ideas you come up with past us first."

A tiny smile softened the line of Wendy's mouth. "Yes, sir. I'll have that information for you shortly."

Lin tipped her head back and rolled her shoulders. "It's still hard being a woman in some arms of the service. That supervisor she referred to? He was there when I went through my training.

Female students had to be twice as good as the male students, and he hated having to award the top honours to a woman."

"Was that you by any chance?"

Lin didn't answer, but looked across to where Wendy was in deep communion with her computer. "Looks like he'll have another tough graduation ceremony this year."

"Let's add this latest information to our timeline. I want to see a chain of cause and effect before we leave the building."

Chapter 15

Less than thirty minutes later, Lin slipped her phone into her satchel and stood. "Rimmer, you need to come with me now."

He looked up from his screen. Perhaps he saw something of the anger rising within her, or maybe he was learning to read her better. Whatever the reason, he closed his computer and pushed his chair back. "Everybody, you're to continue under Wendy's supervision until I or Agent Tan return. Is that clear?"

Wendy's mouth dropped open and as quickly closed, but her eyes were bright as she sat at her desk. "Perfectly, sir."

"Order in some dinner if it gets to eight o'clock and we're not back." He followed Lin out, refraining from speaking until they were in his car. "Where to?"

She opened the GPS on her phone and typed in their destination. "Take a left out of the driveway, first right, third left, and I'll fill you in as we go."

Rimmer turned out of the driveway and drove in silence, waiting for her to speak. He flicked several glances her way.

She couldn't bear to meet his eyes. Rubbing a hand over her chest above her angry, beating heart, she looked straight ahead. "A shipping container has been opened for inspection at the docks. Inside are the bodies of fifteen young women and one who is alive, but comatose and severely dehydrated."

The car jerked to a stop at a traffic light. "Shit." Rimmer thumped the steering wheel with a fist and expelled a harsh breath.

Did he feel it too, this sense of having failed those women? A visceral spike struck deep, cramping in Lin's stomach. The fact they'd been working the case for too short a time to have stopped the container leaving port made no difference. They had failed to prevent more deaths in their pursuit of Chan, but Chan was involved. She was sure, even without further proof.

"What else do we know at the moment?" Rimmer eased off the brake with more care than he'd pulled up at the lights. How did he exert such steely self-control?

Lin opened her fists and set her hands palms down on her legs and took a deep breath. Allowing her emotions to cloud her thinking would not bring justice for the dead girls, and justice was all she could offer now.

"Not a lot more. The container came in from the Philippines. Ships usually take between five and eight days to make that trip, but the *Santa Rosa* was delayed by storms and heavy seas. Customs officers chose to open a particular container after they checked the manifest. It was listed as carrying soft furnishings, but they don't usually stink. This one was bad. My contact at the docks let me know as soon as she learned what was going on."

"Is your gut feeling that this is one of Chan's shipments?"
Absolutely.

"Could be. It's a method we suspected him of using to stock his brothels." Lin tipped her head back but angry, futile tears slipped from the corners of her eyes. "Sorry, I'm not usually emotional like this." She wiped away her tears and sniffed, the sound defiant and determined to her ears. "We've got to stop him, Rimmer."

He reached a hand over and covered hers where it lay in her lap. "Don't be so hard on yourself. You just said goodbye to your sister. Remember, we're doing everything we can."

" I know, but how many more girls will die before we succeed?"

By the time Rimmer turned into the docks and parked, she was in control of her emotions. Grief for Kim would not stop her from doing her job, not after she'd assured Rimmer that she would use it to make her more focused, more determined.

But as they neared the cordoned off area, the stench wafting on the breeze nearly undid her resolve. Gagging, she turned her back, pulled out a hot pink and red Isadora scarf and fashioned a crude mask. There was nothing she could do about her stinging eyes, except settle her sunglasses over her nose.

Looking grim and a little desperate, Rimmer covered his mouth and nose with a hand. Ahead of them, a makeshift screen hid the open container from any passing view. He hailed a masked police officer who pointed out the official in charge of the gruesome site, and then strode to where a group had gathered upwind of the worst of the smell.

Rimmer stepped into a gap when the group parted and flipped out his ID.

Lin followed, fumbling for hers in her satchel and withdrew it several beats late. Behaving like an emotional junior assistant instead of the experienced field officer she was, was unacceptable.

Looking at the expressions on the faces of the group, she noted one who was green around the gills. He was probably responsible for the puddle of vomit several metres away. She turned her attention to the badged officer answering Rimmer's questions. " . . . fifteen dead. Only one alive, barely. She's been taken to hospital already, unresponsive. It will be touch and go if she survives."

There was nothing new so far.

"I want a guard posted at her door. Notify us if she wakes."

Concentrating on facts, Lin spoke up. "What are the names on the cargo manifest?"

The officer's gaze flicked to Lin for the first time. "Agent—?"

"Lin Tan."

He held out an iPad. "There. Do you want me to send a copy of it now?"

She ran her gaze over the details. The sender and receiver company names on the screen were ordinary, common, unfamiliar, and probably aliases, but they'd have to be investigated. "Yes please. Is it okay if we take a look now?" Two protective-suited attendants walked past the group carrying a litter. The shape within the body bag was small, barely raising the thick material of the covering. A fresh wave of anger roared within Lin's mind.

"Go ahead. Grab a mask and goggles from the paramedics. You'll need them." The officer took the iPad from Lin. "Turn on Airdrop and I'll send the details now."

Rimmer gave the officer a curt nod. "Thanks. Come on, Lin, coveralls and protective gear are this way."

Lin waved to show she'd heard then thumbed on her phone and waited for the ping announcing the arrival of the promised information before she caught up with Rimmer. "Got it. I'll send this to Wendy to start checking while we're here."

As soon as they had donned coveralls, masks and goggles, they headed back to the container. Another small body bag was carried past them before they reached the open doors and Lin had to force herself to take the last few steps. She stood beside Rimmer and looked into hell.

The interior of the container presented a grim picture, like a macabre full-sized version of a medieval painting of plague victims. Bodies, scantily clad in cheap shifts, lay on mats or bare metal.

Except for the varying stages of putrefaction or rigour mortis, they might almost have been asleep. Every one of them was young; most probably in their teens. The body closest to Lin appeared to still be stiff, her hand stretched towards the doors.

Swallowing bile, Lin squatted and examined the girl's hand. Broken nails and raw fingertips painted a wretched picture of her desperate clawing to escape.

Lin closed her eyes, but the image was burned into her

memory. This poor girl had probably died while the container rested on the deck within sound of rescue.

Rimmer touched her shoulder. His touch grounded her, reminding her she wasn't alone. "The police photos will be sent to us shortly, but, bad as this is, we need to see it firsthand. Ready?"

Speech wouldn't come so she nodded and stepped further inside, her phone raised and videoing the scene from left to right.

Slowly, she recorded the horror, blanking her mind and viewing it through the small screen. Later she would have to analyse the material and deal with being in the presence of death on this scale. Now, she needed to record and then gather clues.

Rimmer's voice was tight as he catalogued the non-human contents for the video. "Primitive toilet facilities, half a dozen mats—they must have slept in shifts or huddled together—" Rimmer squatted beside a pathetically small pile of empty plastic bottles in one corner. "Barely enough water here to last four days let alone a crossing that took much longer than planned."

Outrage sharpened his tone and she glanced at him as she finished recording the general scene and switched into photo mode. "Can you see any signs of food?"

Rimmer frowned above his goggles and turned a full circle. "Nothing. Looks like the girls were starved on the voyage."

"Starving girls are too weak to attempt escape and more receptive to orders." If the dead girls weren't Chan's doing, Lin would make it her life mission to catch whoever had perpetrated this abomination as well as bringing Chan to justice. She photographed each girl's face, hating the thought that these would be the last images of young lives. When she had finished, Rimmer jerked his head towards the opening.

She followed him outside, but he kept walking towards the edge of the dock before he removed his mask and goggles. Far enough so that the smell from the container didn't make her gag as she removed hers. She sucked in a breath of diesel-laden salt air and stared over the water, looking without really seeing anything.

Small waves slapped against the pier, the rhythmic sound soothing.

"You okay?" Rimmer sat on a low bollard marked by the many chains that had held ships at anchor there. His shoulders slumped and he lifted his head with what looked like an effort to meet her gaze.

"No." She tipped her head back and looked past the security lighting now bathing the docks. Somewhere up there were stars and open skies and freedom from what she had witnessed. "Man's inhumanity to man, or in this case, woman. Nobody could see that and be okay."

"We should get back to the office." He stood and reached for her hand. "With luck, Wendy might have found our source and—"

The breeze gusted from behind Rimmer and Lin stepped away, gasping. "You stink, Rimmer. And I probably do too."

Rimmer lifted one shoulder and turned his nose into his shirt. Quickly he turned away. "Showers first before we inflict this on anyone else."

"You can't walk through your hotel lobby stinking like that."

"What do you suggest I do? Dive into the oily waters of the docks?"

She shook her head. "You can shower at my place."

"And what will I do for fresh clothes?"

Running a practised eye over his body, she nodded. "I have something that will fit. Not very well, but it will do until you can get back to your room. The bonus is, you won't knock out every person within a twenty-metre radius."

***

Paul drove with the air conditioning on full blast and the rear windows open. Whether it was that combination, his mouth breathing, or the lowest setting above Arctic chill that kept him going, they reached Lin's apartment block without his stomach wanting to hurl his last meal. He pulled into a space across the road from the entrance and his eyes travelled up the height of the seven-storey building. The modern concrete and glass affair loomed above them, its harsh lines softened by tiny diagonal balconies cutting across the corners. Planter boxes with vivid green plants softened the grey concrete of several lower floors. This wasn't where he'd imagined Lin living. After seeing her family, he'd expected . . . traditional.

He turned the engine off and climbed out quickly. "I don't usually leave my car unlocked, but is it safe enough here if I leave the windows open to air it while we shower?"

Lin tipped her head from side to side and shrugged. "Leave the stink to grow worse in a locked car versus the slight risk of car thieves this side of midnight? We won't be that long, but I'm going to ride back on Minnie. Your car, your choice."

Paul lowered all four windows and lifted his backpack from the back seat. There was nothing else of value in the car. "I'd almost be willing to risk riding pillion just to avoid smelling myself."

"You say that now, but wait till you've removed the stink. Come on. You can shower first while I find you something to wear."

Lin entered a security code and pushed open the glass entry door, bypassing the lift. "I often take the stairs for exercise, but tonight, it will be doing my neighbours a favour by not taking the lift."

Lin ran lightly up four flights before turning left out of the stairwell.

Paul stayed three steps behind all the way until she unlocked the door to one of the corner units and flicked on a light switch.

"The bathroom is down the hall, second door on your right. Fresh towels are on the shelf. If you drop your clothes outside the door I'll throw everything into the washing machine." She set her sandals on a shoe rack beside the front door and disappeared through the third door along the hall, leaving Paul to his thoughts.

He removed his shoes and set them beside hers. As he straightened, his gaze fell on a small shrine and a photo of Lin's sister. Pretty, like Lin, but with slightly softer features, she wore a necklace like the one Lin's fingers often played with. He leaned closer, zeroing in on the leaf pendant, certain it was one and the same.

A faint scent of incense rose past the stench of his clothing.

Grimacing at his image in the circular mirror beside the shrine, he unbuttoned his shirt and pulled it off, dropping it outside the bathroom door before he entered. Inside, he undressed quickly and dropped the rest of his clothes on top of the shirt before turning the shower water on hard and hot. As steam filled the room he stepped into the shower and lowered his head. Hot water pounded over his head and neck, blinding him as he groped for the plunger on the bottle of body wash.

He scrubbed his face and body and then set to washing his hair.

Lin's voice sounded from the other side of the door, but her words were lost in the hissing water.

He pulled back the plastic curtain and stuck his head out. "What was that?"

The door opened a little way and Lin's face appeared in the gap. "I said I'm leaving fresh clothes outside the door for you." Her gaze met his, dropped and seemed to follow the shampoo suds running down his cheek and down his chest.

Heat surrounded him. Heat in her gaze, heat in his body—

In Lin's cheeks.

She tore her gaze away as though it pained her to do so.

"I'll leave you in peace."

"Thanks. I'm almost finished."

"No rush, Rimmer. If you're riding with me on Minnie I want you fresh as a daisy." The door closed softly.

Paul stared at the spot where she'd turned her heated gaze on him until soap ran into his eyes. "Blast." Turning the hot water tap off, he rinsed his hair and blasted his body with cold water.

Two words played over and over from her parting quip.

Riding—me.

He wished. Attraction had its place, and right at this moment after the afternoon's horror his awareness of Lin was a welcome-unwelcome distraction. The sight of her through the steamy room broke through the images of death rolling in endless procession through his mind. That was the welcome part, but his physical response to her would be awkward on Minnie.

If he hired a proper motorbike, she'd ride behind him, wrap her arms around him, and press herself against his back. He held onto that fantasy until he was clean and dry and back in control of his body. With a towel slung around his hips he opened the bathroom door to look for the promised clothing.

Lin walked towards him, her footsteps soft on the wooden floor. She wore a bright red sarong tied around her neck and carried a shirt and a pair of khaki shorts. "I've put all our clothes into the washing machine. Here, these should fit well enough. No underwear though. Sorry."

The idea of Lin going commando beneath that sarong undid his good intentions in the cold shower. Gripping the towel in one hand, Paul reached for the clothes and held them strategically positioned in front of him. "Commando is fine. Thanks for these. Are they leftovers from an old boyfriend?"

Lin shrugged. "It happens. There are always leftovers from relationships."

"You're lucky these leftovers are useful. My ex left me a

collection of romantic DVDs when she walked out."

Lin grinned. "Don't tell me you watched them with her."

Paul tightened his grip on the clothes between his hands and snorted. It had been one of the few things he'd stood firm on when Katy had moved in with him. "Not in your wildest dreams. I'll get dressed out here so you can get going with your shower."

"There's beer in the fridge if you want one." Lin edged past him into the bathroom, carefully avoiding touching him, and closed the door.

Paul pulled on the borrowed clothes. The shorts were a baggy style and fit well enough, but Lin's boyfriend had been smaller around the chest and the sleeves hugged Paul's biceps. He buttoned the shirt from the bottom up to halfway. It would do.

Sounds of the shower being turned on peppered his memory with reminders of the night in his hotel room. Lin had showered there and . . . Deciding he'd suffered enough Lin-distraction for one evening, he took a can of beer from the fridge, popped the tab and opened the door onto the balcony. A sensor light switched on as he stepped outside, bathing a pair of cane chairs in soft amber light.

Framed by two large trellised plants, city lights above the building opposite Lin's apartment block flooded the picturesque view, but stepping onto Lin's balcony was like walking into a jungle. Tropical flowers sat like jewels amid lush green foliage. Water trickled into a miniature water feature in one corner, the sound soothing and pleasant. Lin must be quite the gardener, another thing he wouldn't have guessed about her.

He leaned on the rolled top of the railing, cool beneath his arms without the tropical sun heating the metal, and sucked down a large mouthful of a local beer. Crisp, lighter and more citrusy than the bitter brew he was used to, it was refreshing in the humidity. Never had he appreciated a beer, a shower and clean clothes as much as now.

Without the stink of decomposing bodies clinging to his clothes, without being surrounded by so much terrible, needless, inhumane death, he could focus again. He sifted dispassionately through what he'd observed, adding a mental note to follow up on girls and young women who had recently gone missing in the Philippines and cross-check details of their disappearances with his list of those closer to home.

"You found the beer, I see." Lin's voice sidled into his mental list making. She leaned on the railing beside him and raised a can of beer to her mouth. The sarong had been replaced by jeans and a long-sleeved pink T-shirt. Both hugged her figure while covering her from neck to ankle.

"It's not a bad drop. Different, but it hits the spot."

"Good." She sounded as though her mind was elsewhere, but her quiet presence was a balm after the day's intense activity.

Relishing this quiet moment, Paul half-hoped her distraction was because of him. Payback for the times she'd affected him would be fair, wouldn't it?

She turned her back on the view and leaned her elbows on top of the railing, pinning him with her intense look, the one that usually preceded her telling him something he didn't want to hear. But the soft balcony light turned that look into one that sent a different message. One that said Paul should put his can of beer down and kiss her until—

She broke eye contact and toyed with the flattened tab on her beer can.

Damn it, had he leaned towards her? Had his intention been obvious? So much for his home-grown reputation as a poker-face.

"Listen, Rimmer, we have to trace the girls who died in that container. I was thinking we should split this investigation into parts. One of us needs to focus on analysing reports of missing girls. That's where our clues will be. And since you've been doing that already—"

"I agree. I'll send a request to the Philippines police. When we get their report we can correlate details with what I've found here. We also need cooperation and increased surveillance and checking at likely ports of departure. I'll do that through the Bureau. But we need to ramp up efforts to find Chan."

"I was thinking about that too. We could install an operative in a building across from each business place we've identified so far, as well as request drone flights over possible residential properties."

Paul nodded. "Expensive and a bureaucratic nightmare, but there's no better time than now. Assuming those girls were destined for Chan's brothels, we can also assume he'll move quickly to make up his losses."

"So we increase surveillance at selected docks for shipments destined for the same company here in Singapore."

"And give our rookies their first taste of covert ops. We have a long night ahead of us."

Chapter 16

One of the interns had curled up under his desk around two a.m. and was lightly snoring. Lin cast an envious look and noted it was Dax. Staring at her computer screen for hours on end left her eyes gritty and dry. She pushed her chair away from her desk, stood and stretched her arms high above her head before bending over and setting both palms on the floor.

"Want to call it a night?" Rimmer moved into the space behind her. Even looking at him upside down, his eyes were red-rimmed and tired.

Lin unrolled her body slowly upwards and perched on the edge of her desk. "Might be wise. I read that last paragraph three times and barely took in a word."

Rimmer raised his voice. "Okay, everyone, let's call it a night and be back here at nine o'clock."

"Make it ten, Rimmer?"

He glanced at her, picked up on her unspoken message, and looked back at their young team. "Ten o'clock. Good work tonight."

Someone toed the sleeping intern who startled awake, sat up and hit his head on his desk. "Come on, Dax. Time to go home and keep sleeping."

Dax looked sheepish as he stood and rubbed his head, and the group quickly dispersed, except for Wendy.

She approached Paul with a neatly clipped set of printed pages in her hands. "Thank you for giving me responsibility for the team today. While you were out I cross-referenced all sightings of Chan with his known businesses and ran a deep analysis of all known family and associates. That first residential property you mentioned— It was bought by Chan's second cousin by marriage in the name of a shelf company. And there's a copy of upgrades made to the security system three months ago."

Closer to Wendy than Rimmer, Lin held her hand out and took the printed pages. "Thanks." She glanced at the top page and passed it to Rimmer.

He looked briefly at the page and nodded. "Good work, Wendy. We'll work this into our operational plan tomorrow—later today."

Wendy gripped the strap of her shoulder bag and backed away. "Just so you know, Dax was in here working at seven yesterday morning. He's a good guy and a hard worker."

"And you know this because—"

Wendy pushed her glasses up her nose and met Lin's gaze. "I was here too."

"Dedication to your work is commendable, Wendy, but I don't want to see you in here before ten tomorrow, got it?" Rimmer folded his arms and tried to look stern, but Lin could see the slight tug at the corner of his mouth. He was impressed by Wendy, both the quality of her work and her work ethic.

"Understood, sir. Good night—um, morning." She blinked before hurrying through the door and closing it behind her.

Rimmer rubbed both hands across his face. "Come on, Lin. I'll drop you off at home."

Lin's lips twitched before she gave up the attempt and grinned at him. "You forget we rode Minnie here because your car stinks. How about I take you home with me?"

Rimmer's hands stopped their movement. He lowered them slowly and pinned her with a look that stirred an answering longing low down in her core.

Her breath caught in her throat. "I didn't mean *take you home* like that, Rimmer."

"Yes you did. Admit it, Lin. We've been circling around

this since we met."

She didn't want to admit it. Or rather, she could admit to herself that she wanted Rimmer—too much. He sparked a fire in her and she wanted so badly to lose herself in him. The problem was she shouldn't, mustn't. "What about not compromising a case by giving in to mutual attraction?"

"One of my rare stupid statements."

He waited, still and silent, watching her with an intensity that refused to let her slide away from the truth. Damn her subconscious for casually letting it slip.

And yet . . . After the horror at the docks, both of them could use a dose of life-affirmation. *Sex*, Lin reminded herself. *Call it what it is.* Whatever name she chose, only one thing mattered.

Several heartbeats passed. Heartbeats that thudded with anticipation and desire and—need.

"My place. Let's go." She grabbed her satchel and slung it over her head, tucking it into her side as she strode to the door.

***

Paul pushed Lin's front door closed behind him and waited, watching her. She dropped her satchel and, with her back to him and her hand resting on the small shrine, fixed her gaze on the photo of her sister. Was she having second thoughts?

Tired as they both were, the sexual tension between them had ratcheted higher on the ride from the office to her apartment. They had sped along quiet roads and where Lin had no choice but to pull up and give way to other vehicles, she had jerked Minnie to a stop with a G-force that plastered Paul against her back. With his arms wrapped around her, his legs bracketing hers and the pressure behind his jeans zipper beyond uncomfortable, every neurone in his body was tuned to hers, primed to party.

By God, he knew what he wanted. Knew it flouted every rule about relationships the Bureau had taught him. But Lin drew him like she was true north to his ship's compass. This moment had been inevitable and why it was so, he neither knew nor cared.

It simply was.

Certain they'd been on the same page when they left the office, the tense set of her shoulders now, as they rode up in the lift, suggested otherwise. Was her self-control better than his, or had the enormity of what she'd accepted kicked in? He knew they shouldn't, but wanted her anyway.

But if Lin had doubts . . .

"We don't have to do this, Lin, not if you've changed your mind."

She bowed her head and drew in a deep breath.

His body ached with unfulfilled need, but he reached for the door handle and cracked it open. "My car's downstairs. I'll let you get some sleep and—"

She turned and their gazes crashed into each other. "You're wrong, Rimmer. There is no more choosing to or not." Sliding both hands up his chest, she stood on tiptoe and pressed her lips against his. Soft as this first kiss was, its restraint took nothing from the urgent need rising within him. Her kiss fed it.

He slid both hands around her hips, holding her body against his. One foot kicked backwards and pushed the door closed behind him. The click sounded loud in the quiet apartment, and released something within both of them.

Lin gripped both sides of his shirt and ripped it open. Buttons pinged onto the floor as she pushed it off his shoulders. In the time it took him to release his arms from the tight sleeves she had flicked open the button and zipper of his shorts.

Paul caught her hands and moved them away from him, and then lifted her T-shirt over her head. While she struggled to release her long hair from the garment, he toed off his boots and stepped out of his shorts. Going commando had advantages.

Lin freed her arms and head from the long-sleeved T-shirt.

As she flicked her hair back over her shoulder her gaze snagged on his erection.

Paul held his breath when her lips parted and her tongue touched the corner of her mouth. "Yeah, I don't think I'm capable of long and slow this first time."

"Long and slow next time, Rimmer." She launched herself off the floor and wrapped her legs around his hips. The pressure on his erection was hard and deliberate, telling him she wanted him every bit as much as he wanted her. Her lips found his and Paul doubted he'd last until they reached the bedroom.

Except there was still the barrier of Lin's jeans between them.

He groaned and lifted his head enough to make it down the hall without walking Lin into a wall. Her bed was queen-sized and neatly made before Paul set her down on the cover and knelt either side of her hips. He slid his hands up and cupped her face, kissing her with all the urgency raging through him.

"Let me just get some protection on—" He lifted himself off her and froze. If he'd been wearing his own clothes, the problem would have been non-existent. "Damn it, I haven't got any with me."

Lin raised an arm and pointed to the bedside chest of drawers. "Lucky for me, I do. Top drawer."

Paul reached across her and reefed the drawer open. He snagged a packet of condoms and ripped it open. With protection taken care of, he looked at Lin.

In the spill of light through her window, her hair made a dark halo around her face. Eyes half closed, she flicked the press-stud on her jeans open.

The momentary interruption had given him a chance to catch his breath and now, seeing her like this, he didn't want to rush this first time with her.

He caught her hands and dropped a kiss onto each palm and

then gently set both hands above her head. "Don't move them."

Her breath hitched and her hips wriggled beneath him. "I need you, Rimmer, now." But she left her hands where he'd placed them.

"Good things come to those who wait." He dropped a light kiss on her lips and slid down her body. If the friction was half as arousing for her as for him, she must be on a hair-trigger. He clamped his jaw, drew a deep breath and met her hooded gaze. "Let me make it good for you." He cupped her breasts and ran his thumbs over her nipples.

Through the soft pink fabric of her bra, they pebbled. He took one into his mouth and sucked.

"I don't want long and slo—oh yes."

Her breathy sigh made him determined to draw every ounce of pleasure from their love making for her.

"Please, Rimmer, just—" She arched up into his mouth and groaned.

The sound almost undid his resolve, but he kept his touch light, his kisses lighter as he made his way over her stomach. Briefly he dipped his tongue into her belly button and her hips rose, but she kept her arms above her head.

Her body quivered with tension as he slid her jeans and undies—pale pink cotton that matched her bra—in a slow reveal down her legs. She had long, lean muscles and he took his time working his way back up from her ankles. Behind her knees he paused, tasting her skin. She tried to pull away.

"Ticklish there, are you?"

"Don't get any ideas about using that against me." Her voice was husky, but her hips lifted again, enticing him to continue his exploration.

He looked deep into her eyes. "You're beautiful, Lin, inside and out." He lowered his head, savouring the musky scent rising from between her thighs.

Suddenly her hands were in his hair tugging him up to her mouth. Her lips crashed against his. One hand felt its way down and caught his erection, the other pushed against his shoulder and she tipped him onto his back.

He rolled, willing to hand over control if that was what she needed. And he loved a woman who knew what she wanted and went for it.

"Enough foreplay, Rimmer. I need you now." And she took him deep into her body.

Chapter 17

Lin woke as the dawn light filtered through her bedroom window. Rimmer's arm lay across her waist and his body cocooned hers. His breathing was deep and regular—still sleeping, whereas she woke fully alert, sated and at the same time hungry for more of what they had shared.

Tears pricked her eyes. Last night she'd needed him. Needed that life-affirming joining of bodies. How she had loved the way he'd made love to her. Such consideration and attention as he'd given her had been unexpected, almost tender. Like he cared about her.

He'd called her beautiful.

Except she wasn't beautiful, inside or out. Rimmer saw only what he expected to see, what he wanted to. He couldn't see the driving need for revenge or know the darkness lining her soul. But she was grateful for the gift he'd given her, for showing her she could still feel—something other than grief and loss and despair.

Easing out from beneath his arm she set her feet on the floor, reached for her silk robe and then tiptoed from the bedroom. The first rays of the sun touched the slice of water between the buildings opposite as she stepped onto her balcony, coffee in hand. Leaning on the balcony railing, she sipped her coffee and squinted into the white-gold ball of rising sun.

What have I done?

Sex with Rimmer had been great—best-of-her-life kind of great. And now it was going to complicate everything between them because, no matter how much she denied it would happen, every time she looked at him she'd be thinking about his kisses, how he'd made her feel, and how she'd fallen apart in spectacular fashion twice before they'd fallen into an exhausted sleep.

"Stupid, Lin. You made the wrong choice. Be smart and don't let it happen again."

But in her head she heard Kim's voice telling her not to be so lost in her work she forgot to live. Kim would have liked Rimmer, and liked that he'd made Lin forget her strict rules.

Behind her, the soft slide of the door alerted her to Rimmer's presence a moment before he leaned on the railing beside her, mug of coffee in his hand, looking far too good after the handful of hours sleep he'd had.

"Morning." Stubbled cheeks and bed hair looked good on him.

"Morning." She stared into the bright sunlight, determined to return to businesslike interactions.

But her traitorous body clamoured for his, turning towards him like he was the sun, not the bright ball of light now clearing the horizon.

He raised his mug of coffee and clinked it against hers. "Brewed ready and waiting when you get up. I like your coffee machine."

"I like my coffee communion watching the sunrise."

"Me too. Clears the head for the day." His tone was sincere and he closed his eyes, savouring the strong brew with focus on it and nothing else.

"You're a hedonist, Rimmer."

"A pleasure-seeker?" He frowned.

Had she insulted him? She hadn't intended to. It was just that she liked the word and the sound of it, and the idea of focused pleasure. "When it comes to food and drink, you are. Pleasure with intent."

He pinned her with a look that eclipsed everything and brought all they'd done in bed rushing back. Memories—and a thrill of pleasure.

Was that what he'd intended?

"I do all *pleasurable* things with intent."

She recognised that, and now she knew what it felt like to be the focus of Rimmer's pursuit of pleasure. Intense and all consuming. "You're a generous lover."

He didn't smirk, not like another man might have, but his gaze dipped to her mouth before meeting hers. "Half of any pleasure is in the sharing. Where would the enjoyment be if all I did was take?" His hand rose and tucked a strand of hair behind her ear.

Like the tide drawn by the moon she could no more stop herself from turning her head and resting her cheek in his palm. This attraction was dangerous, delicious, and impossible to ignore.

Rimmer tipped her face up and brushed his lips across hers. "We have a couple of hours before we need to head into the office. How about we—"

From the dining table, Lin's phone pinged. Dimly she recognised the sound of an incoming message but ignored it. She slid her free arm around Rimmer's neck and deepened their kiss, tasting coffee, tasting him.

Was she foolish to continue what they'd started?

We haven't left the apartment. It's still last night. It's only a single moment of foolishness.

She pressed closer, sensing desperation in her kiss.

Probably Rimmer did too because he raised his head. "What's wrong, Lin?"

Rationalising changed nothing and she refused to lie even to herself. Opening her eyes she met his gaze.

Concerned.

Intent on understanding what had changed.

Understanding her.

Rimmer saw too much, guessed the rest. Needing distance

she stepped away. "Let's not complicate things further."

"It feels simple to me. We're consenting adults, and we both want what we did last night to continue. If you need space, that's fine. But this—" He jerked a thumb between the two of them. "This isn't over."

"Think whatever you want."

"Do you regret giving into our attraction?"

"No." The word shot out of her mouth and she realised she meant it. Softening her tone she set a hand on his chest. "No regrets. I was selfish, but I needed you. Wanted you."

"You weren't alone in feeling selfish. Yesterday was tough in every way, but especially for you on top of losing your sister so recently. There are times when we need connections to remind us we're human and alive. What happened yesterday was one of them."

Somehow she found her head resting against his chest, his heartbeat slow and strong in her ear. Lin breathed in the scent of him for several heartbeats, allowing herself this brief moment of pleasure.

The last such one, she promised herself.

Hearing the ping of her phone again, she lifted her head. Soft as the intrusion was she accepted the reminder. Casework and the outside world were waiting. "I'd better see who's trying to get hold of me." Stepping away, her hand slid down Rimmer's chest, unwilling to lose the contact.

He caught her hand and kissed her fingers. "I'll be here when you decide you need or want me again, Lin. I'm not going anywhere."

But he would leave once they'd caught Chan. There was no way Rimmer would stay after their assignment was completed. Their time together had an end date.

She looked up at him silhouetted against the growing sun's glare and the thought repeated in her brain.

There is an end date. We have only limited time.

Was sleeping with him while he was here such a terrible idea?

Conflicted yet attracted by the possibility, Lin slipped inside and picked up her phone. Sun-blind, it took her several furious blinks before she could make out the message.

Please meet me in Providore coffee shop Orchard Road 10 a.m. Urgent.

Helen Masters

***

"Want a refill?" Paul closed the sliding door and headed to the coffee machine, throwing a glance her way. Lin was staring at her phone as though engaged in a staring match with a deadly snake. He stopped in front of her. "Everything okay?"

Her frown gave him his answer before she lifted her gaze from the screen. "Remember I said I didn't believe Serena Masters had returned home? This—" She raised her phone between them and waggled it, shaking her head. "I think it could be proof. Her mother texted, asking me to meet her. She said it's urgent."

"Any idea what it's about?"

"Other than Serena—no."

"Want me to come?"

"I'm not sure." Lin set the phone on the table and refilled her coffee mug, an air of absentmindedness around the action. "I have a strange feeling. The timing is odd."

"How?"

"Helen could have talked to me yesterday when we visited her husband. I noticed her car being washed out on the apron in front of the garages as we drove up."

"The silver-blue Mercedes?" Paul had admired the sporty car, but any envy he had for its top speed was tempered by his memory of driving in Singapore's traffic.

"Yes."

"Go with your instincts. I always listen to mine. We can see her together if you want, or if you think it's better to meet with her alone, I'll hang out nearby and watch. Sound okay?"

Lin nodded, but he could almost see the wheels spinning in her mind. "What about the team? We told them to come in at ten."

"Is it far from the office to where you're meeting her?"

"Ten minutes to the café."

"I'll call Wendy. She can hold the fort until we get back."

"Rimmer, can we go to the office now? There's something I want to check."

Any chance of enticing Lin back to bed disappeared and Paul switched into work mode. "I'll get dressed. Are my clothes in the laundry?"

Lin's nod was distracted. Clearly she needed space and he would give her that.

By the time he had showered and changed into his own clothes, Lin was dressed and seated in front of her laptop. She glanced up as he pulled out a chair and sat next to her. "I want Dax to dig deeper into Lew Masters' dealings prior to joining the Ministry and I'll ask Wendy to look into Helen Masters' background before her marriage to Lew."

"What do you expect to find?"

"No expectations, but I want to cover all bases. We've focused more on Serena's father's dealings as the most likely reason for her abduction, but what if there's something in her mother's past?"

Chapter 18

Paul kept watch on the balcony coffee shop from the opposite side of Orchard Road, waiting for Lin to appear. While he waited, he pulled out his phone. Lin had been very successful using her device as a prop while scanning their surroundings the day they'd met. He felt like a tourist holding his phone high, but wasn't that the aim?

Setting aside his personal dislike of the stereotype, he turned slowly from left to right playing at taking a panoramic photo. Down the famous road to the left was a park. No one loitered in the car park or beneath the nearest trees. He panned along the street, passed across the building opposite and continued to his right.

Dropping his hand, he pretended to check the screen and then held the phone to his ear as though on a call while imagining he was talking with Gran. He wanted to project a relaxed demeanour and she had always brought a smile to his face. As he talked and laughed at things his non-existent caller said, he scanned the street and outside balconies of the Mandarin complex from behind his sunglasses.

There. First floor balcony.

Lin's bright red dress caught his eye as she approached the coffee shop from the right. Helen Masters stepped through the doors of the café and raised a tray holding two cups.

Paul checked his watch. Ten o'clock on the dot.

Helen led the way and the two women sat at a table off to one side. Sunlight glinted off metal tabletops next to the outer edge and a couple of people in business suits sat at the table closest to the glass panelled railings. The table where Lin sat was in his line of sight, but one of the women at the closer table and a poorly placed potted palm hid Helen Masters from sight.

Paul strolled casually along the shopfront, his free hand in his pocket and maintaining a one-sided conversation peppered with 'yeah' and 'cool', the word of choice last time he'd listened to his young nieces.

A man walking past sidestepped a woman pushing a pram and knocked into Paul's raised arm.

"Sorry."

"No worries." Paul tracked the man until he turned into a nearby shop. He returned his gaze to Lin; the new angle allowed him to see Helen Masters' face. She appeared upset. Quickly Paul raised his phone and zoomed in.

Distraught might be a better word. She gripped Lin's hand between hers and then dived into her handbag. Pulling a wad of tissues from it, she held them over her face and patted her eyes.

Overt displays of emotion had never impressed Paul, but Helen Masters seemed genuinely upset. Her request to meet Lin had to be about her daughter.

A sudden crash and honking of horns drew Paul's attention to his left. A small truck set its hazard lights flashing. Paul craned his neck. He could just make out a car at an odd angle at the front end of the truck.

Turning his attention back to the café, he cursed under his breath. Lin and Helen Masters had gone. He pressed the speed dial number he'd assigned to Lin and waited for her to pick up. When voicemail came on and asked him to leave his name and number, he ended the call. Helen Masters had been so upset he guessed Lin had taken her to a restroom.

Concerned about the time they'd already taken away from their young team, he texted a quick message as he strode to the car park.

Meet you back at office. PR

***

Grateful for the space and seating in the five-star hotel restroom, Lin drew her club chair closer to Helen's and kept her voice low. "Here." She handed over a bunch of fresh tissues and listened as Helen's sobs subsided into hiccups and died away. The woman's eyes were red and her face, blotchy, and other women cast sympathetic glances on their way in and out of the restroom.

"Okay, so you got as far as telling me how you came to miss my visit yesterday. Now tell me what you know and what you suspect."

Helen sniffed and dabbed her nose before scrunching the tissues into a ball and resting her hands in her lap. "You know how determined Lew was to pull every string he could to find Serena? One night last week, he'd been going off about the lack of progress and how useless the police had been and how even the Bureau's top agent hadn't found his daughter—" She glanced at Lin and a different red coloured up her cheeks.

Suspecting as much from Masters, Lin patted Helen's arm. "It's worrying and frustrating, I know. Go on."

Helen bit her lip and nodded. "Sorry. Anyway, in the middle of his rant about incompetent officers he was called away to an urgent phone call. He didn't come back to join me, so I followed him out to the pool deck. I don't know who called him, but he was shaken by whatever they had said. The next day, I heard him talking to the chief of police telling him to call off the search for Serena."

"But she hadn't come home, had she?" Lin was certain the missing woman hadn't returned, but if there was news of her . . .

"No, she hasn't, and I've had no word from her." She drew a shaky breath and Lin feared another bout of sobbing, but Helen shook her head and sat straighter. "I was so angry with Lew, but he cut me down when I begged him not to pull the pin on the search. How could he do that when she hasn't come home? Please—will

142

you keep looking for her?"

"Unofficially?"

"In whatever way you can. Please? I have money of my own. I'll pay you as a private investigator." She clutched Lin's arm, her grip tight to the point of becoming painful.

Lin patted Helen's hand and gently eased her arm out of the woman's fierce grip, certain there would be bruises. "Forget the money, Helen. Did your husband give you any reason for calling off the search?"

Helen shook her head. "I told you he was angry, but underneath that anger was real fear."

"Why do you think that was? Do you have any idea what his caller said to him?"

"No, and believe me, I asked. All he gave me was that she's safe and not to make waves or we wouldn't see her again."

Lin frowned and tapped her fingers on her knee, rapidly calculating and discarding possibilities. How much of the thoughts pinging around in her mind should she reveal? Usually she wouldn't voice them, but watching Helen's expression, it seemed likely some of the same thoughts had already occurred to her too.

"He could mean anything from Serena having left of her own volition and not wishing to return home, to someone holding her against her will to retain power over your husband. Did he truly say nothing else?"

Helen started to shake her head and then froze. Her eyes widened. She slapped both hands over her mouth and pinned Lin with a look that would haunt her nightmares.

"What is it, Helen? What have you remembered?"

Helen's voice was a bare thread of agonised whisper. "He said her return home would be an event—*one way or another*."

An event? Lin considered the possibilities. Weddings were events. The return home of prodigal sons—and daughters—were events, as were significant birthdays.

Unbidden, her mind latched onto the image of scattering Kim's ashes. As sad and as tragic as that was, it too had been an event. She frowned at the image, all too aware of the danger of allowing personal problems to colour responses to ongoing investigations.

But why the ambiguity around the nature of Serena's return unless the form her return home took was dependent on her father doing something for the person who had abducted her?

"Helen, perhaps Lew meant only that you would be celebrating when Serena comes home, but that it must be her choice when she does."

Helen's fingers tightened in the soggy lump of tissues. Red-rimmed eyes stared into Lin's, seeking an answer she didn't know and wouldn't speak with offers of false hope. Finally, Helen huffed a sigh. Her voice, when it emerged, was a thin facsimile of itself, devoid of colour, strength, and hope. "But Lin, what if he meant it would be my daughter's funeral?"

Lin dropped her satchel on the desk and met Rimmer's eyes.

"Well? What did Helen Masters have to say?" He pushed a chair out from under the desk with his foot and sat back, looking like he welcomed the break.

"I expect you saw her collapse into tears before we left the café?"

"Yes. Was that because you were right and Serena hasn't returned?"

Succinctly, Lin filled him in on what she had gleaned from Helen. "What do you think? Can we continue looking for Serena—unofficially?"

"If we have a credible reason to link her disappearance to

our investigation, there's no reason not to make it official."

"Do we have credible reason? I can't see it if there is any, and I've been formally taken off the case and the file has been closed." Not that that would stop Lin from continuing the search for Serena. Not now, after speaking with her distraught mother. "I'll be disciplined for it, of course, but—"

"Keeping it off the record for the moment is my call. It won't affect you if there's any fallout. I'll make sure it doesn't."

"You can't do that. This is my decision and—"

"Officially, Lin, this is my decision."

He held her gaze in a silent stand-off.

Stubborn, annoying, infuriating man. She glanced over her shoulder. No one was near enough to overhear, but she lowered her voice anyway and stabbed the desk. "This is why sleeping together was a bad idea. Now, you feel connected to me. Responsible. You're not. I'm a grown woman and more than capable of doing what needs to be done. You don't have to protect me, Rimmer. I stand by decisions I make, and I accept the consequences, whatever they are."

"Do I need to remind you who's in charge here? It's simple chain of command. Nothing more."

He turned his computer screen to face her. "What do you think of the surveillance assignments?"

Lin knew enough of Rimmer by now to know—pushing him on this in the office wasn't going to work. She drew a deep breath and exhaled slowly before pulling her chair beside his and leaning closer to scan the assignments. "Are we spreading our resources too thin? Our team is young and inexperienced after all. Do you think we might be better doubling up and concentrating on only four key locations?"

"Four? If we double these guys up, that gives us three with the two of us as responders."

"What if you and I keep Chan's residential property under

surveillance, but stand ready to leave if we get a call from these guys?"

Rimmer's mouth quirked up briefly as he stared at the screen for several long moments. "I've already checked—the house across the road from Chan's is available for lease. Let me see if I can arrange something with the realtor so we can access it."

"Shall we select the three most promising business locations from this list?"

"Sure." He pulled the keyboard towards him.

As they bent their heads to the task, Rimmer's knee brushed hers. Fighting the distraction, she edged her chair to a new angle as they discussed, discarded and chose their top three. Rimmer printed out the list and stood, paper in hand.

"Listen up, everyone, we've got your assignments here."

Heads turned, all eyes pinned on Rimmer's commanding presence.

"You'll need to collect equipment before you leave. You have time to go home and pack personal gear. Pack light. You probably won't be going home for a few days."

Lin looked around the group of expectant faces. "Report to your station within two hours. I'll give you your cover story and contact information when Agent Rimmer has finished assigning everyone. Understood?"

All heads nodded and eyes turned back to Rimmer.

"Agent Tan and I will be back up. If you get into trouble or you have a clear sighting, report to us immediately. Pete, Vic, you're at location one near the docks. Mads and John, you're at location two. Wendy and Dax, you're at location three. That's an apartment above the store opposite number sixty-five, the brothel. Any questions?"

There were none, but the bright eyes looking back at her and Rimmer told Lin how excited their team was. They would learn very quickly, but a pep talk now wouldn't hurt. "Surveillance can be mind-numbingly boring after several hours; worse after a day or more. Do not lose concentration. Do not allow yourself to be distracted. Put your personal devices away and watch. Be alert. Look for any unusual activity, patterns of movement and so on. Your check in times and call signs are on the same sheet as your cover stories if anyone's around when you arrive. Do not miss a check in or you'll be off the team. Understood?"

This time, heads nodded in solemn agreement.

"Ready to go?"

Brief bustle accompanied a scraping of chairs and packing away of laptops before each pair collected their notes from Lin.

As the door closed on the last pair she picked up her bag and turned to Rimmer. "Ready? Your car or Minnie?"

"My car." He slid a laptop into its case and closed the flap. "That means you're with me."

"I got it already. It means you're in charge."

He glanced up at the ceiling as though communing with some higher being. "At last, she agrees."

"Chain of command." She walked ahead, turning back after a few steps. "But that doesn't mean I have to like it."

Chapter 19

As far as stakeouts went, this one was comfortable, and came with a kitchen. Paul lay on the bed, hands folded behind his head, eyes slitted as he watched Lin. He was supposed to be taking his turn to sleep, but his body wasn't complying. Not with Lin in the same room. Silhouetted against the streetlight, she stood in front of a gauzy curtain at the second-floor bedroom window, her binoculars trained on the house they believed Chan occupied.

"Stop watching me, Rimmer. Go to sleep."

She didn't turn, but her soft voice caressed his ears and made him long to pull her down beside him. Under him. On top . . . He didn't care which side of him she chose as long as her body and his met.

"You have no idea what's happening behind your back."

"Of course I do. Ever hear of something called a reflection?"

"There's no light anywhere near me. How can you claim a reflection when all the light is beyond the window?"

Lin snorted, but didn't turn from her surveillance. "Got me. You're right about there being no light, but there's a quality in your silence. It carries weight. I can feel you looking at me."

He was glad his presence affected her, like hers did to him. Most of the time he was also glad she didn't let him get away with anything. It meant she was thinking about him. Especially since last night.

"Good. And can you hear what I'm thinking?"

"I can, and no, you can't do that. Not during a stakeout."

"Spoilsport." Pleased to know they were on the same wavelength, he chuckled. "But you can't stop me thinking about you in bed here with me."

"Thanks for that distraction. Now I'll be thinking about what I want to do to you while I'm scoping out the house. Did you mean to make my job harder?"

Jeez, she was thinking about doing things to him? If he'd had trouble sleeping before, thinking of her in bed with him now was ten times worse. She was thinking about sex too.

In spite of the air conditioner pumping cool air into the room and the fact he'd stripped off his black T-shirt, his core temperature felt like it jumped several degrees.

"Like you were saying to the team about surveillance, it's boring as heck. You can't fault a man for where his mind takes him when he's off duty."

"So long as you're planning something good. It's not as if this is my first stakeout and I don't know how to keep my mind on the job, but you should know, Rimmer, right now I'm imagining you without a stitch on waiting for me to have my wicked way with you."

He could imagine Lin slowly licking her lips as her hand traced a path down his chest towards his burgeoning erection. If he'd thought to tease her, she'd neatly turned the tables on him. "For an agent who can do nothing about a certain itch, you know how to torture a man."

"I'm sure something's hard right now and I don't mean the job." She moved closer to the curtain.

"Will it help if I go into the other bedroom to sleep?"

No answer. His eyes opened fully.

Even across the dark room he could read the tension in her body. His feet hit the floor and he strode to her side. "What is it? Can you see something?"

"The security lights went off and the nearest street lights just blinked out." She leaned towards the window, binoculars glued to her face. "I can't see much detail but a white delivery van just pulled up at the gates. Where's the night vision goggles?"

Paul picked up the goggles, slipped them on and cracked the curtain. "What sort of company delivers at whatever o'clock in the morning this is?"

"The driver is carrying but I can't see much detail without more light. Can you see what guns the guards have? Are they AK47s?"

"Looks like it. Wait, the main garage door is going up. We're not going to see anything else from here. Come on, let's go."

Paul checked his gun and heard a soft click as Lin checked hers. He pulled on the long-sleeved black T-shirt he'd so recently stripped off and slipped his shoulder holster on.

"I'll call for back up." Light from Lin's phone screen lit her face.

He reached over and covered the screen. "No. We do this without the others. Alone, we might stand a chance of getting inside while the security lights are off."

He took the stairs two at a time. Lin followed close on his heels as they slipped through the side door of the house and raced across the darkened street into the front corner of the property adjoining Chan's. The one Paul had tried, unsuccessfully, to negotiate access to, having discovered the owners were away.

Lush foliage poked above the high concrete fence that separated the two gardens. Paul jumped and gripped the top of the fence, pulling himself up high enough to look over the top. He dropped down and leaned close, his voice a bare whisper. "We'll go over here. I'll give you a boost up."

Lin set her foot on his linked fingers, her hand light on his shoulder before he bent his legs for better thrust.

She gripped the top of the fence and scrambled over almost before he had straightened up.

Setting his sights on her disappearing legs, Paul leapt and

followed her over. He dropped lightly into a crouch and pulled his gun from the shoulder holster before tipping a single night lens down and scanning the area beyond the perimeter plantings. Touching Lin's shoulder, he signalled her to move between the fence line and the trees towards the rear of the property.

At the narrowest point of exposure between the garden and house, they paused again. The open garage door had revealed a downward slope and the house plans he'd spent the early part of the evening studying indicated a series of vents along the near corner of the garage. Crouched low, he checked the area and then ran, Lin close on his heels.

Flattened against the bricks either side of a long slitted vent, they looked into the garage. The front of the van was angled towards them; the rear doors were open wide blocking their view of movement at the other end.

Paul signalled Lin to move two vents along. The new angle offered a better view of the unloading. Stacks of shallow cartons were being transferred from the rear of the van onto a trolley. A shaft of disappointment hit his gut. How ridiculous to feel like that, but he'd felt so certain the windowless van carried human cargo that the sight of the shallow boxes was an anticlimax.

Pale bars of light fell through the slatted vent onto Lin's face. She mirrored how he was feeling as she mouthed one word, "Drugs", and raised her phone to record what they were seeing.

He nodded. More than likely Lin was right. The Bureau would have a win from their discovery, but the knowledge offered minimal satisfaction. The grim contents of the container had fired every protective instinct in his body. He wanted to liberate the girls and young women caught by people smugglers. He wanted to do it now.

And he wanted to take down John Chan.

Lin touched his knee and jerked her head towards the van.

The two armed guards stepped close to the vehicle, guns at

the ready. Two others climbed into the van. Whatever they were bringing out was important and definitely not more inanimate cargo.

Paul leaned closer as though that would allow him to see through the side panel of the van. His head met Lin's and he thought they both held their breath waiting to see what, or who, emerged from the van.

The backside of one of the men emerged first as he backed out of the van, his hands wrapped around a pair of feminine ankles. The woman kicked hard and freed one leg.

Caught off balance, one foot still in the van, the man staggered and let loose a string of swear words. The woman continued to kick him as he tried to recapture her ankle. A frantic, powerful kick caught him in his belly. Grunting with pain, he doubled over. One of the armed guards grinned and the other laughed before making a comment Paul needed no translation to understand.

An annoyed voice from within the van brought an immediate response. The laughing guard lowered his gun, nudged the injured man aside and grabbed the woman's legs, backing away and bringing the woman's body into view.

A black material bag covered her head, but she was alive and kicking. That fact gave Paul a great deal of satisfaction.

"Hold her still." The curt command issued in Mandarin came from someone out of Paul's sight.

The laughter stopped. Even the injured man attempted to stand straight as a new person entered the scene. One look and Paul's blood ran cold.

The newcomer carried a hypodermic syringe. He waited until the guards had the woman in a secure hold and then injected her. She gave a single muffled squawk and slumped. At his nod, two men hoisted her inert body between them and carried her out of Paul's sight. Moments later a door banged.

Paul pressed his nose close to the vent and mentally followed the likely path the trio took as the guards slammed the van doors. The engine started, sending a fug of diesel fumes wafting through the vents.

Lin covered her mouth and nose and kept videoing, but Paul's desire to cough grew. He covered his mouth, turning away and trying not to make a sound while his stomach warred against the smell.

The van rolled towards the slowly opening garage door, and Lin slipped her phone away and touched his arm, nodding towards the fence.

Right. They had to get out before the security and streetlights were turned back on.

Eyes blurring as he gagged and swallowed, Paul stayed low and slipped across the open space into the perimeter shadows. A quick glance showed the guards turning back from the closing security gates. Paul grabbed Lin's elbow. They had seconds before the security system was turned back on. Seconds before the lights caught them in revealing white brilliance.

He linked his fingers and boosted Lin up and over the wall. As he bent his knees for his jump, light flooded the garden and cast shadows of the trees onto the concrete side fence. Paul dropped and rolled in close to a thick cluster of tropical plants beneath the trees. A twig cracked as he tucked his legs up and he held his breath.

Through the long dark-green leaves he watched the guards share a few words and then separate. One headed off along the front fence; the other turned down the side where Paul hid.

Raising his gun hand, Paul kept his eyes on the man.

He ambled slowly, casting glances over his shoulder in the direction his partner had taken. When the first guard was out of sight, the second pulled his phone from his pocket and turned it on. A soft glow lit his face, revealing an intent focus on the screen.

Was he sufficiently engrossed that Paul dared scramble over the wall?

From the far side of the wall Paul heard a soft pfft. A crack like glass breaking sounded and the corner security light went dark. A shout erupted from the nearby guard who shoved his phone into a pocket and ran towards the corner of the building.

Paul rose, lunged for the top of the wall and scrambled over, dropping to the ground beside Lin and listening for sounds of pursuit. Adrenaline coursed through his body, his heart thudded in his chest, but he whispered a quick, "Thanks." That had been one hell of a good shot.

Lin tucked her gun back in its holster and slipped into the shadows, leading him by a circuitous route back to their surveillance post.

***

"How do you want to handle this?" Lin tugged the light doona up to her waist and flung an arm above her head.

Rimmer's gaze was fixed on Chan's house while she was supposed to be sleeping, but her mind buzzed with what they'd seen in that garage and the probable implications.

"Our main problem is still who can we trust at the Bureau. I'd like to hit Chan's house and businesses all at once."

"Like you did in Sydney?" She hadn't meant that to come out the way it did; like a reminder of his Bureau's failure to net Chan. She hastened to amend her comment. "I know that was a great success in terms of netting most of the cartel members."

"But we lost Chan. Somewhere in that operation there was a slip up. Whether there was a third mole in my department or for some other reason, Chan escaped. That must not happen again."

"So how do we get that woman out of his house without alerting him?" Lin's eyes closed while she was talking. Some small detail niggled at her brain just out of her reach.

"I'm thinking about it. Now go to sleep. One of us needs to

be firing on all cylinders come morning."

"Yes, boss."

"Remember that phrase for when we're off the clock."

Wishing she could see his face, wishing she could lose herself in Rimmer's body and wrap herself in the safe blanket of his arms, Lin rolled onto her back and focused on her breathing. Yogic breathing in a disciplined mind was the only way she would find any rest tonight.

As she breathed in, held the breath, and breathed out to the rhythm her yogi had taught her, her mind replayed the moments when the guards has struggled as they tried to carry the woman out of the van. At the time she'd been intent on videoing everything and keeping watch for other guards around the house.

There had been a glint of metal around the woman's ankle beneath the baggy pair of oversized track pants she wore. Lin pictured each item—clothes several sizes too big for her, bare feet, and some kind of anklet.

Breathing pattern forgotten, Lin tried to recall more details. Her eyelids flew open. "Damn it, what did I see?"

"Are you talking in your sleep?" Rimmer glanced over his shoulder.

"No. I'm trying to remember something." She threw off the doona and sat up, reaching for her phone on the bedside table. Fast forwarding through video of unloading the cartons, she slowed the speed of the playback as the woman's legs came into view. When the woman kicked the man holding her legs, Lin froze the frame and zoomed in on the woman's foot.

Around her ankle was a fine gold chain with charms dangling from several links. Zooming in closer, she stared as the closest charm took shape. A golden new moon lay against the woman's skin and Lin sucked in a breath.
"Rimmer, we've found Serena Masters."

Chapter 20

"Team three, anything to report?" Paul held the binoculars in one hand and his phone in the other. Behind him, Lin had finally succumbed to sleep. She lay on her stomach, dark hair splayed across the pillow and a sheet pulled up to her waist. A single glance at her sleeping form led to a keen desire to join her and he'd resolutely turned his back and set his sights on the residence across the street. In his mind, the deliveries made by the van, and the level of security confirmed their suspicions: the property belonged to Chan. But Wang would ask for more than Paul's gut feeling to initiate official action.

"Team three reporting," Dax answered, suppressing a yawn by the sound of the long indrawn breath. "Nothing out of the ordinary. Clients going in and out on a fairly regular basis. We've photographed all of them. Wendy noted a white delivery van drove down the lane between numbers sixty-five and sixty-seven and caught a glimpse of it turning into our target backyard. It remained there for three minutes."

"What time did she see it?"

"Um . . ." There was a rustling of paper and a softly spoken exchange in the background before Wendy's voice took over the report.

"The van arrived at one-oh-four this morning and left at one-oh-seven and forty seconds."

"Did you record the make and plates?" Allowing for travel time to Bukit Timah Hill, it could well be the same vehicle. The video Lin had taken would confirm it.

"Yes, sir, both written and video records."

"Were you able to see what was loaded or unloaded?" His

next breath stalled, the ache of it in his lungs a real pressure. But whether Wendy had seen anything or not, their investigation was making progress. Sometimes he needed to remind himself of that, when the driving need to catch the bad guys seemed to operate in a slo-mo time frame.

"No. The rear of the vehicle was behind the building line."

He released his pent-up breath slowly. It had been too much to hope for confirmation in the same evening they'd stumbled across the minister's missing daughter. "Pity. Never mind. The sighting is a good start, and getting the number on the plates."

"Do you want me to search for street camera footage? The rear entrance to a pharmacy is just down the lane from number sixty-five. It's on the corner of the street that runs parallel to ours. There might be footage from its rear security camera." There was just enough hesitation in Wendy's question to remind Paul he was working with interns. Bright and motivated as they were, they still needed guidance and supervision, and the occasional word of praise when they thought beyond their assigned task. Like now.

"Good thinking, Wendy. Look and see if they have a better angle into the back of the brothel. Well done, both of you. Stay in position until further notice and don't miss your next report." He signed off and considered what their combined surveillance had uncovered. Given the lack of activity at the first two locations it was beginning to look as though the brothel was a channel point for both drugs and smuggled girls.

But the problem of *who* at the bureau they could trust with the information remained.

Several hours later, as early dawn lightened the sky with tinges of deepening orange and hot pink, he heard the soft noises of Lin stirring. He imagined her stretching her arms high and the bare expanse of skin below her cami-top. Soft skin that he wanted to kiss all over right now. Suppressing a groan of frustration, he blinked gritty eyes, resisting the urge to turn and look.

He heard nothing of her approach, but suddenly she was sliding her hand up his back, across his tense shoulders and slowly running a finger down the length of his spine. "Morning, Rimmer. Fancy a coffee?"

"Yes, please."

"Any action?"

For the briefest of moments, hope, fatigue and frustration turned her question into an offer. Action with Lin on the bed behind him.

If only it were possible.

He rolled his neck and shoulders without taking his eyes off the house across the road and shrugged. "Since the van left, nothing at Chan's house or in locations one and two, but Wendy and Dax spotted a white van stopping briefly at the brothel. She sent some video of it. Can you check if it's the one we saw carrying Serena Masters?"

Glancing down he saw Lin was already opening the attachment from Wendy. She zoomed in on the van's number plates and then switched tabs to her recording from the garage. "Same van, and the time stamp on Wendy's recording shows the van called into the brothel before it came here. This is progress, Rimmer."

"I wish I could say the same. I haven't come up with a viable plan to spring Serena." Each hour the young woman spent as Chan's prisoner shredded Paul's sense of honour. Each hour grated roughshod over his need to bring justice to the women who had died because of Chan. The man was a soulless monster and the world would be better without him.

Paul caught himself.

Damn, but he was beginning to sound like some airy-fairy do-gooder.

"You didn't get any sleep last night. I'll make us a pot of

coffee and we can brainstorm if you like. And then maybe you'll get some sleep."

Lack of sleep. That's all his dip into maudlin waters was.

"Fine. I'll begin the next round of check ins. I'm keen to know if that van or any like it have been seen at other locations."

"I won't be long."

"Thanks." Paul would have liked a ready supply of coffee throughout his watch, but if Lin brewed a fresh pot now he could just about stay awake through the day to come.

He picked up his phone and pressed the second speed dial number. Lin's occupied the first spot.

Vic answered within two rings. "Team one, all quiet here. No sightings to report."

"Any vehicles picking up or dropping off anything?"

"No, sir."

Similar responses came from the second team.

He pressed the number for the third team as Lin came through the door carrying a tray. The aroma of freshly brewed coffee preceded her, teasing his taste buds and more enticing than the packet biscuits on a plate between two mugs. Reaching for the mug, he inhaled the aroma of a strong dark brew before taking his first sip. As he took his second sip, he realised his call was still ringing at the other end.

"Damn it, if they've fallen asleep I'll give them a right bollocking."

Lin's gaze collided with his, her hand frozen in the act of raising her coffee mug. "Who are you calling?"

"Dax and Wendy."

"If Wendy hasn't replied by now then something's wrong. Come on."

Paul gulped a mouthful of coffee, grabbed his keys from the table and followed Lin out. "Damn it. I'll drive. Keep trying their number on my phone and check if there's any CCTV footage front or back of their location with yours."

They jumped into his car and he backed out, forcing himself to drive normally and not squeal the tyres. No matter how great his need for speed, drawing attention to themselves would be stupid and dangerous. And it could blow their covert operation in this exclusive suburb.

Lin cradled his phone between her shoulder and ear and tapped into her phone as they left Chan's home behind.

The faint sound of unanswered ringing made his gut clench. Lin was right. If Wendy, the most reliable and conscientious recruit he'd encountered wasn't answering, plenty was wrong at location three.

"Got an email. Wendy sent video footage taken from that pharmacy camera she mentioned. It was sent an hour ago."

"Can you see what's going on behind the brothel? Does it show if they carried Serena out from there?"

"No." Disappointment leached from Lin's voice.

"No, you can't see, or no, Serena didn't come out of the brothel?"

"Those wretched rear van doors concealed her if she was loaded in there. All I can see are the tops of two heads. They could be facing each other and the distance between them could be the length of Serena's body, but it's moot because the doors hide everything."

"But the time stamp fits with that being their final stop before we saw the van arriving at Chan's place."

"It does."

"So we need to get inside the brothel. Can you arrange a search warrant?"

"I can." She hesitated, and her indrawn breath told him there was more she wanted to say.

"But?"

"But we still have the problem that if there's a mole in my

department, he or she could let Chan know what we're doing before we make it through the front door."

"Do you trust your boss?"

"I do, but I'd hazard a guess you also trusted the agents in your Bureau before they were flushed out."

His fingers tightened on the steering wheel as he pulled into the kerb at the end of the street where both the brothel and Team three were. "We're stuck between a rock and a hard place."

"What about going in undercover?" Lin closed both phones and handed his to him.

"Let's keep that as a last resort." He got out of the car, and reached into the back seat for a light jacket to cover his shoulder holster and gun. "We'll take the rear stairs to the apartment. Final check for texts from either Wendy or Dax?"

Both checked their phones. The lack of communication was of concern. Paul set it aside and focused on the task ahead. The rear entry to the second storey apartment had seemed a bonus when they found the available unit, but now he worried it could be the reason they had been caught unawares.

He slipped along the alley past stinking industrial garbage bins reeking of piss and decay. At the rear of the seafood restaurant, fragments of prawn heads and shells floated in a pool of water extending in both directions from a closed door. At the second gate past the restaurant, Paul stopped and punched in the security code for tenants. The gate squeaked as he eased it open.

Flattened against the dividing wall he scanned the small rear courtyard and concrete stairs that led to the second storey. The apartment assigned to Wendy and Dax was at the front of the building, along a narrow central walkway that opened like the top arm of a T-shaped corridor. He climbed the stairs with a soft tread, pausing at the top to listen. Lin followed close behind, covering their rear. In the shadowy walkway a light blinked off and on and Paul lowered his gaze to avoid the distraction.

At the end of the short walkway he branched right, keeping close to the wall.

The door to the apartment where they'd set up Dax and Wendy was ajar.

Anger and concern vied for dominance. Ruthlessly he suppressed both. His reaction was irrelevant. The reason for the breach would be revealed in a few seconds, but his gut ached. Something had gone wrong.

Leading with his gun, Paul peered through the crack of the open door before nudging it open with his shoulder. To his right, the door to the tiny bathroom was open and the light on. He peered inside. Empty.

He continued down the short tiled hallway, stepped around the corner and swept the one-bedroom apartment with his gun. Empty.

Lin stepped around him, leading with her gun past the black sofa . . . and stopped. Her expression tightened before she dropped to one knee.

Paul moved around the other end of the sofa.

Dax lay on his back, sightless eyes staring at the ceiling, a gaping slash disfiguring his throat. Blood pooled around him.

Lin let go of the wrist she'd been checking. "Defensive wounds on both hands and arms. Death probably occurred within the last two hours." Her nostrils flared as she rocked back, standing in one jerky movement. "No sign of Wendy."

"We're going to have to call this in and involve Wang now. Can you call for—"

Lin nodded. "I'm on it." She moved into the narrow kitchen space, leaning against the sink with her back to Dax as she explained the situation and requested collection of the body.

Guilty, and sick to his stomach at the sight, Paul swallowed his regret for the young man's murder.

Yes, Paul was responsible for his youthful, inexperienced

team.

Yes, he had explained procedure and protocol, with extra words of caution about security and safety because of their inexperience.

No, there was nothing more he could have done to keep them safe.

Except not to involve rookies against such an enemy. But the time for self-recrimination was not now.

Dropping to one knee in an unbloodied patch of the rug beside Dax, Paul examined the fatal wound. Deep and wide, made by a large heavy knife. Not the usual weapon of choice of Chan's men.

He amended his thinking. At least not the usual weapon back in Australia. That this was Chan's work he had no doubt.

That Chan had ordered this death also suggested that Paul and his team were getting too close for comfort. But how had Chan known? And where did that leave Wendy?

He patted down the body. Dax's phone was still in his pocket. Likely he and Wendy had been taken by surprise with no time to call for help. Flipping the cover open, he applied Dax's thumb to the home button. The screen lit up with several missed calls from Paul's phone, all within the last hour.

Scrolling through recent outgoing calls, Paul spotted one to the nearby restaurant.

"Please tell me you didn't phone for takeaway food, Dax." He turned and his gaze landed on several empty takeaway containers piled in the far corner of the kitchen bench.

He huffed out a frustrated, angry breath, weighed down by the feeling he was missing something important here.

Unit one-oh-one on a stakeout: Do not interact in the neighbourhood and do nothing to draw attention to yourself. Had he not made that point keenly enough to the rookies?

Having ascertained the means of Dax's death, he closed the

young man's eyes and offered up a silent apology. Breathing through his mouth to avoid the coppery tang of blood, he began looking around the open-plan apartment for anything Wendy might have secreted within seconds. Would she have had time and the presence of mind to hide a clue to the killers' identities?

Methodically, he quartered the small apartment, reading what few signs remained of the surprise attack, looking for anything, no matter how small. Hoping that Wendy—bright, quick-thinking Wendy—had been able to leave them any clue was a long shot, but in the absence of a second dead body, he had hope she was still alive.

A shattered pair of binoculars lay on the floor in one corner beside the bed. Paired with a ripped curtain, half pulled from its rod, it seemed likely Dax had been on watch when the killers entered. Taken by surprise, had he flung the binoculars as he tried to grab a weapon?

Paul scanned the floor and the top of a narrow cupboard next to the window. Where was Wendy's phone?

He moved into the second quadrant, which centred on the bed. The top sheet trailed on the floor, pulled completely out from the bottom corner on the far side. Assuming Wendy had been off duty and asleep, had she been pulled from the bed when the killers broke in?

His search through the kitchen and bathroom offered nothing new. Once he'd observed what there was to be seen, he set to work photographing the apartment from several angles, conscious of distancing himself through the screen of his phone.

Having recorded what he could, and itemising the sparse contents, he began searching for Wendy's phone in the disturbed bed linens. As he pushed his hand down the back of the mattress on the near side, his cheek pressed against the headboard. The new angle revealed drops of blood in a spray pattern low on the wall, too light and too far from Dax to be blood spatter from his killing.

Paul straightened slowly, his gut tight and knotted. Blood-red drops danced in front of him.

Not Wendy too.

Losing a team member was always tough. Tougher still was losing two—both young and inexperienced. What did this discovery of blood mean?

Lin approached the far side of the double bed. "Found anything?"

He jerked his head towards the blood on the wall. "I want that tested and cross-matched to see if it's Wendy's." Savagely he dug his hand down between the headboard and the mattress.

His fingers closed around cool metal and glass. Gripping the slender device, he pulled Wendy's phone free. "Looks like she had just enough time to thrust this out of sight, but why?"

Lin finished searching the other side of the bed and backed off the mattress and stood, hands on hips. She nodded towards the phone. "Knowing Wendy, her password won't be easy to break. Vic and Wendy are pretty friendly. She might have some idea."

"I'll call her and ask."

Lin raised one hand, catching his eye before he hit the speed dial button. "Rimmer, do you think it would be better to bring the others back into the office? This is shocking news to get, even for more experienced agents."

Paul glanced at Dax's body and gritted his teeth so hard his jaw ached. The death of a young and promising man was a tragedy, but how much worse would it be for the classmates with whom Dax had been training?

As for his decision to use rookies on what he knew was a dangerous mission . . . Now wasn't the time for soul-searching or self-blame. He had killers to find and bring to justice, and a missing agent to recover. Recriminations were a luxury that would have to wait.

"Yes, do that. Call them and tell them to leave everything

where it is and return to the office. I'll arrange to meet with Wang face to face. I want to see him when I deliver the news."

Chapter 21

Rimmer sat wearily on the chair behind Lin's desk, his expression shuttered. But when their eyes connected, she saw the pain of loss in his stark gaze. So many deaths to lay at Chan's door: the women who had died to satisfy his dark perversions, the girls in the container. Dax.

And Kim.

Separating her grief for her sister from the other deaths was too hard. Timing and blind fate bound them together, and right here and now, at this moment, Lin felt overwhelmed.

She sucked in a ragged breath, and another.

Distance. Perspective. Objectivity.

These were her weapons and her tools, but she needed to sharpen her wits to wield them.

From a distance she heard the ding of the lift arriving on their floor. Her boss was on his way.

At the sound, or maybe in response to her reaction, Rimmer sat forward and flattened his hands on the desk. "You know Wang better than I do. Watch how he reacts to the news when I tell him."

Lin dragged a wooden chair beside his and dropped onto it. The weight of failure sat on both their shoulders as though a mountain had fallen on them. "He rarely gives anything away. You know that old saying about inscrutable Orientals? That's Joe Wang."

"Nevertheless—"

"Agent Rimmer, Agent Tan." Joseph Wang, Bureau Chief, Singapore, shut the office door behind him. He was of only middling height, but his presence—the sense of a powerful man in total control—filled Lin's office.

She rose and indicated the chair she had drawn up to the desk between them. "Sir, please take a seat."

Joe nudged the chair with his knee and angled it so his back wasn't to the door before sitting.

You can take the agent out of the field, but never the training out of the agent. Joe had shared that with her on her promotion to second in charge, when he'd reassured her she would still work selected cases.

"Care to tell me why you've chosen not to operate out of the main office?" Resting his elbows on the chair arms, her boss linked his fingers and pinned them with eyes that gave nothing away.

Rimmer gave nothing away either; not in his expression. But the rigid line of his shoulders and the jut of his jaw were as clear to her as words spoken aloud. He hated the news he had to deliver. Unlike some agents she knew, fame-seekers at any cost, Rimmer cared about his team. No one was expendable and the failure to bring everyone safely through the operation haunted him.

Joe's eyes narrowed. "Calling me here means you either have good news about the case or there's a storm about to break."

Rimmer met her boss' gaze, drawing his whole attention. "The latter. We've made progress, but the price we paid for it is too high."

"You've lost someone. What's interesting is that you requested no other agents to assist on this case, nor were any listed on this file, so who did you lose."

"I chose to operate outside regular assigned agents."

Clipped words. Colourless tone. Bureau-speak.

It disguised what to Rimmer was difficult, indefensible, unthinkable.

"I see." In the lengthening silence, her boss looked at Lin.

Her suggestion. Would Joe see that? Rimmer could claim full responsibility for the decision until he was blue in the face.

She knew it lay with no one but her.

Realising only now that she'd contributed nothing to the interview, an oversight Joe had picked up on, Lin opened her mouth. Besides, she refused to let Rimmer take all the blame. "It was my suggestion, sir. I believed Agent Rimmer's concerns were justified and accessed the Bureau's current crop of interns. We selected six and—"

"You think my department has been infiltrated and you co-opted interns?" It was the first time she'd seen Joe's nostrils flare, the first time she'd seen any hint of emotion escape through his professional demeanour. But what surprised her most was the hint that he felt betrayed.

"Lin, I'm surprised that you, of all people, went behind my back on this."

His disappointment in her was like a blow from behind. Joe Wang had trusted and encouraged her to reach her potential and push boundaries. Joe had supported her application for the position as his deputy. *I repaid his trust with distrust.*

Rimmer held up one hand. "Chief, I take full responsibility for the decision and the consequences. Agent Tan followed orders: nothing more, nothing less. You're aware the Sydney branch had two corrupt agents who caused chaos within the investigation into John Chan a couple of years ago?"

Joe nodded once, the action slow, but he listened without making further comment.

Rimmer's voice lacked emotion as he recited facts. "My partner and I had gone undercover. When that shitstorm broke, we had no idea who to trust. We're in this situation today—and I've made the choices I have—because we believe there may be another agent who helped Chan escape our multi-target operation."

"I see. So by not sharing your suspicion, you didn't discount even the chief of the Bureau might be the mole? I can't say I'm flattered, but I understand your caution." Joe glanced through the window in the door as the mobile phone on the desk—Wendy's phone—vibrated, the screen flashing the caller ID.

Vic was trying to reach her friend.

Lin looked through the window at the scene within the main work area. Four rookies gathered in a huddle, their expressions, for the most part, curious. Vic alone of the group had her phone out, texting and casting anxious glances down the hall towards the silent lift. All of them must be wondering by now where Dax and Wendy were. Why they hadn't joined the group, and why the station chief was sitting in an office with their team leaders.

"Who have you lost?"

Rimmer sat straighter, rigid as a statue in his chair. "Dax Doepker is dead and Wendy Cheung has disappeared. I found her phone shoved between the mattress and the wall."

Joe's forehead creased into a deep frown and it was several moments before he spoke. "Dax had the potential to become a good agent. Wendy—she's aced every exam and is shaping up to be an excellent analyst. Her weakness is in hand-to-hand combat."

That Joe knew about both rookies' progress shouldn't come as a surprise.

Rimmer nodded. "That's her. It appears she's been taken, although why is less certain."

"Right, you can fill me in along with the rest of your team, and then we'll find where they've taken her, and why." Joe stood, walking towards the door. He stopped with his hand on the handle and turned back to them. "This is still your case—for now."

***

". . . so you'll be returning to your surveillance posts, but with additional security protocols in place. Any questions?" Paul looked around the group. Shock and grief he'd expected, but not Vic's determined expression.

"Sir, if there's any way I can be of use to help find and

rescue Wendy, I'm volunteering now." The willowy blonde was dressed more like a model than her classmates, with enunciation and an accent Paul had heard in Sloane Square in London. Unlikely as it seemed, Lin had said Vic and the more studious Wendy were good friends.

"Thanks, Vic. We'll let you know." He didn't add that her appearance probably precluded her from undercover work in this city. That, and her upper class British accent which persisted, despite having been born in Singapore to ex-pat parents still living here. Her background had made for interesting reading compared to the rest of the group. "Actually, can we see you in the office before you and Pete leave?"

Vic's eyes widened, but only for a moment. "Yes, sir."

Pete stepped forward. "Me too, sir?"

"No, but you can start filling in the forms for you and Vic to be issued with firearms before you return to your post." Regret that he hadn't issued each of the rookies with a gun before they took up their posts was pointless. Not arming inexperienced operatives on their first surveillance had seemed one of those *good idea at the time* decisions.

He led the way back to the private office and closed the door behind Lin and Joe Wang. Leaning against the door, he folded his arms across his chest and looked from Wang to Lin. "No real surprises in their reactions."

Wang moved the chair he'd first occupied closer to the wall and settled into it, the better to look at both of them. He seemed to carry a great weight on his shoulders since the news of Dax's death and Wendy's disappearance.

Paul rubbed his thumb across his lower lip. "Although I'm curious about Victoria Purvis' offer."

Lin perched on the edge of the wooden chair and set her linked hands on the desk. "Those two young women have been friends since they first met in training. We're going to ask Vic if she has any idea what Wendy's phone password is."

Wang's gaze flicked to the mobile lying on the desk. A muscle ticked in his cheek. "What are you hoping to find?"

Paul scratched his stubbled chin. "Wendy's phone was shoved down between the mattress and the wall. Hidden. It was too tight a squeeze to have simply fallen and lodged there, regardless of how fierce a struggle took place. There must be a reason why she did that. I'd prefer not to alert anyone to the fact we have it by accessing the phone company through your work computers."

"Indeed. Now, bring me up to date with what you didn't tell your team; then we'll put our heads together. The more I think about the way this case is developing, the more I agree with you, Paul."

Paul. Wang's change in tone and the use of his first name were telling. Informality was more Jake's style. Every interaction with Wang had been formal and professional. Paul weighed this shift against not knowing who the mole might be. Wang could be playing a deep double game, but at some point Paul had to decide to trust someone other than Lin and their rookie team. "In that case, do you have any suspicion who the mole might be?"

Wang shook his head. "We need to match a list of people in the know at the beginning against a timeline of events. Who was involved, or in a position to know, right from the start?"

Soft tapping on the keyboard drew Paul's attention to Lin. Light from the computer screen lit her face, highlighting high cheekbones and the heart shape of her delicate features. She spoke without shifting her attention from the screen. "We should go back to the abduction of Serena Masters. Somehow, it links in with this case. Sir, do you know who closed that file?"

"I didn't know it had been." Wang took out his mobile and gave it his full attention as a quiet knocking sounded at Paul's back.

He turned, saw that Vic waited outside, and let her into the office.

"Pete's registered the forms. We're to go by the armoury on our way back to our post." Vic stood quietly beside him, raising a hand to tuck in a loose strand of hair.

A subtle fragrance drifted across to him—hints of lime and thyme, and something that reminded him of Italian cooking. Dammit, if even a woman's perfume reminded him of food, he needed to eat. They couldn't afford any distraction on top of a night with little sleep.

Shaking his head as though that would clear it of his focus on food, Paul picked up the mobile and showed it to Vic. "Do you recognise this?"

Her lips parted in recognition and she lifted her hand as though to take it from him, pulling back at the last second. Her gaze flicked up and met his. "That's Wendy's. I teased her for days about her choice of protective case. How—"

Paul turned the phone over and glanced at the back cover. "Mulan. Interesting choice." His young nieces would love to have the Chinese warrior daughter on their own phones. "More importantly, did Wendy share her passcode with you?"

Vic nodded, her gaze snagged by the phone. "Yes. One day while I was visiting and she was cooking, she needed to check a recipe and her hands were covered in oil so she told me. It's the date she was accepted into the Bureau."

Paul handed the phone to Vic. "Unlock it, please."

Her hands shook a little as she took the phone and ran a finger over the figure on the back cover. "Where was it?"

"That's not your business, Victoria." Lin's tone was sharp, whiplike.

Vic's cheeks turned pink and her lips rolled inwards, keeping a tight rein on what was probably embarrassment. She turned to the screen and keyed in six digits then silently handed the phone to Paul.

"Thanks, Vic. We'll check in with you and Pete at 12.30 p.m. Remember the protocols. No sending out for food, no personal phone calls, no—"

Vic's fingers twined so tightly, her knuckles were white. "We will not be taken by surprise, sir. But please, if there's something—*anything* I can do to help Wendy . . ."

Paul opened the door and ushered her out with a gentle hand on her shoulder. "We'll let you know."

He shut the door behind her, watching through the window as Pete picked up some papers from the printer and swung a backpack over his shoulder. He said something, the words indistinct.

Vic shook her head, picked up a large shoulder bag and stalked down the hall. Moments later, the ding of the lift sounded.

Paul glanced up from Wendy's phone. "I want the team's phones monitored."

Lin simply nodded and picked up her mobile. "I'd already thought the same thing." She spoke quietly to someone and added, "He's here now."

Wang's eyes narrowed. "Tell me you're not suspecting a rookie of sabotaging a Bureau operation? It's not possible. They don't have that level of access."

"Joe?" Lin held out her phone. "The controller requires your personal pin code to be entered to allow the surveillance to happen. Trust us. Please?"

Their gazes clashed, held, and then the head of the Bureau plucked the phone from Lin's hand. It wasn't a power play between them; Paul had seen a couple of those in his early days in the Sydney office. What he saw between Wang and Lin showed mutual respect overcoming Wang's reservations about the rookies.

Lin took her phone back and slid it into her pocket. "Thanks, Joe. I hope we're wrong."

Chapter 22

Lin raised the binoculars and trained them on Chan's mansion across the street. "I know a way to get inside, and you're going to hate it." Behind her, Rimmer was intent on studying a plan of the building and formulating how to rescue Serena Masters.

"Hmm, if it's got anything to do with sneaking in by using that white van, forget it."

She gasped and turned from the window. "How could you possibly guess that?"

Rimmer's mouth quirked up. "I'm getting to know how you think, Lin. Scary, isn't it?"

Turning back to her task, she shrugged one shoulder. "Assuming they haven't moved her while we were away, we could manufacture our own blackout."

"What about backup power to the house? They'll have a generator. Chan wouldn't put up with lack of power for any length of time, regardless of what his security team were doing."

"Taking that as a given, where is the most likely place to locate a generator? It won't be anywhere within sound of Chan's living quarters. My bet is in that garage." Training the binoculars there, she scanned slowly along the outside. Not that there was anything to be seen, but the action helped as she reviewed the layout in her mind.

"I didn't see any sign of it when the van was there."

"We weren't looking for it then, but at the far end from where we saw the van, back behind that stairwell, that would be a good spot. Isn't that back corner below the kitchen?"

There was a pause while Rimmer checked, and she imagined him leaning closer to the laptop, enlarging the plans and considering her suggestion. Intense focus and attention to details made him good at his job. Caring about people made him great at it.

"You're a good team leader, Rimmer." Words, not intended to be spoken aloud, slipped into the silence.

There was a sharp intake of breath—his—and she bit her lip. There were so many reasons why giving voice to those words, today of all days, was a bad idea. Timing, for a start. Dax was dead and Wendy, missing, and Lin had stupidly shared her thoughts about Rimmer. "I'm sorry, I didn't mean to—"

"You're right—about the kitchen." His voice was cool, distant, and she felt the solid weight of the wall he'd thrown up between them again. Only this time, she recognised it as a defensive move. This time, she wasn't going to let him get away with it.

"I'm right about you too."

"No, Lin, you're wrong."

"You only think I'm wrong because you can't see what I see. A good leader does everything he or she can to ensure the safety of the team and help each of them be the best they can. You've done that. You've seen opportunities to challenge and extend our team and you've let them do it. Sometimes, things go wrong, things that no one could have foreseen. But that doesn't mean you aren't a good leader—"

"Enough. You're wrong, end of story. Now let's focus on how we rescue Serena."

***

He'd lost two team members in one disastrous failure. One dead, one missing. In nobody's book would that make him a *good leader*. Wishing he could get out, walk, run, push himself physically until his mind numbed him to the losses stacking up against him, all he could do was stop Lin arguing with him and focus on finding a way into—and back out of—Chan's mansion.

"Have we got approval to use the thermal imaging drone for a fly-by of Chan's property?"

Without taking her eyes from the mansion, Lin picked up her phone, thumbed it on and held it out to him. "Here. There's movement on the roof of the second building. You can check if the notification has arrived."

He took the phone from her. "Yep, it's here. I'll give them the go-ahead as soon as it's fully dark. Now tell me what you can see."

"One man, one woman." She leaned forward, adjusting her focus.

He stood behind Lin, feeling the warmth of her body, the flick of her high ponytail as she moved her head. He should move away from her. Leave space between them, not reach out to touch her. His hand froze an inch from her shoulder. Touching Lin would make him feel better, maybe make both of them feel better, but her words—meant to tell him she trusted him—pierced him to his core. He hadn't made the right call when he'd opted not to arm the rookie surveillance teams.

The mistake would haunt him. It didn't matter that the suggestion had been Lin's. He'd made the call to implement her idea. The buck stopped with him.

He lowered his arm and shoved his hand in his pocket out of temptation's way. *Concentrate.* He leaned forward at the same time Lin lowered the binoculars and glanced over her shoulder at him.

"They've gone. She was young, pretty, and scared as hell when they appeared. The guard had an arm around her shoulders and the other hand holding her elbow in a controlling grip. After he said something to her, she *smiled.*"

"What sort of smile?"

"Teeth gritted, lips stretched wide like those clowns in the old arcade games, and then she untied her sarong and bared her

177

breasts in the direction of the mansion. He held her there for a couple of minutes, perving down at her breasts, before he looked towards the mansion and gave a nod. Then they disappeared through that corner doorway. But the whole time they stood there she looked terrified."

A memory of the stage in the Sydney brothel flashed into Paul's mind. Young girls forced to *display* themselves for customers. His memory of the stage morphed into that flat-topped roof. How many more women would be hurt or traumatised or killed before they amassed the *right sort of evidence* to bring Chan in.

If we can catch him this time.

There would be no more *if* it happened. Only *when*.

"Did you recognise the girl? Have you seen anyone else on the roof?"

"No, to both questions. Jeez, Rimmer, whose benefit was that for? It reminded me of a show and tell."

"My guess is that sick bastard just picked his next bed mate."

Lin was silent, but her neck was a rigid line. Anger rolled off her in waves, merging with his own like two white-hot streams of lava.

"As soon as we have details from the thermal drone mission, we'll move into phase two with Wang and—"

Paul's phone vibrated and he pulled it from his pocket. Unknown caller. He pressed the green button and held it to his ear.

"Agent Rimmer? There's someone here wants to say hi." The male voice was smarmy, upbeat, unknown.

"Who is this?" He pressed the speakerphone button and Lin turned, her eyebrows arching up at his question.

A second voice, female and soft and familiar, replied. "Please, they want me to tell you—"

"Wendy, is that you?"

Sniff.

A male voice in the background said, "Tell him, just what you were told to say."

A ship's horn sounded in the background. By accident, or a deliberate ploy to mislead? Paul left speculation for after the call ended.

"If you attempt a rescue—*any* rescue—we'll both be killed."

"Who's with you, Wendy? Is it Serena Masters?"

"I can't—"

The male voice took over. "Got that, Pansy boy?"

The connection went dead.

"At least we know she's alive, Rimmer."

"Alive, yes, but for how long? They know we're planning to rescue Wendy, but how did they know that we know about Serena?"

Within seconds, a ping sounded from the laptop. Paul dropped into the chair in front of the screen and clicked into the secure VOIP connection. "What have you got for us?"

The dispatcher's voice was the same one he'd spoken with when he'd added his phone to the list of monitored numbers. "Caller located in Marina Bay Gardens, near the eastern entrance. We're locked onto and are tracking the phone. He's heading towards the casino."

"Get the closest officers down there now."

"Yes, sir."

Lin abandoned her post by the window and gripped his arm. "If the person who called has Wendy, how is he walking about in such a public space with her? She'd raise the alarm somehow if she were there."

Paul thumped the table. "Dammit, we've been one step behind all the time. It's like they have a ear in all our discussions and an eye on everything we look at." Frowning so hard he felt the tightness over the bridge of his nose, he glared at Lin.

And the phone in her hand.

"Unless—"

Was it possible? Had he been played for a fool after all?

Chapter 23

"Unless what, Rimmer?"

He didn't answer. He didn't move.

He glared. At her.

"Is the answer written on my face or are you back to not trusting everyone, including me? Because if you go down that road again, Rimmer, I swear I'll—"

"Never that, Lin." His eyes narrowed on the phone in her hand and an idea, so bizarre that she almost blurted it out, jumped into her mind.

Silently he held out his hand and nodded at her phone.

"I'm glad to hear it." She handed the phone to him, cottoning on to his idea when he picked up a paper clip from the table and used it to open the case. Rimmer had caught hold of it first, but the same idea had occurred to both of them—about strange possibilities and who to trust.

"So, what do you think we should do now? About Wendy and 'the other person' she indicated is with her."

"Just keep watch. That call is a setback to our plans. Give me time to think some more." Rimmer carefully opened her phone case, tipping the back up a bare inch and peering inside. He turned it to her and pulled a *don't-say-a-word* face.

Inside nestled a small, slim microphone dot attached by a short wire to the case. She nodded that she understood. Every word they'd spoken, every plan they'd made, the night they'd spent together . . . Everything had been heard by whoever had tapped her phone.

With a flick of her eyes down to where Rimmer's phone lay on the desk, she raised her eyebrows.

Carefully closing her phone, he set it aside and opened the back of his. It was clean.

Lin pressed her lips together and frowned. It wasn't like she carried the phone everywhere when she was in the office. Often, it sat on her desk beside her keyboard.

Since she hadn't *lost* her phone, the bug had most likely been planted by someone close enough to her to access the phone without raising suspicion. Did that narrow it down? In the office there were other agents, legitimate visitors and cleaners. Then there was the rookie team in their secret office.

Had she been anywhere else since the case began? When had the case actually begun? With Serena Masters' abduction?

Stepping quietly towards the window, phone in hand and possibilities whizzing through her head, she spoke again. "Why don't you take a break and have a shower?"

Miming water falling and people speaking, she conveyed her idea to Rimmer. They had to create a safe space away from the bugged phone.

How could I not have thought to check my phone?

Had grief over Kim's death distracted her? Or worse, made her careless?

Rimmer pushed his chair away from the table, letting it bang against the end of the bed. "Yeah, good idea. I'll bring some coffee when I've finished." Signalling her to leave her phone where it was and join him, he opened the bedroom door and closed it behind them. Taking her hand, he led the way to the main bathroom and turned on the shower, running the water full pelt.

Then he pulled her close.

Was this necessary or overkill? Or a move driven by mutual need?

She sank against his chest and breathed in his scent.

Rimmer lowered his head and spoke softly in her ear. "We can use this to our advantage. We'll give them a fake plan, and hit them when and where they don't expect us."

She nodded and set her lips near his ear. "The surveillance teams—do you think the others are safe?"

"For now. Otherwise they'd have been eliminated when Dax and Wendy's position was hit." Rimmer's voice held a hard edge. "I still haven't figured out why she hid her phone. There was nothing new on it. That security footage was the most recent item sent."

"Maybe she thought she'd protect her contacts by hiding it? Protect us by keeping the phone link out of their hands?"

They held each other for several heartbeats, moments in which the noise of the falling water and their breathing were the only sounds. The bathroom filled with steam. Reluctantly, Lin released her hold on Rimmer and backed away. Feeling behind her for the handle, she opened the door. The last thing she saw was Rimmer's intense blue gaze through waves of steam.

***

When the door closed Paul reefed off his shirt. The water was running and he might as well take advantage of the break. Turning the hot tap off, he dropped his clothes in a pile and stepped under the cold spray.

The *Lin-effect* on his body slowly subsided as he dragged his fingers through his hair, down his face. God, he was tired. Aware of the need to make everything appear normal to whoever had bugged Lin's phone, he resisted the urge to stand under the water too long.

Ten minutes later, he entered the front bedroom with a pot of coffee and two mugs on a tray and the beginnings of an idea. He set the tray down beside the laptop and filled both mugs. Black and strong, it would keep them going. "Coffee, madam?"

"Thanks." Lin sounded distracted. Her body was relaxed— well, as relaxed as holding a pair of binoculars and keeping Chan's mansion under surveillance allowed her to be. It wasn't hard to

183

guess what preoccupied her.

"I'll let Joe know what's happened and see what ideas he's got. Are you okay for now?" He set a mug down next to her, taking delight in pushing it across the wooden surface beside her phone. He hoped the scritching of cheap mug on wood was magnified a hundredfold in the hidden bug. *Hope that hurt your ears, you bastards.*

"Sure. Only, can you call from somewhere else? I'm trying to think."

He picked up the second mug, sipped it, and smacked his lips. "I'll get the latest update about the girl from the container too. Don't let your coffee go cold. Back soon." Dropping a kiss on her bare shoulder, he went down to the kitchen, hyper-aware that bugs could be listening from both near and far. Was it feasible a directional mike was aimed at them?

Turning on the extractor fan over the stovetop was a start. He filled the electric kettle and plugged that into the power point beside the stove. Satisfied he'd made eavesdropping on his conversation as difficult as he could, he rang Joe.

Listening hard, analysing every word, every pause, heck— every breath the Bureau chief drew—Paul recited the bare facts before adding his own commentary. Skewed it most definitely was, but now they were certain there was a double agent, and he'd returned Joe Wang to their list of suspects.

The only people not on the list were him and Lin.

"We won't give in to threats, Paul." He could almost see the Bureau chief stabbing the desk with his finger. "From Wendy's call, it sounds as though Chan's people have moved the Masters girl elsewhere. If you think the brothel is the likely holding cell, that's where the assault team will hit."

"It's impossible to be sure. I heard a ship's horn during the call. Tracking indicated the caller and Wendy were between the Marina Gardens and the casino, but Agent Tan and I wondered if they might be closer to the docks?"

"Do you want a second team down there?"

"Agent Tan and I could take a look down there. I feel further surveillance of Chan's home can wait. Our priority now is extracting Wendy and Serena." Despite what he was telling Joe, if this gamble played out as he hoped, Chan's people would be focusing on other locations, leaving the mansion, if not exactly open, at least with limited guards.

And if the thermal drone revealed what he expected it to, he and Lin would be free to break in and liberate not one, but two young women.

If he'd guessed right.

Chapter 24

Lin hardly dared to breathe. Crouched in deep shadow behind a line of hibiscus bushes, her eyes were closed to preserve her night vision. Beside her, equally silent, Rimmer wore night vision goggles. Through the thick concrete wall separating their hiding place from Chan's mansion, her ears strained for sounds of the guard patrolling the ground between them and the house. Each pass differed in length, from thirty to thirty-five seconds.

That five-second difference worried her, as did the possibility he might stop in the middle of their chosen crossing point and look at his phone. She held her breath, listening harder.

Crack.

A twig snapped and she tipped her head. The guard was approaching their crossing point and heading towards the rear of the property.

Rimmer's knee brushed hers. She peered at him through a single slitted eye. He held up five fingers.

Five seconds.

She nodded, closed her eye, and mentally counted down. Right on cue, the streetlights went out. Through her eyelids, grey became black. Shouts erupted from the two guards as the main power grid shut down the whole Bukit Timah area.

Lin opened her eyes. Rimmer was holding his hands ready to boost her over the wall. She sprang up, levered herself over and dropped into a crouch. The night was dark, but she could see. The mansion and trees were grey-black against a deep grey sky. Rimmer landed beside her with a soft thud and then they ran, low and fast, in a repeat of their first foray into the heart of enemy territory.

Reaching the relative safety of a bed of large-leaf tropical plants, Lin tracked the garden, her gun and gaze in sync, while Rimmer slipped along the wall towards the far corner of the building. She moved past him into another pool of deep shadow. The far corner of the building was five metres ahead and their entry point, directly above.

Behind her, a generator engine spluttered and kicked into life in the corner where Rimmer had said it would be. Light spilled from two windows, but the kitchen above remained in darkness.

She pulled out the miniature launcher, checked the attached cord, aimed and fired. The soft *pfft* was lost in the throbbing of the generator. She tugged on the cord. When it held, she tested it with her body weight before securing it to the metal on her harness.

Signalling her intention to Rimmer, at his nod, she flicked the switch on her harness and rose silently into the air. Her ascent took her past the kitchen windows. A faint glow of light spilled through an open doorway onto stainless steel benches and then she was rising towards the third storey, rising beyond that to a narrow attic window where she stopped, swinging gently in her harness many metres above Rimmer.

She eased a knife into the close-fitting window groove, prayed the security plan was accurate and complete then lifted the window latch. Holding her breath, she waited for an alarm or flashing light to give away the breach.

Nothing happened.

She set one soft soled boot on the wall and pushed herself to one side.

Fingers gripping the sill, she eased the window open and scanned the interior of the dark room, listening intently. A soft rustling of material came from her right, followed by a muffled moan.

Bingo!

Giving the cord below her a quick double twitch—her

signal to Rimmer—she slipped her legs over the windowsill and eased into the room. The thermal imaging drone had revealed two bodies in this space and a third figure outside the door to the room. Perimeter heat sources were most likely guards, and they were stationed on the lower floors.

Convinced the smallish adults on the top floor must be Wendy and Serena, Rimmer had chosen to go it alone with Lin, try for a rescue earlier than the sting scheduled to hit the brothel around two a.m..

With luck, they'd have the two kidnapped women far away from here and safe in time to call off Wang's part of the operation if need be. She thumbed the switch of her pencil light, aiming the narrow beam towards where the moan had come from.

Wendy squinted and raised her handcuffed hands to shield her eyes. "Agent Tan, is that you?" Her voice was a whispered croak, but she struggled into a sitting position. As she peered up at Lin, the dark bruise blooming on one side of her face and a cut lip suggested how the blood spray beside the bed had happened.

"It's me." A lick of relief ran through Lin at the sight of a living captive. She flicked the torchlight around the room in search of the second body they'd seen on the thermal drone surveillance. The room held only Wendy. Treading softly to the door, Lin set her ear against the wood.

Wendy's whisper was soft, but carrying. "There's just one guard outside."

Lin moved swiftly to Wendy's side and picked up her hands. She'd learned how to pick standard police issue handcuffs early in her training. These would be simple. "I'll get these off. Where's the other woman?"

"They took her away. I don't know how long ago. An hour, maybe?"

The news was a blow. Instead of the quick rescue and escape they'd hoped for, it was likely she'd have to descend to the next level and seek out Serena once Rimmer had disabled the generator. "Did you recognise the woman?"

Wendy shook her head. "They kept a black hood over her head when she was in here."

Lin bent over Wendy's manacles and set to work with her lock pick. "Was there anything notable about her? Did she tell you anything?"

"Only that he'll punish her if she speaks to me. Her voice wasn't familiar, but the hood muffled the little she said. She wore an anklet with charms on it. I couldn't see much detail."

"That's good, Wendy. Good observation." There was a click and the cuffs lay in her hand.

Wendy rubbed each wrist. Her fingers trembled and she blinked owlishly in the spill of light from Lin's pencil torch. "Are we going out the way you came in?"

"Maybe. Can you make it?"

"I'll do what's needed." She rolled onto her knees, pulled one leg up and groped for the windowsill. "I lost my glasses. Everything's a blur."

Lin helped the wounded rookie to stand and set her back against the wall beside the window. Peering around the edge of the frame, Lin checked the outside garden. Any moment now Rimmer should be disabling the generator. She'd send Wendy through the window in her harness, deal with the guard and then set out to find Serena Masters.

Unbuckling her harness, she whispered instructions to Wendy. "Got it? Tell Agent Rimmer exactly what I told you."

Wendy nodded and fumbled with the harness. In the thin light of Lin's torch, her face was pale beneath the bruising. Was it realistic to expect her to make the descent in her weakened condition and half-blind, or would it be safer to risk taking her down via the servants' staircase?

Guiding an injured operative while trying to find Serena

would put them all at greater risk. But what if Lin stayed to assist Wendy's descent, and Serena was returned to the room while her hands were occupied controlling the harness?

Maybe an hour? Wendy's guess made getting caught in the attic room all too probable.

"I need to find the other woman. Can you make it down on your own?"

"You go. I'll take it slowly. Agent Rimmer will be waiting for me at the bottom?"

"Yes." Lin squeezed the young woman's shoulder before turning back to the door. While Wendy buckled up and manoeuvred herself onto the window ledge, Lin picked the lock of the door and eased it open a crack. The narrow landing was in darkness apart from the glowing tip of a cigarette. It glowed brighter as the guard inhaled and Lin moved swiftly.

She stepped in behind him, injecting a swift acting sedative in his neck. He slid down the wall to the floor, one leg curled back at an angle and his head resting against the doorframe. Soft light filtered halfway up the stairwell.

Waiting, willing Rimmer to hurry up and cut the power, she ran through the layout of the lower level. The light disappeared.

Shouts from several parts of the building reassured her Rimmer had succeeded. The security cameras should be out of action for at least the next couple of minutes.

Transferring her gun to her right hand, Lin pressed against the wall and silently took the stairs down to the next level. Her foot touched the floor at the bottom. She peeked around the corner into a short hall and listened.

Empty. Silent.

Aware of the seconds racing away—they had to be prepared for someone to get the generator working again—she sucked in a deep breath.

Move.

According to the building plans, the master suite lay to her right. Except for Chan's private suite, there were guard posts in each corner of the building. She had no idea if Chan would be inside, but there was a good chance Serena had been taken from her attic prison to his private room.

Praying Wendy had reached Rimmer and delivered her message, Lin widened her eyes and slid her hand along the wall until her fingers found a door handle. It turned silently.

As she eased the door open, a wash of light spilled into the crack.

Muffled groaning—female and distressed—reached her ears. Was Chan indulging his passion for torture?

A bolt of pure hatred speared her gut and sent steel down her spine. Pushing the door wide, she stepped into the room and trained her gun in the direction of the groans.

John Chan held a gun to Serena Masters' head and grinned.

"At last, Agent Tan. I thought you'd never arrive."

Chapter 25

Paul crouched behind the brick foundation pier of the building. The ground at this end sloped upwards, and the low ceiling made it unsuitable for vehicles, but useful as cover. He scanned the area, well used to the distorted vision through his night goggles. A black spider as big as Lin's palm scuttled along a metal joist. He tracked its movement while his old arachnophobia sent a rush of adrenaline coursing through his body.

Forget the damned spider. Soon, a guard would come to investigate why the generator had failed. Paul would silence him and give Lin the time she needed to get the women out.

Flexing his fingers, he took a slow breath, forced his gaze from the spider and peered around the brick pier. Through horizontal wooden slats, the inky patch of shadowed garden three storeys below the attic window was empty. Damn the narrow windows. He should have been the one scaling the wall and entering the building, putting himself on the front line of the rescue. But his body wouldn't fit through the slim opening, as Lin had pointed out, ending the argument about who did what.

He checked his watch, knowing it was fruitless. If the women were in a weakened condition, getting them through the window would take as long as it took.

A soft thud sounded from the shadows. Paul's head whipped back to the landing zone. The figure wore a ripped white singlet top and was slight, but her movements were jerky. Awkward, as though she were compensating for an injury.

Not Lin. Wendy.

She stayed low, hidden from external view by the luxuriant tropical planting. Awkwardly, she unbuckled the harness and gave two short tugs on the cord. Her face turned upwards, but the harness remained on the ground beside her. Where was Lin? Was Serena in worse condition than they feared? Was that the reason for the delay?

He glanced towards the internal staircase into the garage. Why hadn't anyone come yet?

A bad feeling gripped his gut. He slipped across a short exposed stretch of concrete floor and through a gap between the wooden slats and the concrete and block wall of the stairwell towards Wendy. He approached silently, conscious that she was probably nervous enough to shoot first. Lin had carried a second gun to give her if the rookie was in a fit state to use it.

"Wendy." He whispered her name. Frightened people were as unpredictable as wild animals and he held out one hand, palm up. It stretched pale from the black sleeve of his commando gear.

A swift intake of breath, a rustle of body against leaves and he was face to face with the business end of a gun. A gun that shook in unsteady hands.

"It's Agent Rimmer, Wendy. Agent Tan and the other woman, are they following you?"

The gun lowered and Wendy shook her head. From the garage came the sound of the heavy stairwell door opening.

"Wait here for me." Paul slipped back into the garage, his back pressed against the concrete block wall. A guard walked past him, his semi-automatic weapon slung across his back and a torch beam trained on the generator. He approached the machine, cursed it and kicked the trolley on which it sat.

Paul checked the guard was alone then stepped in behind and injected him. The sedative acted immediately, and Paul flipped the guard's body so the weapon didn't clatter on the concrete. Stripping the semi-automatic gun from the body, he slung it over his shoulder and then dragged the inert guard deeper into the low-ceilinged end of the garage and dumped him behind the furthest of the brick piers.

He looked back to where Wendy crouched in the garden. If he moved her to safety, he'd lose valuable minutes before finding another way in to help Lin. But if he left Wendy in the garden and things went pear-shaped inside, would she be able to get herself over the wall and away?

Torn by conflicting and equally pressing situations, Paul acknowledged his need to go after Lin was driven by their relationship. Without her in the equation, he'd already have been halfway across the property with Wendy.

"Damn it." Steeling his resolve, he returned to the rookie, took her elbow and drew her towards the narrow crossing between the building and the lush garden fronting the wall to the neighbouring property and relative safety.

Beyond the wall, lambent light from a quarter moon revealed shapes in a palette of grey. But amongst the border of trees it was inky black, only the night vision goggles keeping Paul moving forward.

Wendy tripped over a low, decorative log and stumbled against him. "Sorry, I can't see anything."

"I've got you." He gripped her arm tighter and drew her to the dividing wall. The thought slid through his mind that it was the first time he'd seen Wendy without her glasses. Wang had noted that one on one combat was her weak area. Why didn't she wear contact lenses? "I'll give you a boost over the top. Find yourself a place to hide in the garden and stay put. Agent Tan or I will find you."

"Thank you."

He knelt beside the wall and offered his linked fingers. Wendy's bare foot settled on his hands, one small hand gripped his shoulder and she steadied herself against the wall with the other. "Ready."

Paul rose quickly, pushing her up and onto the top of the

wall.

She half-fell, half-rolled over the top.

He waited only to hear the thud of her landing before he turned back and scanned the grounds and mansion from his deep cover. The harness still hung, empty and untouched since Wendy's descent. A single glance up the wall to the attic window revealed nothing more than the thin rope.

No movement. No Lin. No rescue.

Yet.

Somewhere inside Chan's mansion, Lin was working to free the kidnapped girl.

He'd promised to wait outside for Lin. Training told him to stick to the plan. Training, rules, common sense . . .

Gut-wrenching certainty told him her failure to return meant trouble.

***

Cool, calm, steady, Lin trained her gun on John Chan.

One shot. That's all it would take to give Kim justice.

One shot—

Chan would be dead and Kim would be avenged. Calmly her mind assessed the risk. One shot would end his life, but his finger could jerk on the trigger of the gun held to Serena Masters' head.

The risk is acceptable.

Her finger touched the trigger and every muscle in her body tightened. Vengeance. Justice. The world would be better without Chan in it. She could take him out without risking Serena's life. She knew she could.

Can you have him in your sights and not pull the trigger? Can you promise me that, Lin?

Paul had extracted the promise from her.

Serena moaned, her eyes wide with fear.

Chan's grip around her tightened. He grinned, lowered the

gun and pressed it into Serena's stomach then rubbed his cheek against his captive's. "Not sure about your ability to hit me without killing her, Agent Tan?"

Sweat slicked Lin's hand but she held her grip firm. "I could take you with one shot, Chan, but knowing you'll spend the rest of your life in prison holds a certain appeal."

Rimmer will be pleased to know I kept my promise. I won't fail him.

"Is it enough to know you had me in your sights and failed to pull the trigger? I thought you were supposed to be the brave one, but maybe that was your sister? Do you know how long she was on my delightful wheel and refused to scream?"

Chan's infamous wheel. Torturing innocent women to help him get a hard on. Torturing and killing Kim.

"Why did you take her, Chan?"

"It should have been you. My men went to your apartment. They were meant to fetch you and found her. I must say I enjoyed her for hours before she died. More than I expected."

Fury took over Lin's rational brain, black and all-consuming as a typhoon.

Kim had died because of her. Because she'd told her sister to meet her at the apartment to save time. She'd been late because she was working on Serena's case. Her finger settled against the trigger. Damn her promise to Rimmer, and damn always putting the Bureau and work first.

"I. Will. Kill. You."

"Go ahead and pull the trigger, Lin. But you'll miss because, deep down, you know the odds of killing my enchanting captive are high. Your bullet or mine—it won't matter. She'll be dead.

"And then I'll show you exactly how your sister died. You'll feel everything she felt. When I look in your eyes you'll give me all your pain and fear. I can't wait. Go ahead and shoot,

Lin. I promise you, I'll be the one enjoying myself after you shoot."

Her finger tightened on the trigger and darkness descended.

Chapter 26

Lin woke in absolute blackness with a pounding head and a mouth drier than a desert wind. The space felt unfamiliar; no noise of traffic or sliver of light around her bedroom blinds, and when she tried to sit up, to press her hands to her aching head, the action wrenched tight muscles in her shoulders and back and she came up short. A dull thud and the impossibility of moving brought her to awareness that her arms were shackled above her head. Her fingers touched cool metal, plastic and wood.

What the hell?

Zip ties locked her hands through a metal ring set in a wall. A fug of diesel fumes filled the room—which for some reason was rocking—and she had a strong desire to throw up.

Where the hell was she? Was the rocking real, or a figment of her addled brain?

She wriggled backwards and rested against the wall, half lying, half sitting, trying to ease the pull of her bound hands in her aching muscles. Closing her eyes, she tried to recall the sequence of events before the darkness. Not that there was any light to shut out, but the action helped her to concentrate.

Painfully, she reconstructed her movements from the attic to Chan's master suite. Chan, his arm tight around Serena's shoulders, his face hard against her cheek. Chan, with his gun aimed at his captive's stomach.

Chan, taunting her about how he killed Kim.

Lin turned her head and threw up. The stink of vomit almost overcame the stink of diesel. Her stomach heaved and heaved and she threw up until she was retching nothing but dry despair, then she spat to clear her mouth. Empty and exhausted, but with her mind clearer, she rested her head against the wall.

Images of Chan and Kim, and Lin's guilt, her complicity in her sister's death filled her mind.

Don't think about that now. Work out where you are and find a way out.

Channelling her grandfather's teachings, she calmed her mind and focused on reaching out with each sense. Darkness might surround her, but she had four other senses to feed her information.

That throbbing, low and regular—she both heard and felt it. And that swooshing noise—waves against a hull? The stink of diesel . . .

Am I on a boat?

"That's unexpected." Her voice surprised her. Croaky and soft as it was, it echoed. She continued speaking aloud, listening to the pseudo-echo, working out the size of her prison—*small.* "Maybe I'm in the bow of a boat."

But why hadn't Chan kept her in his mansion or taken her to the brothel?

Her fingers explored the zip ties and the metal ring constraining her hands. The metal was smooth, cool to the touch and heavy. Taking a deep breath, she gripped the ring and tried lunging forward.

The wrench to her shoulders screamed *bad idea!*

Catching her breath, controlling the pain, Lin turned towards the side of the boat. Setting her feet against the wood, she tried pulling. Over and over she pulled with little hope of drawing the ring from its place, her back arching under the exertion until, needing a break, she turned, half-falling, half-sliding to the floor. As she fell, a soft squeal of metal turning against metal filled the silent darkness.

Hardly daring to hope, Lin turned back to the wall. There it was again; the soft metallic scrape was the equivalent of a triumphal fanfare. Fingers scrabbling in her haste, she felt her way to the top of the metal hoop. Where the ring was attached to the wall, there was a narrow circular indentation slightly larger than the head of the ring.

Turning clockwise, Lin thrilled to the sound of metal unscrewing from its home. Twisting her whole body achieved a single rotation of the ring in its housing, but the promise of success, of gaining even this limited freedom kept her going. At last, the metal ring fell from its hole and she slumped to the floor.

Taking a few seconds to ease her shoulders and neck muscles, she listened carefully. Faintly, as though at a great distance, she heard raised voices. Two or three words in a back and forth pattern that sounded like orders given and repeated.

Following the sound, she felt her way along the wall to a corner, and then along that wall until she touched metal that curved slightly. With growing excitement her fingertips learned the size of the door and the location of the handle and hinges, worked out which way it opened then settled down and listened. Hidden behind the door, she set to work on the zip ties.

***

Fury vied with fear for Lin as Paul paced the faux-wood floor. He reached the far wall, spun around and paced the same five steps he'd taken over and over for the past ten minutes. The faux knot in the faux wood was still where it had been when he started pacing, but his patience was wafer-thin. He fisted his hands at his side, stopped pacing and glared at Joe Wang. "They knew we were coming. How else could they—"

"Just bad luck on your part, Paul. Maybe if you'd trusted me . . ." Joe Wang rested his arms on the desk—Lin's desk, Paul noted—and set his chin at a pugnacious angle. "Lin rescued Wendy and you got her to safety."

He glanced at Wendy sitting in a chair in the corner, a blanket around her shoulders and her feet curled up beneath her. She'd refused point-blank to go to hospital, even when Paul made

200

the request an order, and had sat quietly since they'd arrived at the office.

Her hands gripping the blanket, Wendy looked at him, her gaze intense and her voice tight. "Agent Tan was determined to find the other woman, this Serena Masters. I offered to go with her. She'd given me a gun . . ."

Paul snapped a reply. "Without your glasses, you couldn't see to walk in the garden without tripping over a log. How could you have shot anyone?" Colour flared in her cheeks, but she pressed her lips together. Knowing another agent on the inside might have led to a different outcome ripped Paul's insides to shreds, but snapping at Wendy was wrong. "Sorry. It's not your fault. I should have gone in."

Joe shook his head. "You both decided on the best entry point and you were right. Let it be, Paul. Bad luck happens, even with the best-laid plans. If Serena had been in that attic, Lin would have got both women out."

"And yet, Lin and Serena are both missing."

For a long moment no one spoke. Paul replayed the scene in his mind, desperately seeking details he might have missed. The sudden blinding brilliance of security lights bathing the garden in noon-bright light, a rush of guards into the garden, guns at the ready, the lack of any vehicle exiting Chan's garage . . . His hasty exit over the wall before the criss-crossing beams of torchlight could catch him.

"Where did they go?" Joe's frown probably mirrored Paul's.

"How the hell did they get out of there without our seeing them leave?" Paul resumed his pacing. Damn it, this round and round was getting them nowhere.

"Agent Rimmer?" The rookie was biting her thumbnail, but she looked excited. "I have an idea. That second building on the property, the one you speculated might be for Chan's family—

what if it's connected to the main house by a tunnel?"

"It's not for his family." The words shot out of his mouth before his brain caught up and he thought of the woman being displayed on the flat roof. "There was nothing on the building plans to suggest—" But how had the woman been brought to Chan? Lin had watched the mansion. There'd been no sign of movement between the buildings.

Was it possible?

"Check if there's any street camera footage."

"I'm on it." Wendy dropped her blanket and turned to the spare computer on the desk behind her. She pressed the on button and then turned to Joe Wang with a frustrated groan. "I lost my glasses."

Joe stood abruptly and took his glasses off, walked to Wendy and held out the pair of spectacles. "Here, use mine."

Paul looked from Joe to Wendy and back to the chief, surprised he hadn't noticed the similarities between them.

Joe caught Paul's eye and spread his hands wide. "What can I say? Although Wendy took her grandmother's surname to avoid other students working out our connection, someone was bound to work it out one day. I had hoped it would be later rather than sooner."

"Dad! You promised you wouldn't say anything." Wendy sighed, slipped her father's glasses on and turned her attention to the screen, pushing the glasses up her nose with an impatience he'd seen both father and daughter exhibit.

How had he missed the physical likeness and the same mannerisms? What else had he missed while so wrapped up in Lin? "Now I know how you reached us so quickly after I called."

"Wendy borrowed a phone and let me know the situation as soon as she cleared that wall. I admit I was wondering why you and Lin weren't there when we were preparing for the raid on the brothel. The thought occurred to me that you might have made *alternate plans.*" Joe allowed a quick quirk of his lips, the closest he came to smiling.

"You've already had an unbiased assessment of your daughter's ability from me. She'll be an asset to the Bureau. I'm glad she's on our side."

Wendy stopped scrolling through video footage and looked hard at the screen. "I've got something. A dark SUV with heavy tinting took a narrow track that runs behind the properties on the northern side. You can see the headlights turning out from behind Chan's newer building." Wendy pointed out the location of the mansion and the secondary dwelling whose purpose they'd only recently discovered.

"Is there a closer camera, one that might show who got into the vehicle?" Paul leaned over her shoulder, his gaze tracking back and forth along the front street, while Wendy's father peered myopically over the other.

"Nothing. But give me a few minutes. I can track the SUV via the traffic cameras."

Stepping away with a grunt of frustration, Joe pulled out his phone and held it close to his face. "I'll authorise one team to sweep both house buildings and keep the other team on observation of the brothel. Wendy, don't you keep a spare pair of glasses at work?"

"Of course. In my in tray. Sorry, Dad. I forgot about them." Her focus remained fixed on the screen.

Paul opened the door and called over his shoulder. "I'll get them." He strode across their no-longer-secret office to Wendy's desk and found a psychedelic-patterned case shoved to the back of the lower stacker tray.

Grabbing it, he stood for a moment and gazed through the slitted blinds. Palm trees along the front whipped back and forth in a strengthening wind from the east.

The dread that had sucked breath from his lungs eased.

Lousy weather he could deal with. Losing Lin wasn't an option, but finally they had something concrete to go on. They would find Lin. And Chan.

And when they did, if Chan had harmed a single hair on Lin's head, regardless of Bureau rules, the bastard was dead.

Chapter 27

Paul handed the glasses case to Wendy and she handed her father's spectacles back. "Do we know where they went?"

Wendy pushed her glasses up her nose and nodded. "The docks. From there I was able to switch into the port security system. Several figures got onto a small powerboat and headed towards the marina. One of the men was carrying someone over his shoulder. I'm trying to get into the marina's security system now."

"A boat?" Paul frowned and turned back towards the external windows. "Do you think Chan will make a run for it across the Strait? The wind's getting pretty strong."

Joe had turned on the desk computer and sat, frowning at the screen. "There's a low-pressure system moving in from the South China Sea. Potential for destructive winds, but—"

"If they're heading into the Strait, they'll be heading into that storm. How bad does it usually get here?"

"If you're thinking typhoons, Singapore doesn't get them. We're too close to the equator although—"

"Although what?"

Joe huffed and flicked a quick look at Wendy. "It's not impossible. On the day Wendy was born in 2001, Typhoon Vamei hit us. It's the only typhoon in living memory to reach us, but . . . Let me get onto the Coast Guard." Joe began working his phone contacts while Wendy continued trying to access video footage from the marina.

"Got it. The *Beluga* left port half an hour ago against the advice of the harbourmaster."

"Find me a boat with enough power to catch it." Paul opened his phone and pressed a speed dial number.

Wendy and Joe spoke over the top of each other.

"Surely you can't mean to—"

"I'm coming with you. I'll divert a team. The brothel can wait."

Paul's phone call connected. He gave his former partner no time for pleasantries. "Jake? Chan's heading out to sea in the *Beluga*. He's got Lin and a woman he abducted on board. Do we have any naval ships in the area?"

***

Two male voices were arguing outside the door to Lin's prison. The zip ties still held her to the metal ring, but she gripped it firmly. Her grandfather had drilled into her the secret of making use of what surrounded her. Despite her awkward grip, the ring was heavy enough to do damage. She was trained and had the element of surprise on her side.

Widening her stance and with her bottom braced against the wall, she balanced against the increasingly wild rolling of the boat. The door opened and a narrow bar of light fell across the slatted wooden floor. A curse followed—something about stinking puke—and the door slammed shut. More argument—through tone, not words—raged on the other side of the door.

When it swung open again, wider this time, two men stepped into her prison, each with a hand clamped over his mouth and nose. They stood looking down at the puddle of vomit next to the place she should have been.

Lin swung the metal ring at the closest head, continued the momentum of her turn and kicked high. The first man fell and didn't move again. The second pitched forward into her vomit. He grunted and rolled away. One hand scraped over his cheek and flicked away the disgusting mess. The brief delay was enough.

Lin stepped through the hatch doorway and pulled it shut behind her, locking it. The sound of the metal bar clicking into its slot elated her.

One more step towards freedom.

Silently, she edged along the short corridor to the corner and peeked around just as the boat pitched roughly. She fell hard against the opposite wall, biting back a cry. Her shoulder throbbed, but, seeing a clear path to the stairway, she moved ahead. Filthy weather wasn't stopping Chan leaving Singapore and it wouldn't stop her escape.

It will be a challenge getting off the boat if we're in the middle of the Strait though.

First things first. Ridding herself of her bonds and arming herself had to be her focus, then finding where Chan was holding Serena.

Her gut churned as possible scenarios raced through her mind, but even this luxury yacht wouldn't hold all his *toys*. Probably Chan would have Serena in his suite on the deck above, but she listened at each door on the way to the metal stairs. Silence. All hands must be on deck securing the boat against the storm.

Ears straining to hear, she gripped the door handle to the last berth and pressed it down. A narrow chink of light fell from the corridor onto an empty bunk and a small desk.

Lin slipped inside and gently closed the door before turning on an overhead light. Storm preparations were in place here and the metal ring holding her tied hands made it difficult to undo the desk drawer, but finally she hooked a finger beneath the safety catch. The drawer shot open as the boat pitched, spilling its contents over the cabin floor. Paper, a torch, scissors . . . A Swiss army knife. She grabbed it and sat on the neatly made bunk, wriggling backwards until she was wedged into the corner and as stable as she could be on the pitching boat.

She set the tool between her knees, levered open a serrated knife and set to work sawing through her bonds.

***

Paul ducked under the overhanging eaves of the port office

and pressed his phone to his ear, but hearing Jake was difficult over the thunderous rain.

"You're in luck. One of the Singaporean naval frigates is close enough to assist."

"About time something went our way. What's the rendezvous point?"

"Follow Chan's boat. The *RSS Stalwart* will stop the *Beluga* and assist with recovery of the women."

"Thanks, Jake. I owe you one."

"Make sure you come home to pay your debt in person, mate." Jake ended the call.

Paul sprinted through fat-dropped tropical rain, following Joe and one of the already assembled teams. Up ahead, a Coast Guard vessel rocked against the dock, sleek and new and glistening in the watery light of overhead security lighting. The others were all aboard. Paul bounded across the gangplank. As soon as his feet touched the deck two coastguards dressed in bright yellow rain slickers pulled the gangplank on board. As Paul shut the outer door behind him, the boat's engines shuddered against the stormy waters, reversing the vessel and then heading for the open sea lane.

He ran a hand over his face and blinked, clearing his watery vision. Joe Wang and the captain had their heads together over a marine chart. Edging past team members who sat along two wooden benches, gear stowed beneath them, Paul waited until the captain finished speaking to deliver his news. "The *RSS Stalwart* is heading towards the *Beluga*. We're to follow Chan and meet up with them in the strait."

Captain Vickers' eyes lit up. "The *Stalwart* is one of our navy's newest and best frigates. Top speed is twenty-seven knots. I've checked the *Beluga*'s specs. Her top speed is forty knots, but she won't manage anything like that in these seas."

"How long do you think it will be before we catch them?" Paul's fingers twitched with need. Need to hold Lin close. Need to contain Chan—forever.

Joe shook his head. "More to the point, which direction did they go?"

"As luck would have it," Vickers couldn't contain his grin, "I was with the harbourmaster when the *Beluga* left. He tried to stop them leaving port by citing this weather. When the *Beluga*'s captain refused, he told them his latest information showed the possibility of a typhoon forming in the east. He might also have suggested a westerly direction would be safer—if their destination was flexible."

"Did they take his advice?"

"Let's check the radar and see."

***

Even wedged into the corner as she was, the boat's rocking made precision cutting challenging. Finally, the zip tie fell apart under Lin's determined sawing. Relief was immediate, followed by pulsing pain as blood flowed freely from the cut in her wrist. Rubbing and flexing her hands, she pushed off the bunk and sought a first aid kit. Leaving a trail of blood drops as she searched for Serena would be foolish, but loss of blood on top of the after effects of the sedative she'd been too slow to stop Chan's men from administering was suicidal.

Her search found nothing more than a clean white T-shirt. It would do. Wrapping it around her wrist, she gripped an end in her mouth and tightened the makeshift bandage. The smell and taste of laundry detergent hit her nose and tongue.

Blood coloured a small patch on the makeshift bandage, but the cut no longer dripped. Clutching the Swiss army knife and a small pencil torch, Lin eased the cabin door open and scanned the corridor, listening for voices approaching from the deck above. Her next move was the most dangerous. Being caught in the open on the narrow stairs would trap her in this cramped staff half-deck.

Her bare feet made no sound on the metal treads and she

reached the top without a crew member appearing, but as she stepped into the wide central corridor, a door opened halfway along. Quickly, she slid into the closest cabin, praying it was empty, and closed the door until only a crack remained. A voice filtered through to her—male and chillingly familiar.

"I will return as soon as I've given the captain his orders, my dear."

Through the crack, Lin spied John Chan. Impeccably dressed in tailored trousers, a pale striped shirt, and a cravat, he turned and headed in her direction. Before he reached her she gently pressed the door closed and held her breath.

Had he been speaking to Serena? It seemed unlikely. His tone of voice, the gentle endearment, and the concern for whoever was in that cabin were at odds with how he treated the women he took. So who else was on board?

If Chan was simply going to speak to the captain, he would return to the woman soon.

Finding Serena and then finding a way off the yacht were Lin's only goals; not mulling over who Chan might have brought aboard his yacht.

Take action, she told herself. *There's not much time.*

Chapter 28

Peering over the coastguard's shoulder at the screen, Paul felt tension ratcheting his gut into a tight knot. "The *Stalwart* isn't showing up on the radar."

The fresh-faced operator turned and grinned. "It's a stealth frigate, sir. Hard to observe even when the weather isn't filthy." He turned back to his screen, leaned forward and stabbed a finger at the screen. "There's the *Beluga*."

Captain Vickers leaned over the crewman's shoulder. "Heading west, away from the storm. Good job finding her, Winston."

"Thank you, sir."

Paul breathed a sigh of relief and stepped away from the radar operator. "It looks like your harbourmaster convinced Chan's captain there's a typhoon building."

Vickers nodded. "We're lucky Winston is on duty tonight. He's one of our best operators."

"Does the storm interfere with the signal?"

"Even with both rain and sea clutter suppression turned on, a storm like this makes it more difficult to find and track. But young Winston could find the proverbial needle in the haystack."

"Sounds like we're finally getting a bit of good luck. Can we contact the *Stalwart* and—"

"Sir, the *Beluga*'s coming about."

The two men strode back to the radar operator. Winston had mapped the yacht's progress and he pointed at the blip on the 3-D screen display, then the map on the desk. "She's turned 150 degrees and is heading east. We should intersect in—" He made a quick check of his screen. "Fifteen minutes."

Vickers picked up the radio handset and handed a folder to Paul. "Plans of the layout of the *Beluga*. I'll contact the *Stalwart*. Prepare your men, Agent Rimmer."

***

Lin found every cabin empty before she set her hand to the handle of Chan's cabin. The lock clicked softly as she slowly opened the door.

A seductive female voice almost purred in welcome. "You said you wouldn't be long, darling."

Lin slipped through the narrow opening and pressed the door closed behind her, flicking the lock.

Sprawled across satin sheets, wearing a lacy black teddy and a sultry smile, lay Serena Masters. Her smile faded and she jerked upright. "You. What are you doing here? How did you—"

"Escape? I'd ask you the same question but it seems we have different views of John Chan." Her gaze took in the luxury of the cabin and lack of any restraints. Had Serena succumbed to Stockholm syndrome and fallen for her captor?

Serena's gaze darted to the door, and her tongue nervously touched the corner of her mouth. "He's a monster. You know what he's like, Agent Tan. But if I make myself agreeable and willing when he's around, I can survive. Please, you have to help me escape." Tears glistened in her eyes. "I've seen what he does to other women. I've seen . . ." Her voice trailed off in a sob. She hunched over the side of the bed and bowed her head.

Lin frowned. Which was the real Serena? The sprawling seductress with the sexy voice, or the tense woman before her, pleading for help?

She bit her lip and nodded. "Come on. We'll get out of here and find a way to get off this ship."

"You mean—you're it? Isn't there anyone else coming to help us?"

Lin couldn't afford to drag a fearful, nervous captive with

212

her, but she couldn't lie and let Serena think all would be well. "I'll do everything I can to get you safely off this ship, but we'll have to make do for ourselves. Be brave, Serena. Your parents are anxious to see you again. Together, we can do this, okay?"

Serena covered her mouth, sucked in a deep breath, and nodded. "What are we going to do?"

"I expect Chan will be back any minute. We'll hide out in one of the other cabins. Maybe from there I can find a way outside to the bridge and send out a call for help. Come on." She held out a hand. Slowly Serena reached for it. The woman's fingers trembled in hers.

Quietly they made their way into a cabin across the corridor from Chan's and locked the door. By Lin's calculation they should be just about underneath the bridge. She set a chair beneath the handle. It wouldn't hold for long, but even seconds could make a difference.

Serena sank onto the edge of the double bed and shivered. Shock or cold—it didn't matter why.

Lin turned the bedside light to its lowest setting then opened the closet, pulled out a luxurious bathrobe and set it around Serena's shoulders. "This will help. Now you just sit quietly. I'm going to scout around a bit."

Serena grabbed her arm. "Please, don't leave me alone."

"I'm just going to take a look at where we are." She eyed off two large rectangular portholes. Other than the door they offered the only way out—a dangerous, slippery exit. Waves smashed against the windows and wind whistled eerily. Not even luxury yachts were immune to foul weather. If she ventured out that way, assuming she could open the window wide enough to slip through the gap, the odds of being swept away were high.

A slim silver frame on the back of the door reflected the light. Inside was a deck plan of the *Beluga.*

You are here. The red arrow pointed to their cabin. With

her finger, Lin traced their position onto the top deck. *Bingo*, she thought. Above and a little forward of her lay the bridge. Immediately overhead was a sizable lounge and bar.

Having established her position, she eyed off the ceiling panels. One of them should give access to a crawl space and, if she was lucky, the electrical system. Dragging a chair into one of the inner corners, she climbed up and pressed the panels within reach. The third panel she tried lifted. Pushing it up and into the cavity, she gripped the edges of the manhole and levered herself up and peered into the space.

Two possibilities occurred to her, but cutting power to the engines, even if she were lucky enough to find the right circuit, would be suicidal in this weather. Without power, the ship could easily turn broadside in the big seas and capsize.

I need to reach the bridge and send out a distress signal.

Lightly dropping to the floor, she knelt in front of Serena and gripped her hands. They were cold where she gripped the edges of the bathrobe. "I'm going to head up to the bridge and try to send out a call for help. Will you be okay here?"

"Wouldn't it be better if I waited in John—in Chan's cabin? If I'm not there when he returns he'll know something is wrong. He'll come looking and when he finds me here . . ."

Lin's mind raced. If Chan found Serena had left his cabin, he'd hurt her for sure. "But if you go back there, you're placing yourself at his mercy again."

Serena nodded. "But you're risking everything to help me. I need to do this for you. I need to help. Please?"

"Okay. Go. But be careful."

Serena shrugged off the bathrobe and made her way to the door, lurching and falling onto the bed when the ship bucked wildly. She pushed herself up and reached for the closet, then crab-walked to a hook on the wall, and finally to the door handle. Setting the chair holding the handle aside, she gave Lin a tremulous half-smile. "See you soon." The door clicked shut behind her.

Lin hoisted herself through the manhole and felt for the top of the crawl space before turning on the pencil torch she'd found in the crew cabin. Directing its beam in both directions and calling to mind the layout of the deck above, she opted to head towards the bow. If she could come up behind the bar in the lounge area and use it to cover her exit from the crawl space, she should be close to the bridge.

That's the theory anyway, she told herself. Her head made hard, unintentional contact with a metal beam and she stifled a cry of pain. Escaping off Chan's yacht with Serena was up to her.

It was useless to wish Paul was here. Useless and distracting.

Directing the thin beam from her pilfered pencil torch along the crawl space, she pulled herself along the narrow shaft.

Chapter 29

"The *Stalwart* is five minutes from target. We should be seeing the yacht's lights at any moment." Vickers set his hip against the metal railing and raised a pair of binoculars to his eyes.

"Anything?" Paul flipped the single night vision lens over one eye and peered through the driving rain. Somewhere out there, Lin was at the mercy of Chan. Would he be in time to save her?

I have to be.

"I think I saw something. Hang on . . ." Vickers leaned forward, the binoculars pressed to his face. "Got her! About half a nautical mile, just to portside of our bow."

Paul spotted the lights before the yacht was hidden by big waves. "Stay within range, but no contact yet. I want the *Stalwart* in position when we board that yacht."

Now they had eyes on the *Beluga*, battle-calm settled over Paul. "My team is ready. *Stalwart* will demand the captain stops his ship."

"And if they don't?" Vickers turned from the radar screen and met Paul's eyes. "We're almost in disputed territorial waters with Malaysia."

"*Stalwart* will fire a warning shot. Then they'll send an inflatable out to come alongside and board them. Chan is an international fugitive and head of a multi-pronged criminal organisation. Whatever force is necessary will be used to apprehend him and rescue the women on board."

And if anything had happened to Lin—his hand settled on the butt of his sidearm—Paul would make sure Chan paid dearly.

***

Lin cracked the floor panel above her head, listened

intently then, hearing no sound of crew in the area, peered through the narrow opening. The lights were low in the lounge, but sufficient to reveal a small silver-grey keg on the floor directly in front of her. The sight sent relief surging through her.

Swiftly she curled her body up and out of the tight between-deck space and replaced the floor panel. Sheltered beneath the curved wooden bar, she listened again, straining to hear over the roaring storm.

Lightning flickered, flashed and illuminated her hiding place with electric bright white light. She averted her eyes, protecting her night vision, and prayed the crew on the bridge were intent on watching the storm. Any advantage, no matter how small, could make a difference.

The yacht pitched hard into a trough. Lin gripped the towel rail while bottles crashed to the floor near her feet. Both hands and one knee shot down, and her other leg stretched to the side, balancing her against the boat's wallowing pitch. Looking up, she saw a thin metal bar swinging in a wide arc from a now empty shelf. In the time since she'd escaped from her prison in the bilge, the storm had worsened.

Memory stirred. Eight-year-old Lin with her arms around Kim as the only typhoon ever to hit Singapore raged around them. An icy prickle of fear ran down her spine. Would she survive a typhoon at sea?

Intense aromas of expensive cognac and whisky and a stream of liquid soaking the knee of her black trousers cut through her fear. She was alive and at liberty and she had a rescue to carry out.

Taking care where she set her hands on the glass-strewn floor, she poked her head around the end of the bar. A narrow corridor off to her right led into a galley that would service this lounge. Beyond that, a cross-corridor separated the galley from the bridge. An elongated rectangle of light fell through a glass-panelled door leading to the bridge.

Unarmed, she could handle a couple of men without guns. But Chan's men all carried guns. The galley would hold an array of knives, probably locked away thanks to the storm, but she needed a weapon now. Preferably a gun, but she'd take what she could get. A swift search of the drawers in the bar produced a heavy-duty corkscrew and a pestle. Gripping the pestle, she held it like a cosh in one hand, and wrapped her fingers around the metal handle of the corkscrew.

Armed and alone, she slipped through the galley to the door leading to the bridge. A long pane of glass revealed a slice of the bridge.

Crew manned various stations. One turned to the captain. His tone was fearful, and she caught only a few words above the storm.

". . . ship closing . . . same course . . ."

The captain turned to someone out of Lin's sight.

Then she heard him. Chilling tones, and that voice that sent an army of spiders skittering across her skin. Chan moved across her narrow viewing pane and gripped the safety railing beside the wheel, and Lin pressed herself flat against the door.

"Open fire as soon as they're in range."

"It's a Coast Guard vessel, Mr Chan. Do you really think that—"

"You have your orders, captain."

Lin wondered if there was a stricken vessel this far out of port that the Coast Guard was responding to. Unlikely—not with all the warnings that had been issued. Not on the same course as theirs. In her book, that meant only one thing—*Rimmer's following us.*

And Chan had given orders to fire on the boat.

She tucked the pestle into a pocket and reached for the handle.

"Agent Tan." The soft voice behind her belonged to the woman Chan had kidnapped.

"Go back to—" Lin turned.

Serena held a gun on Lin. Gripped in two white-knuckled hands, it wavered wildly, but at this distance, she'd hit Lin.

"I can't let you hurt John. I love him and he loves me. We're going to get married, despite what my father says."

"Marriage?" Lin's mind worked furiously. "But he kidnapped you."

"We made it look real, didn't we? John's clever. Daddy was being obstinate and hateful. We had to force his hand." Serena staggered with the next roll of the boat. She leaned one shoulder against the wall, but the gun stayed on Lin.

"When did you meet him? You can't have known him for long."

Converse. Reinforce the connection. Wait for her lapse in concentration.

Serena gave a one-shouldered shrug. "Six months ago. We discovered we had similar—*tastes*. And now I'm going to give him a very special present . . . you."

***

Once his team had been briefed on developments, Paul resumed his position beside Vickers. Ahead of them the *Beluga* rolled and dipped, lost to sight in the heavy seas then riding high on a crest. Tuned into the same radio frequency as the *Stalwart* he heard the frigate demand the yacht stop.

There was no response. The *Beluga* ploughed on.

Stalwart repeated the order twice more.

Paul imagined the calm efficiency aboard the ship, the sailors manning the guns, tracking the *Beluga*, waiting for an order to fire. The yacht maintained radio silence.

A warning shot crossed the *Beluga*'s bow and the order to stop was repeated as Captain Vickers brought the Coast Guard vessel within close range. Behind him, team members prepared grappling hooks.

Bright lights sprang up in a lounge on the sundeck and, behind the full-length glass panels, Lin appeared.

She's alive.

Then Chan stepped up beside her and a woman—*Serena Masters?*—stood on her other side holding a gun to Lin's head.

"What the—" Vickers eased back on the throttle but maintained close contact with Chan's ship. "Is that your missing agent?"

"Yes. Patch me through to the *Stalwart*. We need their firepower, or at least the threat of it."

"Under these circumstances, are we boarding them?"

The rule book says yes.

If they did, Lin would be dead before his foot hit the *Beluga*'s deck.

A stark choice that was no choice at all faced Paul. Agents went into the field with the knowledge their lives were expendable. Lin knew that. Paul knew that.

But the order to board wouldn't pass from his mouth. He shook his head. "Give me a minute to discuss the situation with the *Stalwart*'s captain."

***

Lin's gaze found the tall, armed man through the rain-lashed windows of the Coast Guard ship.

Rimmer's here.

The knowledge strengthened her, and flowed through her like the night she'd channelled the power of the dragon. Once, she'd thought Kim was the other half of her soul, but Rimmer had been in the hotel room that night too, and he was here now. For her. With her.

Lin turned her focus inward, seeking, finding her inner power. Something would happen. The smallest thing would tip the balance of power in her favour.

The ship lurched.

Serena staggered, bumping into Lin.

Lin grabbed her arm and the gun, spun around and wrapped an arm around Serena's throat, both of them ending up facing Chan. She pointed the gun at Serena's head. "Stop the boat or I'll shoot your fiancée."

Chan's cold snake eyes settled on Lin. "Go ahead. She's just a woman. Expendable."

Serena gasped and tried to pull Lin's arm from her neck. "John! You don't mean that."

Chan glanced at Serena. "I told you once, I don't say things I don't mean." He met Lin's gaze. "Remember what I told you, Lin? What I will do to you?"

Serena tugged on Lin's arm, and Lin pressed the gun to the woman's temple. The breath she sucked in was fearful and desperate. "But you love me. You told me so. We're getting married."

"I said we would marry. The rest is your imagination. Your father's position in government will be useful, but I can control him in other ways." Chan's nostrils flared.

Lin remembered that nostril flare. It matched the snake-like glitter of his eyes. *He's a psychopath. There's no emotion to appeal to.*

"She doesn't matter, but *you*, Lin—you are strong, a fighter. You will make a fitting mate for a man of my power."

Revulsion made her skin crawl. Bile rose and her hand tightened on the gun as she pointed it at Chan.

Warm tears splashed onto Lin's arm and Serena sagged against her.

Lin fixed her gaze on Chan. Loathing laced her response. "That will never happen."

"You're here on my yacht and your so-ordinary lover has

not attempted to board us. He's breaking every rule of his training—for you. You're my ace, Lin. I will not be defeated by you or your weak Australian agent. Death before dishonour—did you know that is my family motto? I will slip from everyone's grasp *again* and then I will possess you."

"Over my dead body."

"Or hers." Chan pulled a gun from his pocket and fired.

Chapter 30

Two flashes burst from two guns and the *Beluga* dropped out of sight.

Lin!

Paul's insides crumpled, and contracted like a black hole. He couldn't lose Lin. He should never have waited, never have gone against his training. If they'd boarded as planned, Lin might be safe. Alive.

But a little voice in his head knew better. *She'd be dead.*

"What happened? Did you see?" Vickers peered through the binoculars.

When the *Beluga* reappeared, the interior of the room was hidden. The same rogue wave that had turned the yacht broadside caught the Coast Guard vessel. Paul gripped a grab bar while the helmsman battled the wheel, holding the ship on course with difficulty.

When the wave had passed, Paul scanned the interior of the yacht. The room where Lin had faced off with Chan was empty.

No. Not Lin. She can't be—

"Move in. We're boarding the boat." Paul's sharp order sent his team to action stations. On the *Stalwart*, a naval boarding party had already lowered a RIB. The rigid inflatable boat peeled away from the side of the frigate and a Seahawk helicopter rose from the rear deck. It moved into position above the *Beluga* and sent a burst of gunfire across the yacht's bow.

Trapped between the frigate and Coast Guard, with a naval helicopter hovering overhead and teams of military personnel approaching, the yacht slowed. A rappel team exited the open sides of the helicopter, manoeuvring around the wide arc of the yacht's twin masts onto the bridge.

Vickers brought the Coast Guard vessel alongside the yacht's port side while the RIB came in on the starboard side. Paul jumped onto the portside freeboard at the same time the first member of the naval team landed on the starboard side. He raced up the steps towards the sundeck where he'd last seen Lin.

Two shots fired. He could only pray one hadn't hit Lin.

***

Serena slumped in Lin's arms, blood streaming from a bullet wound in her shoulder.

Lin lowered the unconscious woman gently, but her gaze was fixed on John Chan, spreadeagled on the floor, his head propped up against the table, his eyes staring at her. Unblinking.

Her gun pointed at his chest as she stepped carefully across the cabin towards him. It didn't matter that part of her brain—the well-trained, logical part—knew he'd never rise again. Not with a bullet to the head, weeping blood like a third eye. No, what mattered was that she didn't trust him not to suddenly stand and proclaim he'd won.

She toed his gun out of reach then stood looking down at the man who had killed Kim and left her family to mourn. She looked—and waited for a feeling of triumph to fill her.

Her enemy was dead. Kim now had justice, and Lin felt—

Nothing.

No triumph, no fear when she looked up and saw three crewmen with guns aimed at her.

Not even relief when Rimmer appeared at her side, or when a team of naval personnel streamed into the lounge and the crew dropped their weapons and raised their hands high.

She spared a single glance for Rimmer before turning back and staring at Chan, dead on the floor at her feet.

She'd achieved justice at last and she felt nothing.

Not one damned thing.

***

Paul led Lin off the bridge to the *Stalwart*'s mess, the quietest place aboard the naval vessel. The prisoners were in the brig and several naval crew had taken charge of the *Beluga*, sailing Chan's yacht between the Coast Guard and the frigate as the three vessels returned to port. The storm hadn't abated, but a following sea meant a quicker journey home.

He couldn't wait that long to talk to her.

Coiled like an overwound spring, she hadn't spoken, at least nothing more than simple responses: *I'm not hurt, yes, sir, don't fuss.*

It wasn't normal behaviour, not for a highly trained field agent like Lin, not even after killing their quarry. As the door closed behind them, he wrapped his arms around Lin and held her.

Chan wasn't an ordinary criminal. Lin's sister's death had changed everything and now, with Chan dead by her hand, Lin seemed to be lost in her own personal hell.

"Are you okay?"

Her eyes met his and her gaze was focused and clear. *Finally!*

"I will be. Just hold me."

He could do that, for as long as she needed and then some. "I never want to feel like that again."

"Like what, Rimmer?" Lin tipped her face up to his.

A red smear remained on her forehead and the sight chilled his blood.

It could so easily have been Lin lying in a pool of blood on that deck.

"Rimmer, tell me."

Jagged words filled with a sharp remembrance of pain were torn from him. "Like everything that makes life worthwhile had been taken from me."

She raised a hand to his cheek and rested it there. "When

did you feel like that? When I didn't come out of Chan's mansion?"

He shook his head and kissed the top of hers. "No. You must have known I'd move heaven and earth to rescue you. But the *Beluga* dropped out of sight just as you and Chan both fired. I thought I'd lost you." He shuddered and held her as though he'd pull her inside and never let her go. "I love you, Lin, too much."

Her frown turned the smear on her forehead into a choppy-waved sea of red. Like a strange ritualistic mark. "How can love ever be too much?"

"It fogged my thinking. I didn't follow the rules and made a bad call in not coming alongside sooner."

"You made the right call. Serena was nervous. She'd have shot me if you'd tried to board earlier. By waiting, you gave me time to turn the situation around. You trusted me to find a way and I did."

"Lin, I underestimated your skills early on, but it wasn't about me not trusting you. Not this time. This was me frozen into inaction because your life was in danger. I had to—" He sucked in a breath and tipped his head back, unable to look at her as he said what must be said.

"I needed to hold you and reassure myself you're real. That you're okay, that you're here and alive, no thanks to me. One last time . . ." He cupped her face and kissed her.

Such an achingly sweet kiss.

Why did she think that when Rimmer's kiss held so much love and tenderness? It was like coming home.

Losing herself in the heady knowledge he loved her, savouring moments she'd feared she might never know again, Lin put all she had to give into that kiss. She was alive, Chan was dead . . . and Rimmer had told her this kiss was their last.

She broke the kiss and pushed him onto a bolted-down bench then, sitting on his lap, took his face between her hands.

"This will not be our last kiss, Rimmer. Not by a long shot. You can't tell me you love me and in the next breath, tell me that's it. I love you. We're good together and we'll go on being good together."

He wrapped his hands lightly around her wrists and bent his head, kissing each palm. "We *were* good, Lin, but this assignment is over now Chan is dead."

A slow pall of dread moved in and took over her mind. What a stupid moment for feelings to show up. She'd killed Chan and ended the hunt and she'd felt nothing. But Rimmer used past tense about their work, about *them*, and she felt . . . desperate.

"There's a lot of tidy up work to do and dismantling his network will take time. *We* have time."

Why was he shaking his head?

"You'll lead that team, Lin. I won't be part of that mop-up operation."

"I'll ask for you to remain on the team. And if you find the idea of being *under* a woman too difficult to cope with, you can be in charge." She slid him a look intended to convey so much more. Her love, her passion, her *need* for him.

He turned his head towards the door, just a little, just for a single heartbeat. Setting his hands around her waist, he lifted her off his lap and stood just before the mess door opened. A sailor stepped through the doorway, saluted, and gave a short message.

"Sir, ma'am, the captain's compliments. He requires you on the bridge. Messages have come in for you."

"We'll follow you."

"Rimmer, I—"

"We'll talk later."

A hand at her back nudged her towards the door. She'd lost the chance to convince him. For now.

Chapter 31

As meetings went, the Chan inquiry was the longest and most draining she'd sat through. So many interested parties and law enforcement agencies from different countries were involved, the gathering felt like a mini United Nations.

Lin pushed her chair back from the elongated oval table in the Prime Minister's boardroom and walked softly to the drinks table. She poured a glass of iced water and stood, sipping the drink and letting the current report wash over her like white noise.

Rimmer wasn't here and, from what she'd gleaned, he'd already returned to Australia. She'd seen him only once, emerging from Joe Wang's office the day after the storm.

The day after she'd shot and killed John Chan.

Can you face Chan with a gun in your hand and not shoot him? Rimmer had doubted her ability to bring Chan in.

Had she proved him right? Had her need to avenge her sister's death at Chan's hands pulled the trigger?

Over and over she'd replayed those moments on the yacht. Each time, she asked herself what she could have done differently. Each time, the answer was the same.

Nothing. Or was that rationalisation at its worst?

But there'd been no time for thoughts of vengeance or weighing up justice for Kim. There had been only Chan pulling out his gun. Neither Chan nor Lin was capable of backing down. Not in that moment of truth.

Poor Serena—caught in the middle. Maybe her father could pull strings to get her a reduced sentence for her part on the yacht.

"Agent Tan? Your report please?" Joe's voice pierced her musing.

She nodded and moved back to her place and set the glass of water on a coaster. Picking up her folder, she presented her report succinctly and dispassionately. When she finished, she looked around, checking the faces of the people at the table. One woman was making notes on an iPad, but the rest were looking at her with varying degrees of interest. "Are there any questions?"

The woman who had been taking notes raised her iPad stylus. "I'm Second Minister Tang and I have a few. Your mission was to capture John Chan and bring him in for interrogation. The international community was looking to us to succeed in capturing him, but he was killed and the daughter of one of our Ministers was injured. The delay in boarding the *Beluga* was a grave error of judgement on the part of Agent Rimmer in not following protocol and boarding as planned. Is there any mitigating factor you know of, why he shouldn't be reprimanded or stripped of his position?"

The impulse to surge out of her seat and defend Rimmer powered through her body. Lin gripped the edge of the table and tightened her muscles, staying seated by sheer force of will. How dare this junior minister blame Rimmer for Chan's death?

Swallowing her anger, she schooled her voice to maintain a tone of reasonableness. "Madam Minister, rules are made to maintain order; they serve as protocols, but in the field, in the heat of battle, they should be used only as guidelines. Agents with the level of experience of Paul Rimmer have to make the final call."

"Rules should not be broken, Agent Tan. If we all treated them as mere *guidelines*—" Her voice sneered around the word. "Society would fall apart." The minister pinned Lin with a gaze that held more than a need to get to the bottom of the operation's finale. The woman exuded dislike.

A frisson of danger prickled Lin's scalp. There was another agenda at play here; what it was, Lin couldn't guess. But what she knew was that this junior minister must have the ear of someone highly placed in government and could make demands that affected Rimmer's—and her—careers.

Across the table, Joe's gaze warned, *Tread softly*.

She took a delaying breath and looked at the minister. "With respect, only those of us who were there can say whether the delay was justified. While it is true that written rules exist governing what to do in a range of circumstances, there are unwritten understandings that override them—like 'trust your partner'. Agent Rimmer and I worked together, led a team together, and caught John Chan—*together*. We learned how each other thinks and to anticipate each other's moves. Paul—Agent Rimmer read the situation aboard the *Beluga* and gave me a small window of time and opportunity to turn things around."

"That delay lost us the chance to interrogate Chan and led to Minister Masters' daughter being shot. I fail to see any advantage coming out of the delay. Can you?"

Joe Wang leaned forward and opened his mouth to speak.

Lin held up a hand, stopping what she thought he was going to say. "Storming the yacht when the Coast Guard first reached us would have led to me being shot. Serena Masters was holding a gun to my head—"

"A ridiculous assertion, Agent Tan. The poor girl had been kidnapped and held for several weeks and abused by Chan. *You* failed to rescue her during that period."

"That's true, but when you have Ms Masters' testimony, you'll see that she was in love with John Chan, and a co-conspirator to her own fake kidnapping. She didn't need or want to be rescued, and actively helped to set a trail of false information."

"That's not what she says in the statement from her hospital bed." The minister held up a slim folder. "She claims she was so frightened by Chan that she did as he told her, and that when you unarmed her, you used her as a shield against Chan."

Frowning, Lin glanced at Joe. Was that the information he'd been trying to offer? When had he learned what Serena said?

"So, Agent Tan, would you care to tell us the *real* story? The one in which you and Agent Rimmer were more *intimate* partners. The story where he chose to value your life over his real mission."

Ambushed, annoyed, and worried all at once, Lin pressed her feet into the floor. Not by so much as the twitch of a finger would she offer the minister's claims any validation. Steeling her spine, she raised her chin and stared the woman down.

"Agent Rimmer delayed because he read the situation correctly. He gave me time to turn it around and then moved in. You should know the outcome would not have been different, no matter who did what or when, because John Chan refused to be taken alive."

"I beg to differ, and I will be formally requesting your dismissal from the department, and removal of Agent Rimmer from his country's Bureau." She turned to the chairperson. "I think we're done here."

***

The view of Darling Harbour was framed by tinted glass as Paul dropped into a chair across from Jake. He pinned his former partner, now second-in-charge at the Bureau, with a fierce glare. "Go ahead, say it. Say, 'I told you so'."

"No need. Knowing you, you've already beaten yourself up over what happened. We both knew taking Chan alive was a tough call, and he had nowhere to escape to in that storm."

"He wasn't going to come quietly for anyone. The choice I made—"

"Was the right one. Hell, I know you, Paul. The choice to delay boarding was solid. You don't make mistakes like that."

Looking at his hands gripping each other on Jake's desk, Paul shook his head. "I saw Lin with a gun to her head and pulled back."

"I doubt that. You trusted your partner, like any

experienced agent would, and she came through."

"She'd have been dead before we grappled the *Beluga*'s railing if I hadn't, but Jake, it was more than that. I froze. I'm no good in the field anymore."

Jake sat quietly, but Paul was aware of his friend's scrutiny. "You fell in love with your partner." It was a statement, not a question and there was no point denying it.

"Am I that transparent?"

"Probably not to other people. What are you going to do about it?"

"Nothing. Her life is in Singapore, mine is here."

Jake's mouth twitched as he picked up a printed page off the desk. "She's been suspended from duty pending the outcome of an investigation. She may not have a future as an agent when that's over."

"What? She's brilliant. Their best agent!"

"One minister in particular is shoving the knife in deep." He read from the page in front of him. "'Failure to find and secure a kidnap victim; dereliction of duty; failing to follow departmental rules'—I'm guessing that covers both lying to her department head and falling for her partner—and finally, the big one, 'shooting and killing the object of a major international operation'."

"Those charges are one hell of a stretch. I was in charge of the operation. I'm the one who should wear any blame. Without Lin's bravery and sacrifice, Chan would have got clean away." Anger roiled in his gut. "It's total bullshit."

"Even the part about her falling in love with you?"

Paul shook his head. Guilty as charged on that one. But the other accusations—something else must lie behind this attack on Lin. But what? "The only thing she's guilty of is following my orders."

"So what are you going to do about it?"

Chapter 32

Paul parked in front of Lin's apartment block and looked up. Light spilled onto her fourth floor balcony, lush and alive with greenery. As soon as his flight landed at Changi Airport, a phone call to Joe Wang had elicited the information that Lin was most likely at home, along with a stern warning not to make things worse for her.

How could things be worse, he wondered? Lin's work meant the world to her. Honour and her sense of identity were inextricably bound together to bring justice to an often unjust world. Her suspension had stripped that from her. What could possibly be worse?

He picked up the pack of Singha beer and the bottle of red wine he'd bought before leaving the airport and locked the hire car. Lights on in her apartment made him hopeful he would find her there. Making his way to the entry of the building, he hoped she'd let him in. He wouldn't hold it against her if she blamed him for the mess he'd left her in. Not that he'd wanted to leave her, but Chan's death had automatically released him from the joint investigation. Jake had called him back and reassigned him before his plane landed in Sydney.

As he approached the glazed front door a woman opened it and stepped through holding a young child's hand.

"Going in?" She smiled when he said yes and held the door until he reached it.

"Thanks."

The floor display above the lift showed it was already heading up, so Paul took the stairs. It gave him a little more time to think.

He grimaced. He'd had plenty of time to prepare for this meeting during the eight-hour flight from Sydney. His steps slowed as he approached Lin's apartment. The metallic apartment number reflected the soft light of the hallway before he stopped in front of her door.

Should he knock, or turn around and leave her in peace until tomorrow?

But Jake's observation that there was more to the allegations against Lin than appeared in the charges saw Paul raise his hand and knock—three firm, loud raps at her door.

He strained his ears to listen for approaching footsteps.

The door opened with no warning and Lin stood looking at him—beautiful with her hair loose around her shoulders, wearing the sarong he remembered from his first visit to her apartment.

His gut was twisted in knots and his mouth felt dry. It wasn't as if he'd wanted to leave her, but Jake had summoned him home. He hadn't seen her before he left, but surely Joe would have told her? What if he hadn't? What if she thought his last words to her on the *Stalwart* meant he'd drawn a line under their relationship? What if she wanted nothing more to do with him?

Nothing would be achieved until they talked.

"Hello, Lin. May I come in?"

"Rimmer—" She took hold of his face and pulled his head down, locking lips for one brief, glorious moment.

Abruptly, she released him and frowned. "What the hell are you doing here?"

*****

Why had she kissed Rimmer? She was angry with him. It didn't matter that her anger—both fierce and sad at the same time—had carried her through the first days of her suspension. He'd left without a word and what did she do?

She kissed him the moment she saw him. *Silly woman!*

She turned away but left the door open. Letting him in

234

grudgingly, without conceding anything. But still—letting him in.

"Can you bring yourself to share a drink with me?" He sounded tired, maybe a bit on edge, and not sure of himself.

She glanced sideways at him. Rimmer was always sure of himself and his place in the world. She should have asked Joe if he knew what was happening in the Australian Bureau. If Minister Tang's threats to end Rimmer's career as well as her own were making headway. Why hadn't she asked?

He stood in the doorway—not quite in, not quite out of her apartment—balancing a plastic-wrapped four-pack of beer on one large hand. The other gripped the neck of a bottle of red wine as he waited for her to decide.

She shrugged. "I'm thirsty. Open whatever." Holding onto her anger, reminding herself *he'd left her without even a goodbye*, still, she couldn't stop a thread of pleasure running through her. *He came back.*

Arms folded, she rested her hip against the sofa, watching Rimmer move with the ease of familiarity around her kitchen, finding glasses, opening two bottles of beer. He knew her well. Her eyes drank in the sight of him, more pleased than she should be that he was here in her home.

"So—" Leaving the word hanging, she lobbed the onus of conversation firmly into his court.

Rimmer handed her a glass and touched it with his. The clink suggested celebration, but there was nothing to celebrate. Not really. He'd left the day after Chan had died and she'd faced the inquiry alone.

"How have you been, Lin?"

"What do you think, Rimmer? Suspension isn't a holiday."

"I know that. I meant—"

"Tell me, have you been suspended? Has your career been threatened?" Hurt and loss and frustration bubbled out in angry tones, swamping any joy at seeing him again. Knowing it wasn't fair still there was nothing she could do to stem the flow. "Were you even rapped over the knuckles for Chan's death?"

He lowered the glass, beer untouched, and met her gaze. "I was lead on this operation and I take full responsibility for everything that happened. That's one of the reasons I came back to Singapore—to set the record straight. I've officially requested to be called to give evidence at the hearing. You won't lose your job, Lin."

"You can't stop them if they want blood. Someone has to pay for the loss of direct information from Chan about his network. The minister has decided I'm to be the sacrificial lamb."

"Chan would never have given up any details. And I won't let them do that to you."

"You have no power here."

"If they want someone to blame, that's on my shoulders. If they want blood, I'll tender my resignation."

She stared at him, at his tense jaw, his white knuckled grip on the beer glass. Rimmer meant it. He would take full responsibility for what happened. But even as a sense of lightness filled her that she wasn't fighting this battle alone, she shook her head. "You didn't tell me to pull the trigger and shoot Chan. That choice was mine alone and nothing you can tell them changes that. Think about it; you raised your concerns about that precise scenario as soon as you learned what Chan did to Kim."

"You had no choice. It was him or you aboard that yacht. And to the best of my recollection, he fired first."

"You weren't on the yacht. Serena Masters was, and her evidence doesn't match yours." That was the crux of the matter. Serena's evidence was coloured by the fact that Lin had shot the man she loved. The man who had betrayed her moments before his death, but she'd chosen to forget that when she made her statement.

Rimmer frowned. "Serena has testified already? But I

thought—"

"They took her statement from her hospital bed. Apparently I used her as a shield against Chan."

"That's not what I saw. I'm sure the Coast Guard captain's evidence will back up mine."

"They aren't calling Captain Vickers or any of his crew."

Rimmer's eyes narrowed and he frowned, his gaze turning towards the window. His thumb brushed his lower lip and she knew he was analysing what the news meant. Rimmer always deep-thought that way, as though the light touch on his mouth triggered a focused state of mind.

"If they aren't calling the captain or any of the coast guards, it's because the truth doesn't suit their objective, but why?"

"I have no idea and I can't access department files to do any digging. Joe removed my access when I was suspended." He'd only followed protocol, she knew that, but it still stung that, along with her suspension and access to files, Joe had barred her from all contact with her rookie team.

With an absorbed-in-his-thoughts expression, Rimmer reached for the hand she'd pressed against her stomach. His touch was warm, welcome, and so familiar she instinctively stepped towards him.

His frown stopped her in her tracks. "Someone's hiding something. You're the distraction and we have to find out why."

Her fingers tightened around his. They were a good team—a *great* team—and, for the first time in days, a tingle of optimism lightened her mood. If Rimmer had an idea, she trusted him to find what the Minister was hiding. "What do you have in mind?"

"It's a back way in, but—" His gaze met hers, sharp, and bright with the light of battle. "It's better you don't know."

Chapter 33

Joe Wang's office at midnight was the last place either of them should be without permission, but Paul figured it was the best place to start digging. Thanks to Wendy, they'd been given an easy way into her father's office. Did Paul trust the chief? Yes—no—maybe. Instinctively he felt Joe was trustworthy and he'd staked a lot on a his belief that Joe would be keeping private dossiers on key players.

Lin slipped behind Joe's burled-walnut desk, a thing of beauty and highly polished. She picked up a neat pile of papers and leafed through them.

"You shouldn't be here. It's a bad decision." How had Lin finagled her way into joining him? Her answer to every objection had been the same and in the end, he'd given into her. He looked around the midnight-silent office and sighed. They *were* a great team, but more than that, they were stronger together. Resistance had been futile. Leaving her behind while he searched by himself was never going to happen.

"Can it, Rimmer. I'm here, deal with it." Lin aligned the pages she'd been looking through on Joe Wang's desk so not even her boss could tell they'd been touched then picked up a slim paper-clipped file from his in-tray. "Wendy will be back soon."

Paul wanted to sigh. No, what he really wanted was to find incriminating evidence on someone—like the junior Minister who had it in for Lin—and clear Lin's name. After that . . . well, he hadn't thought any further.

Except he had.

He wanted a future in which Lin worked with him and shared every part of his life. Just how that might happen he left to fate. And Jake, who had been unsurprised to learn Paul had fallen for his new partner. A partner who was supposed to be temporary, but when he'd thought Chan had killed her, he'd known pain so searing he knew—he couldn't let her go.

Leaving her the night after she'd shot and killed Chan was the hardest thing he'd had to do, but Jake's summons had been urgent and brooked no refusal.

As he reached in front of Lin and switched Joe's computer on he caught the familiar scent of orchids in her hair as she bent over a folder. "Anything?"

"I don't know . . . It may be nothing but why would Joe have kept these notes if it wasn't something?" Offering a page to him, she continued reading.

One glance at the page explained the reason for Lin's uncertainty. "Most of these visits to Malaya by Lew and Helen Masters seem to have been made individually. I get why Joe might keep an eye on the Minister, but why Helen? What did he think was—"

The outer door snicked shut then a light tread approached the office. Moments later Wendy entered and closed the door quietly behind her. She still walked with a slight limp, but the bruising on her face was barely discernible now. "My father wasn't surprised when I said I was going out so late. He told me to turn the lights off when I was finished so I'm guessing he knew I was coming here. He muttered something about *fresh eyes*. I think he hoped you'd do something like this. What do you want me to do?"

Wendy seemed to have picked up right where the team had left off and that in itself was enough to set Paul's mind at ease. That, and the fact Joe seemed to have given their break in his tacit blessing.

Glancing at Lin, Paul asked, "What do you think? Do we start with Helen and her visits across the Strait?"

"It's an oddity, therefore it's of interest." Lin looked at

Wendy. "Check where Helen Masters went, where she stayed, and see if you can find out who she saw, and why."

Wendy nodded and set her capacious shoulder bag against the wall then sat at the second computer screen. "I'm on it."

Silence filled the office for a while, aside from the rustling of papers and the tapping of fingers on keyboards and then—

"Oh wow! You're not going to believe what I just found in hotel lift footage during one of Helen Masters' trips." Wendy leaned back to allow Paul and Lin to view the screen.

Lin rewound the video and pressed play again. The display showed Helen Masters in the arms of a man who wasn't her husband, pressed hard against him and kissing him enthusiastically. The man's back was to the camera, but Paul knew who it was.

"Are you certain it's him?" Of course it was, but if they were going to make this case watertight, they had to have clearer evidence than just a back view.

"I'm sure. I'll take the tape forward a little and then you'll see just before they exit the lift he turns and looks at the camera."

They watched as the floor display lit up. 'P' for penthouse. "That suggests this was no accidental meeting." Lin leaned in closer as though willing the man to turn.

As the lift doors opened, the man put his arm around Helen's hip, grazing it possessively, seductively, then looked at the camera and smiled—a smile Paul knew and loathed. The smile of a snake that had caught its prey.

The face of John Chan, gloating.

***

Lin leaned back from the screen and stretched. A tingle ran down her spine. "Someone's been paying Lew Masters large sums of money to a bank account in the Caribbean after every government meeting about border protection and maritime boundaries."

240

Rimmer pushed the single unlocked drawer in the filing cabinet closed. His hands were empty as he stood beside her and looked at her screen. "We need to access minutes of those meetings and find out what Masters was doing, how he voted if there was a vote taken, and what his decisions might mean for Chan's network."

They were onto something, she knew it, but could they dig far enough past security protocols without help to get at the whole truth?

"We need to find enough to join the dots and take it to Joe. There's plenty to suggest wrongdoing by Masters, but we need concrete links between Chan and his meetings with Helen, and Lew Masters' voting pattern and the money that went into his offshore account."

Rimmer sat on the edge of the desk and folded his arms. "There's another possible player we haven't looked at yet—Minister Tang. Why is she so set on getting rid of you that she's willing to run an investigation into Chan's case that any appeal court would call unfair?"

Lin wanted to know the answer to that one too. Her gaze connected with Wendy's. "Have you seen or heard of any connection between John Chan and Minister Tang?"

Wendy shook her head, looking thoughtful. "No, but what if they connected through a third party, such as Helen Masters? It doesn't make sense that a man like the Minister would turn a blind eye to his wife's affair unless there was a need for the connection."

"Are the women friends?" Typing quickly, Lin clicked into the news channels and set simple search parameters. Within seconds, images of Helen Masters and Minister Tang at various government and society events filled the screen. Scrolling down the page, Lin frowned as image after unremarkable image rolled past. "We need something less public."

"Go back." Rimmer's request held a note of urgency.

"How far?" Lin scrolled slowly back up.

"That one." He tapped the screen over a photo she'd dismissed.

Enlarged, the image focused on the Minister and the young winner of a popular singing competition, but in the background, Helen Masters was handing something to Minister Tang and glancing furtively over her shoulder towards her husband.

Lin zoomed in on the women and the paper in Helen's hand. "Can you read what that says, Rimmer?"

"It looks like a bank account. I think it's time we brought Joe in and show him what we've got."

Chapter 34

". . . and so this inquiry into the lawful shooting of John Chan concludes that Agents Tan and Rimmer acted lawfully and with the sort of initiative expected of top operatives. We commend them and their team for the work done in bringing the head of the Chan cartel to justice and breaking up an international drug and people smuggling operation. This board also commends the department for uncovering corruption at high levels of government. A separate inquiry will be established to look into . . ."

Beside her, Joe was relaxed, arms loosely folded over his stomach and confident in the strength of the material he'd presented to the head of the inquiry. Perhaps he'd been given the news earlier, but the finding Lin had waited so long to hear was now public. The rest of the summation she'd happily wait to read later.

Phone held low in her lap, she quickly texted Rimmer with the news. Pity he'd had to go back to Sydney before the finding was made public. She fancied celebrating with him. Somewhere private. Quiet and secluded and out of contact with everyone.

Her phone vibrated and she glanced at the incoming message.

Want to celebrate with me?

She grinned and typed her reply:

Of course. How soon can you catch a flight?

Three dots rose and fell, dancing below her question then his answer appeared:

No flight required. Turn around.

She sat forward and turned slightly, trying to look without

appearing to do so. Press scrutiny had been intense this morning, and she'd been besieged by news crews as soon as she left her apartment building.

Joe's lips twitched. He seemed to be focused on the speaker delivering the board's findings, but leaned towards her and murmured, "I think you've heard enough. Your suspension is over, you and Paul are in the clear and you're on holiday for the next two weeks. Get out now before the press knows you've gone."

Quietly she got to her feet, collected her handbag and slipped out of the row near the back of the room, wondering if Joe had chosen these seats for this very purpose. At heart, Joe was a secret romantic.

Rimmer was standing unobtrusively, partly shielded by a potted palm next to a side entrance. She doubted any of the journos had spotted him, or her quiet departure from the audience.

He opened the door and slipped through behind her, closing it quietly behind his back. They were in a deserted hallway that led into the working heart of government offices. She reached up on tiptoes, but all she managed was a brief brush of her lips over his before he tugged her hand and drew her towards the fire exit stairs.

Only when they were inside the echoing stairwell did he draw her into his arms and nuzzle her ear. "Unofficially, Joe let us know the findings last night. I caught the midnight flight so I could be here when you heard and do this—"

This was a highly satisfactory kiss that left her breathless and not caring about drawing another breath, so long as Paul's kisses were the reason for her lack of oxygen.

"I've got a car waiting below and a boat all ready to take us away to a very quiet, very private beach house."

"Did Joe tell you he's given me two weeks holiday?"

"He agreed you're overdue for some leave when I said I was taking you away, regardless."

"There are times when you're overbearing and then there

are times I like your caveman style. We can stop off at my apartment on the way to the boat and pack."

"Hmm, about that . . ."

"Rimmer, I'm not going away with nothing. I promise I won't take long."

"Wendy packed a bag for you. She didn't trust me to remember essentials like moisturiser and sunscreen and—"

"I trust Wendy to pack. Okay, lead the way."

***

Delighted with how smoothly they made their escape, Paul thought about the rest of his plan as the small yacht made its way to the smallest of a remote island group and dropped anchor in the clear shallows. Tiny fish darted around the anchor and sand stretched in ripple formation to a wide white-sand beach edged with luxuriant foliage.

Lin held his hand as they strolled behind the porter carrying their bags. As they rounded a shallow point, their bamboo cabin came into view. Built over the water, it was accessed by a suspended walkway, and there wasn't another building in sight.

"It's an eco-resort. There are only five cabins in total, each on its own small stretch of beach. We can order food to be delivered, or a water taxi will pick us up and take us over to the main island for dinner, if you prefer a glamorous night out."

"Sounds like heaven to me. You know how to spoil a woman, Rimmer."

"There's more to come."

"What?"

He dropped a light kiss on her forehead. "You'll have to wait and see, Ms Impatience."

They found swimming costumes but left the rest of their unpacking for later. "Come on slowpoke," Paul called and dived into warm, clear water from the deck that jutted into aquamarine sea. They swam until the sun was low in the sky.

Paul hauled himself onto the deck while Lin climbed the ladder and he handed her a huge beach towel. "Do you fancy champers and caviar with your sunset?" He stepped into the wide-open cabin and picked up a bottle and two glasses cooling in the ice bucket.

Lin tipped her head to one side and rubbed the long fall of her hair in the towel. "Yes, please. Are we eating in tonight?"

Paul popped the cork and filled a glass, handing it to Lin before he poured one for himself. "I thought you'd probably like to relax and star gaze the first night. Was I right?" He hoped he was right. He had a plan to put to her. Champagne and softly shushing waves beneath a starry night were part of his strategy to convince Lin of its merits.

She raised her glass. "To a successful operation."

He tapped his glass against hers. "And to a great partnership."

"Better than with your boss, Jake, or your friend, Tamsin?"

He swallowed a mouthful and suddenly waiting any longer to set the scene wasn't an option. He set his glass on the bamboo table and placed Lin's beside it then took her hands in his.

"The best partnership I've ever had . . . and one I don't want to end—ever."

Lin went very still and turned wide eyes up to meet his. "How can we continue it beyond this precious time together? My work is in Singapore, yours, in Sydney."

"Our department heads have been conferring and it seems they think our combined skills are suited to running more international operations in our part of the world." He brushed his thumb over her knuckles and waited for her response. "Would you ever consider taking on a role like that?"

"You and me together? In charge of our own sub-department?"

"Yes. Just think about it, Lin. You don't have to decide for a while, but there are lots of positives."

"Where would we be based?"

"That's up to you. Singapore, Sydney—wherever you choose."

"Where I choose, Rimmer—no, that name doesn't feel right anymore. Paul. That sounds less like a job choice and more like a—"

Paul tried to read her expression, but she lowered her gaze to their joined hands.

"What do you think it sounds like, Lin? Because you're probably right."

"It sounds like you want us to live together all the time."

"I do. At least, that will do for starters."

She pulled her hands from his and leaned on the balcony, her face turned to the rapidly disappearing sunset. "I can give you my answer now."

He stopped himself reaching for her, or kissing her, or trying to convince her to give it—*him*—a chance, but held his breath, waiting for her next words. He should have taken more time to lay the groundwork, given her more time to relax. Except—she sounded sure of herself and her choice. "Tell me."

"You're part of this deal, aren't you? There's no chance they're offering this and somebody else will come in and fill your place, is there?"

He swallowed. Had he misinterpreted something important here? "No chance—unless you prefer not to work with me again."

"I'm just making sure . . . because I can't think of anything I'd like more than to work with you and live with you."

Relief released the tension holding him away from her. He pulled her into his arms. "I can think of one thing I want more right now."

He lowered his head and kissed her as the deep purple tropical night fell around them and Paul knew he'd come home, because home was wherever Lin was.

The End

Thank you for reading *Singapore Trap*.
If you enjoyed this story, please consider leaving a review on Goodreads or wherever you purchased this story.

If you'd like to keep up to date with new releases and occasional deals, visit my Website or sign up for my newsletter.

Tamsin's story is coming in 2022.

Acknowledgements:
With special thanks to Henry C. for all things maritime.
And, as always, huge thanks to Annie Seaton, editor extraordinaire, and SE Gilchrist.

Born and raised in Toowoomba, Susanne is an Australian author of contemporary and rural romances set in Australia and exotic locations. She adores travel with her husband, both at home and overseas (and hopes to do more one day when the world opens up again).

Her heroes have to be pretty special to live up to her real life hero. He saved her life then married her.

She is published with Harlequin Mira/Escape, and has written several self-published rural series. A popular guest speaker, she has been invited to speak in libraries, book clubs, and to community groups.

Social media links

SUSANNE BELLAMY

Facebook   Twitter   Website   Pinterest
Bookbub

Head on over to my webpage and find out more about my rural series and other stories:

Website:

BOOKS BY SUSANNE BELLAMY

Rural fiction

Hearts of the Outback (6 book series)

Individual titles – Hearts of the Outback
Just One Kiss
Heartbreak Homestead
Long Way Home
Winds of Change
Wild About Harry
The Cattleman's Promise

Home to Lark Creek
A Promise of Home
Hard Road Home
Turn Left for Home
Home from the Hill
Book 5 coming 2021

Bindarra Creek Romance
Second Chance Love
Pearls and Green Beer (novella)

<u>In the Heat of the Night</u>

<u>Through Escape Publishing</u>
<u>Starting Over</u> (Also appears in print bind up: Heart of the Town - four book anthology)
<u>Engaging the Enemy</u>
<u>Her Christmas Kisses</u> (Also appears in print: Christmas Among the Gum Trees)

<u>Contemporary romance</u>:
<u>White Ginger</u>

<u>Romantic suspense</u>:
<u>The Emerald Lei</u> (originally published as Winning the Heiress' Heart)
<u>High Stakes</u>
<u>Singapore Trap</u>

<u>Novellas</u>:
<u>A Taste of Christmas</u> (in A Season to Remember)
<u>One Night in Tuscany</u>

<u>Regency:</u>
Four Calling Cards (in <u>12 Rogues of Christmas</u> anthology) – to be released in novella form soon.